Edward and Charlotte Ryan

Manchester

December 21, 1964

Books by Katharine Scherman

SPRING ON AN ARCTIC ISLAND

THE LONG WHITE NIGHT

The Long White Night

The Long White Night

by Katharine Scherman

LITTLE, BROWN AND COMPANY · BOSTON · TORONTO

*Published simultaneously in Canada
by Little, Brown & Company (Canada) Limited*

PRINTED IN THE UNITED STATES OF AMERICA

For Axel

The Long White Night

*J*acques Davitt lay back in the old easy chair staring absently *at* a year-old news magazine. The radio was tuned low, and the thin nervous sound of dance music emphasized the quiet loneliness of the little chintz-curtained living room. A muted voice interrupted the music to announce the weather in New York and give the time — five A.M. Ought to go to bed, thought Davitt, and still he sat, aching with sadness familiar as an old wound. A dog howled outside, then another and another, until the wild voices were entwined in barbaric harmony. A breath of cold air touched him, and with sudden urgency he pulled himself out of the deep chair. I've let the stove go out, he thought guiltily. In the half darkness of the kitchen, its windows curtained too against the bright Arctic night, he could see the stove glowing red at the seams. Yet the current of air was stronger, and he walked around the corner of the ell, to see the outer door open.

A small dark figure stood on the threshold. Around it streamed the pale gold of the spring morning. Davitt blinked at the light and moved forward, but the man lifted a hand as though to warn him off. A low voice spoke without expression: "Constable Davitt, a man is dead in the rocks behind Splaine's River." Davitt had a disquieting moment of clarity, as if he had been through this before and knew what would happen next. He blinked again to shake off the sense of nightmare. When he opened his eyes the bright oblong of door was empty.

Unhurriedly the constable gathered food, primus stove, gun, cartridges and sleeping bag and stowed them in a wooden box. He pulled on a white wool anorak and over it the loose, dark blue, gold-trimmed policeman's parka. Carefully he banked the stove fire and closed the drafts, then stepped outside. The sky was thin blue and the sea ice glowed. Sun touched the top of a hulking black mountain that jutted far out into shining Aurora Sound, and its wrinkled flanks seemed to absorb the new light, forbidding the day.

The village was asleep, its cluster of white tents and small stone houses tightly shut. It seemed that the cold Arctic dawn held only two live beings, himself and the Eskimo hunched on the broken sea ice over the traces of three prone dogs. The bitter emptiness of the neat house behind him smote Davitt, and he shivered. I've been here too long, he thought; a good policeman wouldn't react this way. He shook himself and went on down the beach.

The three dogs lay exhausted in their harnesses. "Stake them," ordered Davitt. "We'll take mine." Gratitude lighted the man's somber face for an instant. "We'll have to make a fast trip," the policeman continued. "Constable Ide's been taken outside with burned eyes, and I have to go and come back in a day." His face tensed as he spoke, and he glanced back at the curtained house.

Together they unharnessed the tired dogs and tied each one to a separate rock spaced far apart. The precaution seemed unnecessary — the dogs were apathetic. Patches of fur had fallen out, revealing stark ribs and haunches. Hopeless hunger stared out of their dull eyes. Davitt went to the shed behind his house and brought back the carcass of a seal.

"Tiggak — old male," he said with a grimace. "All we have left." He and the man laid it open with long knives, cut it into pieces, and threw the fetid flesh to the dogs. They gulped it with horrible haste, then reared to the limits of their lines, gasping snarls, trying to reach one another.

Davitt watched them curiously. "They're all old," he remarked.

[4]

"Why did the young ones die? Starvation should have taken these first."

The man bent over the discarded harnesses. His face was hidden. "The young ones did not starve," he said in his expressionless voice.

The two men harnessed Davitt's ten big dogs to the long police sled. They pushed the sled over the frozen sand and tumbled ice at the beach edge, Davitt calling to his dogs. The traces tautened and the sled moved smoothly over the sea ice toward the crouched mountain.

Time and space stretched before them, immeasurable, over the long sea and the slow-rising hills beyond it. It could have been two hours or two days later that they led the dogs through a wilderness of rocks littered in a crooked maze of valleys high above the inlet. Davitt looked at his watch; they had been gone six hours. When he had to find the place again he could guess it only by time. The Eskimo walked ahead with assurance, but the policeman had long since lost track of their direction. Sharp ridges cut them off from sight of the inlet below and the mountain above. They might have been anywhere; away from the sea all landmarks were deceptive. The tall gravelike slab of rock before them could just as well have been the one in the valley behind them.

They turned the corner of the slab and came on a crude shelter of boulders with an old caribou hide stretched over it. The body lay just outside the shelter. It seemed to have shrunk; a featureless, primitive giant form was outlined in gray mud around it where the body's first warmth had melted the snow. But it was cold now, and blood was frozen on its lips.

Davitt surveyed the wasteland. No early flowers grew here, no bird sang, the snow held no tracks of fox or weasel. They were two hours inland from the sea and the natural haunts of men. "How did you know where it was?"

The eerie conviction swept over him again: he knew the answer before it came. "I killed him."

[5]

1

I T WAS a year earlier, in June, that a red and white plane had circled through the clouds above Aurora Sound and come finally to rest on the sea ice a mile away from the settlement. It carried supplies, mail and a passenger named Douglas Ewen Michel. Before its propellers stopped turning a dozen or more dogsleds were out on the ice, loaded with Eskimos. Only three families lived at the Aurora Sound Police Post besides the two constables. But Davitt had told them that a plane was coming. The news had fled around the inlet, and in a few days tents had gone up all over the terraced hillside, filled with brothers, cousins and uncles. Children tumbled in and out of the tents, chasing one another.

Now they crowded around the closed door of the plane, chattering and laughing softly and touching the gleaming metal. Michel, in his seat on the other side, could neither see nor hear them. He was still tense from the erratic flight through clouded mountains and the low-flying search for a landing place on sea ice like frozen surf. When the motors were finally shut off it seemed that all sound and motion had stopped and the earth no longer turned. Outside was gray fog, endless and unshadowed. Only one form was visible — a long hunched mountain dimly outlined and enormous through the fog. It was a treeless mountain, all rock and ice, and it looked like a vast prone man. The titan who was to create the world, still asleep. He hadn't yet got around to creating this world. A sense of aloneness touched Michel. The isolation he had successfully spent his life avoiding might await him in the silence outside the plane.

He caught his random thoughts and pulled them together. He could use his own faint fear. The well-known D. E. Michel touch, the instantaneous feel of a place that so pleased his readers, was already in operation.

Then he looked out the window again. As a traveling journalist for a wide-circulation magazine he had reported from jungles, mountains, ships and strange cities, and in all these he had never been at a loss. There had been landscape and people. Here was nothing. Michel was not at all sure he was going to like it. The country was not specific. He would have to look into a void to seek his story.

The nothingness quivered into sound, weird and wild. Howls rose one after another, intertwined, to a high tremolo, swelling until their pulsation filled the ears, the head, the whole body, and it seemed that the blood itself echoed the savage counterpoint. Slowly they died down to a sigh, then lifted again. He had never heard anything so lonely. It was not so much a sound as a definition of the still uncreated world. He himself was not really there; he was only a dream of the sleeping titan and the voices were its unconscious speaking.

Mentally he recorded the similes. The writing would go on anyway. He didn't have to enjoy the place.

Unfastening the seat belt, he walked unsteadily down the sloping floor to the still bolted door. He wrenched the bolt back and pushed open the door, ready to step out into the primitive mist. Instead he looked down on a murmuring sea of dark faces and reaching arms. Recoiling, he bumped into the co-pilot, who was carrying a wooden landing ramp.

Michel laughed, embarrassed. "I didn't expect so many people."

"They always show up," said the co-pilot casually. Then he noticed the pallor of the tanned freckled young face and the white-knuckled hand still gripping the door, and added apologetically, "It was a rough trip. Anybody would feel shaky. We have to fly through these gorges to see where we're going. There's not much in the way of radio signals and half an hour ago we could have dropped a bomb on the magnetic pole. Nothing's any use but eyes — and we might as well be blind in this . . ." He gestured at the ground fog that made sky and sea indivisible.

"All I need is about five minutes of solid earth."

"You'll have more than that." The offhand words struck an unsuspected answering chord. Michel looked beyond him, over the heads of people and still howling dogs, to the untouchable wilderness of tundra and mountain. Definitely, he thought, I liked the other places better. It's pretty empty around here.

The co-pilot turned and waved at the crowd. "Hi, kids. I've got your tobacco." A shout of delighted laughter went up, and some of the men waved blackened pipes. "There are just two reasons why they're here," he told Michel. "The first is tobacco. The second is they'd like to take this plane apart to see what makes it fly, then put it back together again, better."

Michel looked again, wondering, at the huddle of upturned faces. Even laughing, they were expressionless, and the eyes were flat black stones. Was there even so small an emotion as desire for tobacco behind those impassive masks? Could those onyx eyes look at an engine with anything but blankness? These people were anonymous, like their scenery. Michel, at ease in the certainties of predictable information, recalled snatches of secondhand knowledge of the kindness and gaiety of Eskimos. The faces before him registered nothing. He would have to think of something else to write about them.

A late sled arrived, longer than the others and pulled by ten large wolflike dogs. Its driver, a white man in the uniform of the Northern Police, called a long-drawn-out syllable, quiet-voiced, and the dogs instantly lay down in their traces. Behind the driver sat a small Eskimo woman in a snowy white parka, lavishly wool-embroidered, white fox fur around her delicate brown face, silver sealskin boots on her tiny feet. He dismounted and held out a hand to help her but she evaded him, laughing, jumped off the other side and ran to join a group of whispering young women.

The man, tall and big-boned, moved with slow grace to the ramp, where he met Michel descending. There was an instant of searching wariness before they spoke, the practiced scrutiny of men accustomed by their duties to looking below the surface.

The two were of even height. Michel looked straight into smoke-colored eyes deceptively sleepy. Waving black hair, ivory skin, features so handsome as to be almost soft, lazy slouch of the wide shoulders — the man looked like a resting puma. He's at home here, thought Michel; this is his territory. He may talk to me openly and he may not.

The other saw a bright blue gaze, a mobile face alight with interest, a long-limbed athlete's body leaning slightly forward, a suggestion of tenseness in the pose. Stiff sandy hair twisted up at the top of his head in a cowlick, and he had the thin fair skin which reddened easily — no doubt, thought Davitt, to its owner's annoyance. He looked like a very large small boy, friendly and naïve and impatient. He would probably always be surprised.

The dark-haired man smiled and offered his hand. "I'm Constable Jacques Davitt. You must be Michel of *East-West Review*. We've heard of your travels. Even here," he added with a glance out at the immensity of sea ice.

"I've heard of you too. Kindest and toughest policeman in the Arctic Territories. Half the reason for my assignment." He followed the policeman's gaze. "Not even a journalist could feel important here. Isn't this the place the sailors came to when they fell off the edge of the world?"

"It grows on you," said Davitt mildly.

Michel flushed. "That's what I was sent to find out," he said. "Why."

"You can write down a thousand facts and not have the answer. But we'll give you the facts. It's not often we get to talk to someone besides each other."

Michel put a question mark in his mental notebook about the dressy Eskimo girl who had come on the sled and had now vanished. Then he filed her away and watched the men unloading the supplies. Small and slight-appearing as they were, they lifted cartons with one hand and heaved sacks as if they were filled with feathers instead of flour. A running patter of conversation accompanied the work. They appeared to have gathered by the plane only for a gossip, and the division and stowing of the loads on the sleds was so casual as not even to be a distraction. Michel wandered among them, avoiding the large slit-eyed dogs, and noted with surprise that each sled was expertly balanced, its load distributed with mathematical precision.

In less than a half hour the loads were lashed down. One by one the drivers flicked long heavy whips in the snow and shouted, pushing their sleds roughly against the rear animals. The dogs rose without enthusiasm, strained in their harnesses against the burdened sleds, then padded toward the shore, heads and tails low. Grunts, growls and sharp howls of pain accompanied the irritable yells and the booming cracks of the whips. Michel closed his eyes and pictured an African slave pen, then a cage of lions with a tamer.

Definitely he would have to revise the happy picture his readers expected, of merry little men living chilly but utopian lives insulated from the frenetic stresses of the twentieth century. Doubt flickered: this assignment might be, incredibly, for the first time, beyond him. No quick assessment fitted.

Davitt had loaded his own sled and Michel added his slight gear. The constable had a whip too but he did not use it. He spoke a name quietly. The lead dog turned his head, wagged his tail and stood up. The other nine were on their feet immediately. Davitt

[II]

and Michel slid the big sled out of its ruts and it glided effortlessly over the rough ice. Plumed tails waved like flags.

"What do you do that they don't?"

"I talk to them politely and feed them every day. But it isn't the fault of the people. They have to overwork their teams hunting and trapping. When they've finished feeding their families there isn't much left over for the dogs."

"They don't even seem to like them."

"They don't pat them and invite them into bed." Neither would I thought Michel — they smell. "It's one of those facts — " Davitt's gray eyes appraised him — "that I mentioned before."

"A little ordinary kindness," Michel remarked, "wouldn't hurt either the dogs or the people."

They came to the edge of the beach, an untidy litter of tide-driven pressure ice, dismounted, and let the dogs pick their way across it. Then Davitt set about unharnessing and chaining them to stakes set far apart on the beach. Michel tried to help. But each dog, when he approached, lay down solidly on its trace and stared at him with wolf eyes, lips slightly lifted over the long teeth. Embarrassed, he turned to survey the shore.

From a narrow arc of white beach the land rose in shallow terraces, older beaches abandoned by the receding ocean. On the highest terrace was a clean white frame house with green trim and a red roof. From its chimney came a comfortable plume of smoke. Beside it were several smaller outbuildings, and around all of them wound pebbled paths lined with whitewashed stones. One path led to a little river icebound between its curving graveled banks. A round hill rose behind the terraces and on its slope more white-painted stones proclaimed *Aurora Sound* to the unheeding wilderness, presumably to inform lost airplanes that they were not in an identical part of the Arctic a thousand miles away.

The scene had the natural grace of a softer land. Half closing his eyes, Michel pictured rippled blue-green water, striped beach umbrellas, grapevines on the gentle terraces, cypresses along the river, a small temple on the hill. He opened them to the reality of ice debris at the ocean edge, dogs huddled on the sand, ancient beaches slippery with mud and rotting snow, a cluster of primitive stone dwellings and ragged tents, and beyond all, dominating by its vast nullity, the deadened sea. He remembered uncomfortably that the little white villa was a police post so isolated that it could be reached only once a year by a trading ship, and rarely, when the fog lifted and the sea was safe, by plane. His eyes clung to the bright-painted plane abandoned far out on the lonely ice. It looked as if it were grounded on the far side of the moon.

"Not exactly cozy, is it," he said.

"It's beautiful," said the constable with unexpected feeling. "But I know how you feel. When I first came, five years ago, I used to think about trees all the time. Now when I go outside trees look unnatural, sticking straight up in the air with no boulders and guy lines to hold them there. It takes a while to get used to the bareness."

"I don't have to get used to it. I'm only staying twenty-four hours." He smiled boyishly and Davitt smiled back. Good thing, thought the policeman; very likely he wouldn't get on here at all. This peripatetic newspaperman was not one who would fathom the static Eskimo mind.

They walked up the terraces toward the house. Scattered over the lifeless mud were unlikely clumps of clean purple flowers. A small black and white bird perched on top of an aerial poured out cascades of song. The sun appeared briefly, almost touching the ridge of the heavy mountain; the edges of the dark low clouds were fiery and haze shimmered pale yellow over the sea.

It was an erratic, illogical beauty, a teasing promise on the desert of snow-splotched brown earth and paralyzed ocean. Davitt seemed to neither look nor listen, but strode, calmly indifferent, over the mud. What made him so content?

Inside the house Michel found part of the answer. The warm

smell of baking bread greeted him as he followed Davitt through a cold entry porch. The clean kitchen was dominated by a fat black coal range. Shining pots hung in rows over the sink, and a glimpse of the pantry showed well-stocked shelves and a variety of herbs and spices. In the living room faded chintz curtains covered the windows and electric lights glowed softly under old-fashioned fringed lampshades. Easy chairs held the impress of relaxed heads and bodies. Two small bedrooms, a closet of an office and a bathroom were separated from the living room by a hall lined with books. The heat from the coal range found its way into every corner of the house and the drawn curtains hid the bleakness outside. He could be anywhere. He could pull aside a curtain and see green fields and cows and birch trees.

The constable's voice interrupted: ". . . so you can have his room." Michel put a sharp brake on his thoughts. If he were to live up to his reputation of lightning-like perception he had to stop thinking about cows. Whose room, anyway?

"Thanks very much," he said, "but I don't want to put anyone out. I expected to pitch a tent."

"I expect you'll be more comfortable here. Ide won't be back from patrol for three or four days." Of course, the other policeman. They went in pairs, like nuns. "Besides," continued Davitt, "nobody pitches a tent this time of year unless he has to. Particularly nobody from outside."

"I've pitched a tent before," said Michel, bristling.

"I know," said the constable soothingly. "First ascent of Mount Thomson. 'Intrepid reporter reaches Camp Five. Helps in crevasse rescue. Spends night on cliff bivouac roped in upright position.' All the same you'll be happier in here than perched out there on the mud."

Michel laughed. "How right you are. My father and I camped and climbed when I was a kid, and since his death I've expanded it into a business. I was seeing subheads: 'Night in an ice igloo. Reporter turns Eskimo on frozen sea, eats raw whale.' I didn't

[14]

expect electricity, fresh bread, indoor plumbing . . ." his eyes strayed to the kitchen . . . "or a maid who looks like a miniature *Vogue* model."

Davitt whirled. The young woman who had jumped off his sled was clearly at home in his kitchen. Her sealskin boots made no sound as she moved gracefully from oven to table, lifting out loaves of bread and setting them to cool. Davitt's face showed distress and he arranged a self-conscious grin.

"I didn't know she was . . . quite likely to come in at midnight and scrub the floors . . . but sometimes she . . ."

Michel broke in politely. "Please introduce us."

Davitt frowned. "Nina," he said reluctantly, "can you leave the bread?" An entrancing smile lit her face as she turned to him. She had the native features, small flat nose, wide-spaced slanting eyes, high sculptured cheekbones. Her skin was gold-brown and her hair black and sleek, drawn into two shining braids behind her ears. Davitt spoke in her language, his voice changing from the flat Midwestern drawl to a rising and falling lilt, deep in the throat. She gave a low merry laugh and answered, her voice musical. As she spoke she looked sideways at Michel.

"I told her you were going from one Arctic post to another to see how her people lived and write about them for a big magazine. That this was your first stop because here they still hunt seals with harpoons and cook over stone lamps and soften animal skins with their teeth. She answered that these are ordinary things, and that her people will be more curious about you than you are about them. She means that *she* will — Nina thinks everyone from outside is a god from heaven and she wants to know all the details of what heaven's like. Don't paint too rosy a picture." His voice held warning.

"I would consider it a kindness if she could show me the houses of her people," said Michel, carefully formal. Davitt spoke to her; Nina smiled dazzlingly at both of them and slipped back into the kitchen.

A few minutes later Michel looked and she was gone, as quietly as she had come. He wondered what the constable had said. It was evident that the visitor from outside was not meant to see her again. Davitt, however, could not know the depth of his disinterest in this or any other native girl. Entanglements, no matter how alluring, seldom occurred in Michel's nomadic life. It was safer that way.

The three men of the plane crew came in, busy with plans, and ranged themselves around the kitchen table while Davitt began opening cans and setting water to boil. "King George's Bay tomorrow night," said the engineer, "if the weather breaks. Then Seven Islands and two days later Storm Head."

"If we get in," said the co-pilot. "Worst fjord in the north for landing. Pulls in every breeze like a wind tunnel."

"We have to get in. There's a sick kid there. Then we clear the Archipelago and drop a few supplies at Spruce River — caribou's low over there, they say."

"Sounds like Jules Verne," murmured Michel.

"Spruce River — tree line — then, by God, home," said the pilot fervently. He was a gray-haired man in his fifties; in his faded blue eyes was the look of years of sighting into distance and sunlight and moving clouds. "There's a rumor around I have a grandchild. I'd like to confirm it, maybe even get introduced to him before I have to take off again. You coming all the round trip with us?" he asked Michel.

"If you'll have me."

"Plenty of room on the flour sacks. I wouldn't stay here if the Governor left me the whole Arctic in his will."

Davitt, serving an acceptable canned beefsteak, smiled at the pilot. "But you never stop coming here."

"Makes me appreciate my semi-detached," said the pilot with a laugh. "Mortgage and all."

They left immediately after dinner. "Have to stay with the

[16]

plane," explained the co-pilot, "or the kids will have it apart by morning."

Their going left a loneliness. Michel drew back the kitchen curtain. Heavy fog was rolling in from the invisible ocean. The mountain across the inlet was gone and the crewmen walked toward a blurred hump of plane that seemed to rest on cotton wool. Even as he watched, that too disappeared. It seemed that the plane and crew, coming from outside, had already gone back outside, taking their cheerful humdrum talk with them.

He turned to Davitt, who was slouched comfortably in one of the big chairs, a coffee cup balanced on one knee. "Why do you like it here?" asked Michel.

"Don't have to dress up and go on parade," answered the constable lightly.

"Doesn't the solitude get you?"

"It's less lonely here than outside. When you've been here a long time you find it noisy and crowded anywhere else. Too many people, and none of them care for you or each other. You could lie dead on the street and no one would look around at you. Here, if you burn your finger it gets on the radio schedule and a guy four hundred miles away asks you how you're feeling."

"How about the natives? Do they ask you how you're feeling?"

"I don't think of them as 'natives.' They're men and women. Yes, they ask me how I'm feeling." Michel flushed and Davitt went on quickly. "You're right, they're about two thousand years different from us. But I get along with them. They make me feel at home."

"Home," echoed Michel. "It's not in my vocabulary."

Davitt looked at him curiously. "You're missing out."

"No I'm not," he began emphatically, then stopped. He'd never cared to talk about his beginnings in the small, pretty, bitter town on the north Atlantic seaboard. The Scotch mother and French father he had loved had died young, leaving him as heritage a taste, unfashionable in the neighborhood, for literature and music and

[17]

mountains and wild animals; a heritage, too, of village prejudice against his double nationality. Half his schoolmates had despised his last name, the other half had disliked his first two. At his parents' death he had sold his father's small fishing fleet and left the town that couldn't accept him. He seldom looked back on these facts and even more rarely spoke of them. "I didn't care much for the overgrown crossroads I was brought up in," he continued, "and towns are all the same. I've been a reporter since I was sixteen and I've kept moving because that's how I prefer it."

"Maybe you prefer not to take a chance," murmured Davitt. "Permanence might be dangerous."

"I wouldn't know. My life is enjoyable and the assignments have been good. The excavation of the Temple of Snakes in Guatemala, the reconstruction of Cook's New Zealand explorations in a sailing ship, first ascent of the third most difficult mountain in Nepal — they're all entertaining. There are always new places and new people to talk to. I can go anywhere I please and get well paid for it. Why should I settle down?" Particularly here, he added silently.

"You'll have all day tomorrow. That's not too permanent, is it?"

Michel laughed. "It's about right. I still don't understand why you don't lose your reason here. Five years, you said. That's a long time for a man to be away from his own kind."

"I don't need company that badly. Winter patrol is about two months and it's the best time of year. Then there's a real chance to be alone. The solitude and the space out on the sea ice give a man time to think. Even here at the post I don't have too many distractions. The Eskimos in this area are mostly a good lot. They know too little about our civilization to have problems and they don't ask much. I hope they stay that way." He added seriously, "I intend to keep them that way."

"Can you?"

"I don't think I have to try. If you like we'll take a trip tomorrow and you can see what I mean. I can leave the post for a few hours even though Ide is off. We'll go down the inlet and see how the Splaine's River people are making out. They didn't get in to see the plane — you were a few days early and they're the farthest out of our people. Likely they didn't care to see it anyway. They're pretty old-fashioned. Only one rifle in the village. You can get your whole story in one day. You may even find you like them." Michel glanced at him, but the serene, soft-featured face told him nothing.

"Thank you, I'd enjoy that," he said politely.

Michel was nearly asleep in Ide's bed when he heard the clatter of dishes in the kitchen sink. Then came the ring of cup against saucer and the low steady murmur of voices. The hired help had come to do the housework and have a cup of tea with her employer. Before he dropped off again, Michel wondered dimly about Ide.

2

THE RUNNERS whispered over snow-covered ice and the loose-jointed sled swayed and creaked like a little boat. Snow was falling, gentle and slow as if the fog itself were disintegrating into flakes. In the hushed twilight they seemed to travel neither on land nor sea nor sky, going nowhere. Michel sat at the end of the sled gazing sleepily back at the uneven bluish tracks of its runners and the spatter of dog prints, quickly erased by the snow. The fantasy came over him again that it was too soon for people; the world was still an unformed cloud. But this time it was a tranquil fantasy. They *were* here. The occasional grunt of a dog, the quiet creak of the leatherbound slats, and the dim tracks under his eyes were brave and comforting and soporific.

Cacophonous honking shocked him awake. Startled, he turned to Davitt, who pointed upward. The mist was disturbed, then a wedge of ten snow geese broke through it, proud and purposeful, not more than twenty yards above them. The great black-tipped wings beat slowly behind outstretched slender white necks, and harsh voices challenged the sleeping, shrouded earth.

They stared after the big white birds until all sound had faded. "The runners of spring," said Davitt then, with awe. "You wouldn't think, them so haughty now, that in a month they'll be waddling around a puddle like barnyard fowl, short-tempered and fussing over eggs."

"At any rate they seem to know where they're going, which is more than we do."

"Yes we do. Look at the snow." Michel did so; it was as featureless as the fog. "See those long wavering ridges? They're wind marks. The last wind was day before yesterday and it came from the southeast. We have to go west, so we cross the lines on a diagonal. We should hit Splaine's River within a quarter of a mile. Actually, with the dogs, we'll probably hit it on the nose." A far-off howl punctuated his last word. Michel suddenly felt humble. For Jacques Davitt this still white world was far from amorphous; it was a lively place where even the drift of snow had a voice. For the first time Michel appreciated, even envied, the constable's oneness with the isolated life he had chosen.

The Eskimo village was a huddle of eleven small stone houses. The beach below it, like that at Aurora Sound, was crowded with large dogs, ears erect, bodies tense, muzzles turned toward the sea in a fugal howl. Why did they sing? Were they welcoming the newcomers; were they saying, Go away, Stranger, don't tangle with us; were they simply chanting because they liked the feel of it, like people in church? Whatever they meant, the stranger noted with approval that they were all tied to rocks.

Between the huts stretched lines, hung not with clothes but with polar bear, fox and weasel skins gleaming white through the fog, and dark silver ring-patterned seal hides. The houses themselves, built into the hillside, looked more like cave dwellings than twentieth-century cottages. They were only three or four feet above the ground, oval in shape, composed of rough rock slabs. The roofs were of overlapping flat stones, mud and grass, and looked like large birds' nests. The doors were holes out of which straggled a seemingly inexhaustible supply of identical brown children. A few shabby adults followed. Davitt approached one of the men, shook hands and delivered a long speech, to which the man replied at equal length.

This one was just as short-statured as the others, just as poorly dressed, just as sallow-skinned. But he spoke with grave formality, and the ring of authority was in his voice as he turned to two women who stood shyly behind him. As if he had turned a switch, they scuttled into the nearest house. The Sultan, thought Michel, has ordered his women to withdraw. He smiled down at the drab little man and found himself, uncomfortably, the subject of an expressionless scrutiny.

"How do you do?" he said tentatively to the flat black stare. There was no response and the silence grew tense.

He turned to Davitt. "What did I do wrong?"

"Nothing. Nauligak is not sure about you yet. They never say how do you do right off."

"What the hell . . ." Michel gave an irritated laugh. "Does he think I have designs on his harem?"

"His wife and daughter," said Davitt dryly. "No. He sent them in to cook. I think we're to be invited for dinner."

There was another lengthy discourse, and Nauligak's voice took on a stern intensity. His eyes turned to Michel every now and then, though he spoke only to Davitt. He doesn't want me here, thought Michel; he probably doesn't want any outsider here except Davitt, who is not an outsider. That is what he is telling Davitt.

"Nauligak bids you welcome," said Davitt at last, "and hopes to help you in your work. He would like you to share their Sunday meal, although he says his house is poor, his meat is bad and his women the worst cooks in the village. A sort of Chinese politeness."

"Did it take all that time to say that?"

"Oh no — there was some gossip," said Davitt.

Michel looked straight at the dark unsmiling face as he offered a speech of thanks. "I am only staying until the plane goes," he ended. Davitt translated, and the Eskimo's face lightened for an instant.

The two tall men had to stoop to enter. A narrow tunnel crowded with dog harnesses, snowshoes, harpoons and outer garments of indeterminate shape and color led downward into the house proper. A penetrating smell of seal oil and animal skins hung in the dim room. Murky daylight filtered through a small gut-covered opening at the back. Another flicker of light came from a burning wick laid along the edge of a shallow soapstone dish filled with oil. An arrangement of stones and bones supported the big black cooking pot above the fire; a noxious effluvium steamed from it. One of the women crouched by it, stirring with a wooden spoon. The flame's light played on a face scarred with wrinkles, and wisps of graying hair hung over her forehead and ears.

The other woman was on the raised platform at the back, arranging hairless skins and patched blankets. Michel couldn't see her face. In her boots and the shapeless gown of worn caribou hide, she could have been man, woman or child.

Nauligak was right: his house was poor and his food was bad.

Then the woman at the lamp raised her worn face to Michel, and when she smiled the whole room was brighter. For the first time since the plane had landed Michel felt welcomed. She spoke quietly, and the woman on the sleeping platform slipped quickly out of the house, with a sideways glance at the newcomers as she passed. Michel saw a flat yellowish face, hair like patent leather — and merry eyes and a swift sweet smile. She looked young, not more than fifteen. Soon she came back, herding three small boys and an old man. The man was fat, with a crumbling face and knobbed hands. From his tangled hair to his ragged boots he was irretrievably filthy. Nauligak motioned them all to the neatly folded skins on the sleeping platform, except for the old man, who squatted apathetically by the entrance, eyes fixed on the floor.

"Grandfather?" whispered Michel.

Davitt laughed. "Nauligak would never allow a grandfather like that. No relation. A derelict named Saloositak Tana — that means fat lazy one — that Nauligak takes under his wing once in a while to keep him from starving. All he can do is carve stone. Aitu, Nauligak's wife, won't let him sit with the others. She says he has things growing on him." His clothes, indeed, seemed to be growing on him. It did not appear that they had been changed since he had reached manhood. He looked up suddenly, straight at Michel, with sly eyes almost lost in the fall of dark gray flesh. Michel shuddered slightly and bent his head to the prayerbook that had been handed to him.

It was dog-eared with long use. On the left side of each page were the English words, on the right the Eskimo syllabic script that looked like children's drawings. There were no other books; Nauligak's family knew the words by heart.

The service, conducted in the Eskimo language, took an hour and a half. Not one prayer was left out, and the responses were delivered with the ease of long and loving familiarity. The little flame on the cooking dish lighted the peaceful faces of the children and the tired, beautiful mother as they chanted the terrible words: "We have erred and strayed in our ways like lost sheep . . . We have left undone that which we ought to have done, and we have done that which we ought not to have done. And there is no health in us. But thou, O Lord, have mercy on us, miserable offenders."

Between prayers hymns were sung fervently, and Nauligak accompanied them on a battered accordion. His wood-colored face bent sternly toward the rakish instrument; the effect was comic and sinister at the same time, like a medieval carving of a lesser devil.

As soon as the service was over, the smallest miserable offender leaped on his brother, who tried to pull him off by the hair. There were giggles and shrieks, and the house seemed full of writhing small bodies.

Michel asked a quiet question, and Davitt answered, "They weren't born Christians, not even the little ones." The youngest, now standing on his brother's neck, looked about five years old.

"Nauligak was a witch doctor, in fact, and he still holds top rank here because he's the best hunter. But when the missionary came — Splaine, that is, who named the river — they took to the services as if they'd been born in a parish house. Liked the sound of the prayers. Splaine was around for two years, but I think he got them all baptized in the first month."

"Maybe they liked the missionary too. What did Nauligak think of this?"

"You just saw. He never misses a Sunday service."

I'll bet he didn't want the missionary here, said Michel to himself, any more than he wants me.

"Why did Splaine leave?"

"Oh, one thing and another happened," said Davitt vaguely, "none of it important. He really didn't matter. The people are still the same as they always were, even with Sunday prayers."

Davitt evidently didn't care to enlarge on the missionary. But, Michel agreed, it was not important. His story lay with these people — if a few hours could give him a glimmer of what lay behind their masks.

Sunday dinner was boiled seal meat swimming in grease and sharp-twigged roots fried in seal oil. Michel chewed politely for a long time, and when he was through an old smell of seal seemed to come out of his pores. Not even his assignment seemed as urgent as a few minutes of fresh air.

"I'm going for a walk," he told Davitt.

"Be back in a half hour. We'll have a chat with Nauligak, go around the village, and still be home in time. The fog's not rising — the plane can't take off till morning. Go along the beach that way" — he pointed east — "and you'll find some hundred-year-old whalebones big as a house."

There was a hint of command in Davitt's offhand advice. Perversely, Michel turned his back on the shore and followed Splaine's River inland. Its channel deepened, and he walked above it over little round hills. At the top of each one he could see the clouded sea ice and the blur of the seaside mountain he had first glimpsed from the plane.

A fault in the earth split the river. Looking down the smaller fork, Michel noticed a faint track on the high bank of its near side. An animal trail to the sea, he thought as he followed it along the edge of the branch, back toward the shore. The hills became flatter until they were hardly more than terraces. On the far side of the fork a cross was dimly outlined against white sky.

The track dipped here, down to the river, and Michel could trace it on the other side, circling up toward the cross. Curious, he descended the narrow gorge, stepped over thin blue ice, water bubbling beneath it, and climbed the flat-topped hill.

The trail led to a small graveyard, eight wooden crosses standing awry at the heads of stone-piled mounds. Weather had grayed them and erased their inscriptions. Apart, facing the mountain, was a carved white stone with *Splaine* cut on its smooth side. Below it, partly eroded, and scrolled with a delicate tracery of gray-green and black lichens, were the words: *I will lift mine eyes unto the hills*.

No animal trail would have led to this white stone.

He looked down at it. "Wrong quote," he said. " 'The end of the fight is a tombstone white, with the name of the late deceased; and the epitaph drear, A Fool Lies Here . . .' " Realizing he had spoken aloud, he wheeled as if someone were listening. A black and white bird trilled on the top of a cross, then flew away. The silence was absolute. He thought back to jungle burial places alive with snakes and singing insects, and mountainside crosses surrounded by grass and flowers where sheep grazed and laden travelers stopped to pray.

This graveyard, deserted, facing a mountain of barren rock and ice, above an inert sea, evoked as none other he had seen the total abandonment of life to death. The aloneness caught at Michel;

[26]

he had felt it with his first glimpse of the north, and now it was seeping into his mind, strange — and not altogether unpleasant.

The old trail descended from the graveyard. His investigative sense alert, he followed it around a hill and down into a protected hollow, still high above the sea.

There, bewitchingly stage-set, was a little wooden house with a peaked roof and a porch. It was weathered gray, like the crosses, but flakes of white paint clung under the eaves. One side looked far out over the white sound, a second to the ice-subdued river, here widened to a pond, a third north toward the mountain, guardian against the northwest gales of winter. Early spring flowers, white and blue and pink and yellow, grew alongside the snowdrifts still piled against the house, and traced small rainbows between snow and mud on the protecting hillside.

Peering through a broken window, he saw a shelf of books and records, a wind-up Victrola, an organ and a reading lectern. An open book lay face down on a sagging easy chair and a volume of music stood on the organ. Michel closed his eyes and saw his own house of long ago, where books his father had loved had lain open and music was ready to be played, and his gentle schoolteacher mother had guided his fingers on the piano or sung him to sleep. But his mother had died when he was ten and his father six years later. The cold smell of damp mold reached him. He looked at the room again. It had not been lived in for a long time. The walls were stained and warped, tarpaper fluttered loose at the paneless window and the porch door swung creaking on loose hinges.

An unquiet spirit hovered here. It almost spoke aloud and Michel knew he would have to listen. Someone had liked this house, and even now, for all its lonesomeness, it was extraordinarily appealing. It was abandoned, thought Michel, just as his own home had been deserted ten years before when, the last tie cut, he had gone without a look backward.

And what am I doing looking back now, he said to himself,

dismissing the pull of the silent house. Davitt was waiting for him, to take him back to the plane and the real world.

He walked down to the cove and back to the village along the curving beach. Davitt and Nauligak sat on the sleeping platform smoking black pipes, and a singsong conversation flowed between them, sounding like one continuous word. Contentment was in the air, and the grave and the house he had seen might never have existed.

But the sense of weirdness invaded him even more strongly. These two men knew something — probably everything — about Splaine's short career on the river he had named, and they had implicitly decided to hide it. Professional curiosity was aroused as well: the stubborn inquisitiveness of the journalist from whom facts are deliberately veiled.

"See the whalebones?" asked Davitt.

"I wandered about a little," he answered indefinitely. "The fog is worse and there's no wind," he continued. "The plane won't fly tomorrow, do you think?"

"Unlikely. This looks like a three-day peasouper. I didn't want to depress you by telling you before."

"On the contrary, I'm glad. Do you know if any of the Eskimos here can speak English? If I had an interpreter it would save you trouble. You'd probably like to get back to the post as soon as possible."

"Good idea." He spoke to Nauligak, who nodded and went outside. "There's an excellent one — Nauligak's oldest son, who's nineteen now. Splaine taught him, then sent him outside to Hudsonton for eight months of school. He didn't like it much but he came back modern. He's the one who has the only rifle. It happens he's a fine hunter in spite of his education, and his father sent him out after seals today."

"Education?" put in Michel. "What's the matter with that?"

"Sometimes it mixes them up. Another of those facts . . ." He smiled. "I've asked Nauligak to send someone to get him in."

[28]

Michel settled beside Davitt and watched Nauligak's wife painstakingly patching a hole in the sole of a child's boot already thin as paper. The three little boys slept, one on her lap, the other two curled in one frayed blanket behind her on the sleeping platform.

"They're rather poor, aren't they," he observed.

"It doesn't bother them. They've always done for themselves, not like some of the people who rely entirely on what we bring from outside and go to pieces in bad times. Actually this is the best village in my territory. There's never been any friction here and they all work very hard — except for friend Saloositak Tana. He's an old rogue but Nauligak keeps him down."

"Nauligak keeps them all down, I'll bet."

"Not down, just busy. One more northern reality."

Michel reddened. "Your project for today — to make it clear I'm an outsider."

"Everyone is," said Davitt disarmingly, his leisurely gaze traveling to Michel's face. "It's usual. No need to be impatient. The motives here are hard to catch on to at first glance." He looked around as the hunter himself came in with his son. The boy was round-faced and soft-eyed and looked like a child, much younger than nineteen, who had been given a harsh adult responsibility. He smiled widely, but his forehead was creased with poignant marks of strain and his temple pulsed visibly.

"I am Ezekiel Okkomikpok," he said gravely. The dark eyes held Michel's with an unreadable plea. "I am glad to help you speak to our people."

"Thank you, Ezekiel. You're a godsend." Michel tried to answer the unspoken appeal with the warmth of his voice. "I am Douglas Ewen Michel." He flushed and turned to Davitt. "One of the half-and-halfs. No solid society to keep me in one place."

"Like Jacques Davitt," said the constable. "It must be something else that keeps you moving."

Embarrassment deepened his flush. "Sorry. But it had to start

[29]

somewhere." He smiled at the boy. "Nobody ever calls me anything but Michel." Ezekiel's taut forehead relaxed as he took the proffered hand.

Davitt rose, stretching. "It's a long trip home in this weather. You two had better come with me. You can do your story at the post, Michel."

Michel looked around the room, at the enigmatic hunter, the sweet-faced wife, the three sleeping children, his new friend with the unhappy forehead lines. He wanted to know more about this family. There was unease here, some conflict that he could not put a finger on.

He made up his mind suddenly. "If it's all the same to you I'll stay here. Ezekiel can bring me back." Davitt started to speak, but Michel turned to the boy. "Did you get seals when you were out this morning?"

"No. I saw two but they were careful. The fog made me go too close."

"I'd like to write about a hunt, since your people live on seal. Perhaps you would have luck now."

The boy spoke to his father. "Yes, he wants me to go out again. I was not on the sea long enough today."

Michel faced Nauligak with a warm smile. "Thank you for your dinner and your hospitality. I am grateful to have your son with me, and will pay him well." Ezekiel translated and his father shook hands, nodding solemnly, his eyes searching. "It's all right with you, isn't it, Constable?"

"It's all right with me. But you won't have time to get anything here that you couldn't get as well back at the post. Be careful, and don't judge too quickly. As soon as you see the sun, come back. The plane crew will be restless."

Michel laughed. "You're as bossy as your friend Nauligak. Don't worry about me, Constable, I'll try to keep an open mind."

"It isn't that." Davitt frowned. "It's only — well, it's hard for an outsider to know what makes these people think and act the

[30]

way they do. Just keep that in mind." He turned to Nauligak, concern on his face, spoke a few words in a gentle tone, and departed. Soon they heard him calling to his dogs on the beach.

Michel, on his own at last, felt like a boy on holiday.

3

THEY RODE out on Aurora Sound, Ezekiel driving his father's team, and within a few minutes fog closed off the village behind them. They were enveloped in a wet cloud; the waving tail of the lead dog was a blur.

"Zeke — do you mind if I don't use your whole name?"

The boy's face was suddenly younger. The worried frown had vanished. "That's what Father Splaine called me."

"Zeke, any seals we catch today are going to have to come up out of a breathing hole right beside this sled."

He laughed. "We find seals soon. A seal likes to be killed. It is like a drop of cool water falling on his head. Maybe one will come up to look for my gun."

"What did Father Splaine think of that theory?"

"He said it is wrong. But he never hunted a seal."

"What happened to him, by the way?"

"He died." Zeke wasn't smiling any more. "I do not know how. I was not here. He was very good, kind to our people. We miss him. We made a stone for him."

"May I see it?"

"Yes. It is beautiful." There was pride in his voice. He studied the windmarks on the snow and turned the dogs. Zeke was freer with his whip than Davitt, and the dogs raced, hitting the cove and the little fork of Splaine's River precisely.

The missionary's house, deserted in the midst of life, seemed diminished, like a widowed bride. Michel looked a question at his guide. When Zeke said nothing he pulled open the ruined door and entered. The boy followed, walking carefully and silently, as if he were in church. He didn't touch anything, but stood in the middle of the floor, the lines again etched on his forehead.

Michel wandered curiously around the room. The bookshelf held the solider English classics — *The Vicar of Wakefield, Gulliver's Travels, Oliver Twist, Sartor Resartus, Utopia, Paradise Lost.* He pulled one out. It was dry and free of mold, though the wall behind it was damp-streaked. The book lying face down on the chair was a thesaurus, well thumbed. The stack of records on the old-fashioned golden oak table included Bach cantatas, Mozart quartets, a Haydn Mass, an incongruous volume of Johann Strauss waltzes. On the organ was an open volume of Bach chorales. He went into the kitchen and lifted one ring of the small range. It was clean of ashes and had no smell even of long-ago wood burning. On the wall above it hung a polished row of pots. Eyebrows raised, he returned to the living room and laid a hand against the pot-bellied stove. It was dustless, and colder than outdoors.

Splaine's house had been — still was — loved. Again his own house, long forgotten, came back. It had been happy, as this had, and the long days were quiet as here because his mother and father had not tried to break through the social barrier raised by the local antipathy between their parent races. Their only son, content with them, had fled after they died. For the first time he questioned the rootless years since. His previous glimpse of the house had brought nostalgia; now a faint hope rose, surprising him. I could actually live here, he thought.

Zeke was still standing in the middle of the room. Hands thrust into his pockets, shoulders hunched, face a mask of wary fear, he had the look of a small boy in a cemetery at midnight.

"What's the matter, Zeke?"

"Nothing," said the boy almost inaudibly.

"You think someone was here and will come back?"

"No!"

[33]

"But someone *has* been here — since Father Splaine left." Zeke did not speak or look at him. "Zeke, listen to me. Why didn't the missionary's people take his things out?"

"We were his people," whispered Zeke. "He left everything for us. He said if ever he had to go away this was our house. We keep it for him. Maybe his soul will come back and look for things."

"Do you believe this house is haunted?"

"I do not know what that is. But if a man does not like the way he dies his bones will sit up in the grave and his soul will try to come home." He brightened a little. "Come, I will show you an old grave where the bones come out of the ground."

Michel persisted. "Was Splaine unhappy with the way he died?"

"I do not know. Maybe he did not have to die." The boy's eyes were big and he seemed near tears. Suddenly he turned and ran outside. Michel followed slowly, frowning. The snow-stained mud was more alive and the drifting mist less chilling than the house behind him. A hollow voice spoke in his ear and he whirled. A loon flew heavily straight past him out to sea, once more uttering its keening cry. The backs of his hands prickled, and he caught himself up sharply. The place was getting under his skin; Zeke's superstition was infectious.

Zeke was working on the dogs' harnesses and Michel walked to the river. "Where does this track lead?" he called. Zeke didn't answer. "To your beautiful gravestone?" The boy nodded, his head down, his hands engaged in a wet tangle of reins. "You wanted to show it to me, Zeke," he said gently.

"Yes. Please. Soon." He lifted frightened eyes and immediately lowered them.

"Do you mind if I go alone?" Zeke shook his head and Michel left him and walked up the little brown and white hill beside the imprisoned river. Fog lay like a shroud over the graveyard. High and windswept, it was entirely free of snow, and all the bared

[34]

crosses were in an identical state of decay. Among them crept low Arctic willow, its fat leaves tight-rolled, its new catkins bright as silver coins, and deep-pink saxifrage bloomed through last year's dead yellow grass.

Splaine's white stone was tall above the flowers and the leaning crosses. Michel knelt and studied the inscription carefully. The words were carved with a craftsman's perfection and the stone was shapely, cut in a smooth curve. He searched the surrounding hills. They were littered with boulders, all granite. The piled grave mounds were of the same rough stone. Splaine's grave was of marble.

He ran his hand down its flawless side. A snow bunting, brown and white like a small piece of spring tundra, flew out of the stone, brushing his hand, and disappeared into the fog. Another, a brilliantly black and white male, materialized, circled anxiously around his head, then landed on a cross, pouring out an angry tumble of song. Michel felt along the bottom of the stone. His fingers found a broken place, explored, and touched a nest of grass and feathers under the grave. He drew out a tiny bird, its beak opened in an infinitesimal screech. The parent circled him again with a cascade of passionate song, and he put the chick back to nestle, perhaps, in the missionary's hollow eye.

The fog was lifting. Beyond the grave foothills rose steeply to the snow-scarred flanks of the mountain. From the sound it had looked squat, its seaward body hiding twin peaks that soared from the giant mass to lose themselves in shifting clouds. The inlet far below was dappled gray, its horizon merging with the sky. Michel looked at the inscription and raised his own eyes, with a sense of exaltation, toward the icy peaks. Like this the coastal hills had lifted behind his childhood home; how strange he had not remembered it when he first saw this mountain. He had been at ease climbing in rocks and snow from the time he could first scramble up on a rope behind his agile father.

He gathered willow and saxifrage, silver and pink, and laid

them against the stone, beside the entrance to the snow buntings' nest.

Turning, he saw Zeke at the edge of the cemetery regarding him with puzzlement. He felt himself flush, and smiled self-consciously. "To please the soul of Father Splaine."

"Do you like the stone?"

"It is beautiful, as you said."

The boy glowed. "Father Splaine told me where it should be and what to say. My father found the stone. After . . . when I came back . . . I wrote the words on it, just the way they are, and Saloositak Tana cut them. He is a lazy old man but he can cut stone."

"The stone is fine, and Father Splaine picked a noble place to be buried. Is he here?"

Zeke looked startled. "Maybe with the Moon Man, maybe walking around, no one knows."

"Zeke," said Michel severely, "you don't believe that."

Zeke grinned suddenly and looked very young. "I will take you back in the hills to an older place where you can see it is true that dead people sit up. One has hair growing on its head."

"Aren't you afraid of them?"

"They are only bones, and the winter pushes them out of the ground. What is there to be afraid of?"

"You were afraid in the house."

"I get mixed up . . ." He hesitated, his forehead wrinkled . . . "Who is right, the old grandfathers who were always here or the kind people of Father Splaine? I liked him more than anyone but he was not here long. Now you are here . . ." He stopped, embarrassed.

Michel was moved. "Oh, Zeke," he said, "I'm only supposed to be here for a day. That's not long enough . . . anyway this is your country. You live here. We only visit."

"You could live here."

"Could I?" His eyes roved over the mountain again, and the

[36]

wide bare country. Yes, he thought, surprised, I could. Except that the plane is waiting and that's my kind of life — coming and going . . .

He looked around at the desiccated crosses. "These all seem to have been planted at the same time."

Zeke's frown deepened and his young face had a look of old sorrow. "Forget it," said Michel.

The boy smiled beseechingly. "Please, this is not an interesting place. Only the white stone. Come, I will show you the one with hair. It is an ugly old woman."

Michel laughed. All at once he almost understood Zeke. "No thanks. The ugly old woman will keep till another time. My feet are wet." He had borrowed an old pair of sealskin boots from the constable, and they leaked. "Can we go back to your house and dry out?"

Nauligak and his family were busy out of doors, using the wan daylight. He was mending a fishnet while his wife scraped fat off an odorous sealskin and the girl sewed a straight row of small stitches along the seam of a torn jacket. One of the little boys was driving the other two, fastened insecurely in a tattered dog harness. The harness tripped them up and the young driver waved a long boot lace as a whip. They all fell together, giggling, and the girl laughed too, looking at them with love. The dust-colored old man sat at a distance, whittling indifferently at a stone. His eyes were on the sealskin and his nostrils twitched.

Nauligak looked up, impassive as before, and spoke rapidly to his son. Zeke answered dramatically, at great length. The hunter's face grew a little less stern and his wife smiled. The girl's black eyes sparkled and her sallow face was alight with gaiety.

"I told them about the flowers and the birds," said Zeke. "They think you are a little crazy like all from outside. The birds would go better in the cooking pot than under the stone. And dead

[37]

people do not need flowers, they want harpoons and knives. They cannot hunt with flowers." He laughed.

Michel reddened, as always afraid of a snub. Deploring his thin skin, he said stiffly, "I was only being polite — and a little sentimental." Zeke looked blank and there was a short silence. It was broken by the girl's voice, a pleasing ripple.

"She says you are kind, like Father Splaine, and he likes flowers better than harpoons because he does not hunt." Michel smiled gratefully at the girl but she had lowered her eyes. Nauligak spoke gutturally.

"My father would like you to eat supper with us," said Zeke. Michel resigned himself to boiled seal meat and crawled reluctantly through the narrow entrance, followed by the others. After a few minutes Zeke entered, carrying two large bloody livers. Michel sighed inconspicuously.

But the liver, sliced and quickly fried, and eaten with fresh-made bannock, hot and sweet, was an unexpected delicacy. The stranger, feeling now no longer strange, ate with the same zeal as the others. Afterwards Nauligak went outside again, to his fishnet. Zeke and Michel lay back on the caribou skins of the sleeping platforms, smoking pipes in comfortable silence. The girl approached shyly. Kneeling before Michel, she pulled off his slimy-damp boots. She held them over the low flame and kneaded the soles with her fingers. Her flat face was serious and intent and Michel sleepily watched her, comparing her with beautiful, ambitious Nina. Once she looked over at him and he opened his eyes wide as he caught the surprising blithe glance and half-suppressed smile. Immediately she dropped her gaze to the boots and her deft little hands sped over the leather.

Their eyes were not, after all, polished black stones. He thought back with difficulty to half-noticed realities. Nauligak's austere gaze seemed to look right into one's head. His wife's eyes were calm and kind and unwavering, with fine lines of laughter at their

[38]

corners. Zeke's eyes changed with his quick changes of emotion — alert, imploring, eager, always alive. This plane-faced, no-colored girl — if she were not so young he would have been sure the eyes were flirting with him.

The education of D. E. Michel, he observed wryly, was proceeding. After some years he might be able to write about these people.

Covertly he studied the girl's downcast face. The smile still touched the corners of her mouth and her smooth cheeks were faintly brushed with pink. "What is your name, little one?"

Zeke answered for her. "She knows no English. Her name is Mauyak. That means 'soft snow,' because she was born in the second month of the sun, when the snow begins to melt."

"What does your name mean?"

"I do not know. But I know the story." In one of his swift changes his voice deepened and he seemed to look into a distance. " 'By the rivers of Babylon we sat down and wept.' But Ezekiel did not sit down and weep. He was captured and taken to Babylon, and he showed his people in exile how to be strong and worship God only. He saw many visions, of the throne of God and the great Church that would be one day, and the people believed him and followed him."

Michel stared at the slight boy with his proud prophet's voice and faraway eyes. "Do you follow him too?"

Zeke turned young again and smiled boyishly as he evaded the question. "Names mean much to our people, not to yours. Ezekiel is my *baptized* name."

"And your other name?"

"Okkomikpok. It is a good luck name. It means 'goes with the wind.' My father gave it to me with the hope that I would never have the storm in front of me to blind my eyes, and my dogs would always run fast with the wind behind them." Even in English his voice had a singing lilt, and his eyes were soft, with an inward expression.

[39]

"So you had two fathers." Zeke's face darkened with confusion and the pulse at his temple throbbed. Michel went on quickly. "What does Nauligak's name mean?"

"Harpoon. His people have always hunted with spears, not with guns. He is the greatest hunter of Aurora Sound. The seals come up to look for his spear." He was proud again, but shy, as if his father were of a race apart. "His people," he had said, not "our people."

"And your mother's?"

"Aitu — that is, a gift. Her parents had no children, so she was given to them by another family. She was much loved, the only child." The mother looked up when she heard her name, her face transformed by the ageless beauty of her smile.

Mauyak sat back on her heels. The worn boots hung limply from her hands and she surveyed them with her head on one side. The light mischievous expression was still there. Softly she spoke to her brother.

"Your bare toes will soon scrape the snow," he translated. "She would like to make you new boots; Constable Davitt will surely not make them for you."

"If the plane will wait while she makes them . . ." Michel felt a surge of nostalgia for this place he had not yet left, from which he would soon be gone forever. These people might have been the first close friends he had ever allowed himself. He looked directly at Mauyak. "Thank you. You are very kind, little one. I would like new boots."

Again she knelt before him, and laid her little hand along the sole of his foot, measuring. Two and a half lengths barely reached from his heel to his toes. Her mouth grew round and her eyes sparkled. She started to speak, then broke off with a smothered laugh and pulled her brother's foot next to Michel's. The boy's toes reached only to Michel's instep and they all laughed.

"Toonijuk — Mikilakmuit — Toonijuk — Mikilakmuit," chanted Mauyak, pointing at them in turn.

[40]

"You are a Toonijuk," said Zeke, "so big you can carry a walrus on your back. I am a Mikilakmuit, so little that I think rabbits are polar bears." Michel stood up, plucked Zeke off the sleeping platform with one hand, threw him over a shoulder and marched around the room with him, head bent to avoid the low roof.

"I am not a big walrus," cried Zeke, panting and laughing.

"I am not a big giant. I only carry little walruses."

Nauligak came in then. The laughter stopped and Michel put Zeke down carefully, his face red. The hunter looked at each one searchingly. The faintest of smiles lit his face when he spoke.

"He says you are a child, like me and my sister," said Zeke.

Michel glanced quickly at Nauligak. The smile was only a hint below keen grave eyes, and in a moment it vanished.

"You must take me back, Zeke. The constable will think a Toonijuk has got us. We needn't tell him we never did get around to hunting seal."

The mist was dissipating and the sun pale as a daytime moon. The inlet was silver with gray shadows, like the skin of a seal. Riding back through the thin-shining sunlight, Michel felt a plucking at his heart as if he had caught a distant glimpse of something precious, once known and long forgotten. He was not quite ready to put a name to it.

4

THE SHOREBOUND dogs had set up their savage howling long before Michel and Ezekiel came in sight of the white police house, and Davitt was waiting on the beach. He stood relaxed, gazing into the distance, one foot on an ice hummock, a hand resting easily on the raised knee. The low night sun, fiery below a heavy cloud bank, drew fierce shadows on his calm face, and when he turned toward Michel his gray eyes were almost tawny in its piercing light. His voice was cold as the chill spring evening.

"The plane is taking off in the morning. We were getting ready to send out a posse."

"I'm ready when the plane is," said Michel pleasantly. "I'll pay the boy and be with you in five minutes." Davitt nodded distantly, turned and swung up the beach, slow and lazy as a big cat. Zeke stood by the sled looking at nothing, a small frown above his blank eyes.

"Zeke," said Michel, "would you be free to help me if I can stay? I don't mean a lot of work, just talking to people. You could still hunt, do everything your father needs you for."

The look of hopelessness vanished instantly; his eyes lighted and an eager grin belied the formality of his answer. "I am happy to help in any way you wish."

[42]

"Good boy. Now all I have to do is talk the constable into it. It seems he'd just as soon I left with the plane."

"He is a good policeman," said Zeke seriously, "very careful. He always thinks, when someone is here from outside, maybe he will drown, get caught by a bear, get lost on the ice, so he worries. But with me . . ." the smile broke through again . . . "nothing will catch you."

"Of course I'm safe, but I don't think Davitt thinks so. He has something on his mind . . ." Michel broke off at the sudden familiar look of confusion on the young face. "It's all right, Zeke, we'll manage," he finished vaguely, with an encouraging smile.

In the living room after breakfast the next morning Davitt and Michel sat over their pipes, not talking. Davitt's eyes were closed and Michel was occupied with his strange new thoughts: the lonesome grandeur of the country, touched with small beauties; the deserted and appealing house; the people he had seen in their unimportant hours, their faces open to him; the pull of mystery in the guarded eyes of the hunter. "I've never held with the plane-hopping method of journalism," he started. Davitt gazed at him without encouragement and Michel forced his voice to casual detachment. "The picture is a kaleidoscope with no real image to hold the eye. When *East-West Review* sent me on this story my editor suggested an overall coverage but left it to me how to do it — as he always has. I didn't know myself until I got here. In two days I've learned that it takes more than two days. These people are so distant from us they might be on another star — or in the Ice Age, when man was new."

"Some people never understand them." Davitt's words floated slowly in the air like his blue tobacco smoke, and Michel repressed instant resentment.

He went on carefully. "I can do a first-rate story if I stay at Nauligak's village for a while. The ship will be here in about six

[43]

weeks, won't it?" Davitt nodded, looking at the ceiling. "I found a house over there, apparently the missionary's. It's in bad shape but it's livable."

The policeman brought his smoke-colored eyes down to focus on Michel's face. "You've changed quickly."

"Not really. It reminds me of my house. I haven't thought of that in ten years. Now I'm thinking of it."

"It's doubtful," said Davitt, "that the missionary's house is in the least like yours."

"Probably not. But the situation appeals to me."

"This isn't a summer resort," continued the policeman without intonation. "Splaine's house is not for rent."

There was no recourse. Michel's tension loosed and overwhelming sadness took its place. He closed his eyes and saw the soaring mountain and shining sea ice, flowers and singing birds on the still frozen tundra, Mauyak's serious little flat face and laughing eyes, Nauligak's carved features for a moment relaxed as he saw his children playing, Zeke's grown-up frown and boyish grin, the white tombstone. He opened his eyes suddenly and fixed them on the policeman's serene face.

"By the way, I found Splaine's grave. Very touching, the regard his people had for him. You sidestepped my question back there in Nauligak's house. What did happen to him?"

"Didn't think you'd be interested in an old accident. You're writing about present Eskimos, not long-gone missionaries. Splaine died during a starvation winter. He was on his way here to get supplies and didn't make it." His manner was offhand.

"Right," said Michel. "The missionary is unimportant. But something about his death was important." Davitt didn't react. "He seems to have had an influence on Zeke," continued Michel. "The boy trembled like a poplar leaf when we were in the house."

The constable laughed. "Ezekiel wasn't here when the missionary died, and he took it hard. He's probably been telling you stories about walking bones. He's a smart boy, knows exactly

[44]

where he's going — it's in two opposite directions at the same time."

Michel flushed with annoyance and opened his mouth to speak, but at that moment Nina slipped into the room, smiling radiantly and impartially at both of them. Davitt allowed a frown to crease his imperturbable forehead. She sat on the sofa beside him and touched the frown with one slim fingertip. Bringing a carved ivory cigarette holder out of her embroidered belt pocket, she held it toward Davitt; her eyes were like dark pools with starlight in them. He gave her a cigarette, lighted it, and leaned back gazing at her as if she were the sun after the Arctic winter night. Behind her was the kitchen, dishes dirty in the sink, food congealing in the pots on the stove.

Obscurely irritated, Michel spoke into the rapt silence. "Mauyak is going to make me boots."

"I'll see they're sent on." Davitt did not move his eyes from the exquisite face beside him. Like an Egyptian statue, thought Michel — and about as useful. He busied himself with his pipe, knocking out the ashes, cleaning, refilling, relighting with intense concentration, while the sense of loss swept over him again. It wasn't Mauyak, it wasn't Zeke, it wasn't the subtle northern spring — he still could not name it, and now he would never be able to.

A breath of cold air stirred the lazy smoke, and heavy feet stamped in the ell beyond the kitchen. "Hello, Ide, have a good trip?" called Davitt, not moving.

The other constable stood in the doorway surveying the littered kitchen and the wordless domesticity of the living room. He was not so tall as his superior but stockier, broad-chested and heavy-shouldered, his body thrust forward aggressively like a boxer prepared to attack. His fair skin was burned red and peeling, and pale blue eyes protruded below white-blond hair. A pointed nose and receding chin detracted from his belligerent appearance. The nose, red-tipped, now twitched. He looked like a large angry rabbit.

"Uneventful, thanks. I see things haven't changed here either."

[45]

"Have some coffee," said Davitt mildly. "There's a pot on the stove."

"Nina, get me a cup of coffee. She's the maid," Ide explained emphatically to Michel. Nina, unperturbed, tripped into the kitchen, smiling prettily at Ide as she passed. "You must be D. E. Michel," he went on. "I'm proud to meet you. I hope you've enjoyed the hospitality of Aurora Sound." His light eyes flickered coldly over Nina as she handed him a cup.

"I've been over at Splaine's River, and I've enjoyed it so much I'd like to stay there until the ship comes."

"He wants to stay in Splaine's old house," put in Davitt, "and I don't think it's wise. He'd be isolated out there. No way of making sure of regular supplies or help if he gets sick. The ice in the sound will be impassable any day now."

"He won't be isolated at all. There's Nauligak's village a half hour away, and we're well stocked enough to keep one man from starving for a few weeks."

"Being the chief constable of the district," said Davitt quietly, "I am responsible for this community. That includes stray white men. Suppose a bear wandered in his front door?"

"It's not likely there'll be bears this time of year. Anyway I'll give him my spare rifle."

"Hunting is against the law except for natives."

"I've never killed a wild animal and don't plan to start now," put in Michel. They paid no attention to him.

"Protecting yourself against bears isn't against the law." Ide's pale eyes bulged at Davitt. "A first-rate journalist wants to do a story on Aurora Sound. We're going to be real popular with the Home Office when they hear we've thrown him out."

Michel relaxed and leaned back to wait for the end. The wrangling had nothing to do with him. It was the continuation of a permanent and trivial quarrel — but without it he would be on the plane in an hour. The voices hardly penetrated as he took an unaccustomed look into his mind. His piecemeal existence, for all its charms and triumphs, no longer contented him; he now wanted a base. The desire had come unexpectedly and he couldn't fathom the reason. But the result was spectacular: he had been blind and all at once he could see. The North was preternaturally desirable, the new acquaintances were friends.

That was all he needed to know. He tuned in again on the argument.

"The house belongs to Nauligak's people," said Davitt. "There's legal right involved."

"An unwitnessed document that nobody's seen but you. The house belongs to anyone who lives in it."

"It's possible Nauligak may not agree with you."

Ide's anger flared. "You're the one who doesn't agree with me. Nor I with you. He stays at Splaine's River or I'll . . ." He spluttered helplessly.

Davitt's equable voice broke the uncomfortable silence. "You'll do nothing, Ide, because there's nothing you can do." He stood up and walked over to Michel. "Stay here, then, if you want to. I'm deciding it this way because I don't like friction." A slow smile spread even to the serious smoky eyes. "You've just had a private showing of what this country sometimes does to people. I'm sorry. But remember it. This is not an easy place to live."

Michel rose to shake the outstretched hand. "Thank you, Davitt. I've already forgotten it. It's not part of my job to get much involved. The immediate atmosphere is all that counts."

Naïve adventurer, said Davitt to himself, afraid of getting in too deep, looking only at the shallows. "Be careful," he said gravely. "It's all very well to take in the landscape, but you may unexpectedly find you're part of it."

Late in the morning the plane took off. It circled the station twice, dipping a wing in salute. Michel watched until it was a distant star in the blue-white sky.

[47]

"You may think of that a few times in the next six weeks," said Ide beside him. The man was staring hopelessly at the empty sky, prominent eyes watering from the reflected ice glare.

"I doubt it." Michel looked curiously at the unhappy, red-patched face. "If this is such a dismal outpost why did you help me?"

"I wasn't actually helping you. Everything he says I want to say the opposite. He's so damned unruffled and he lives like a native — but still he's a good cop. Maybe it's envy. They don't like me and I can't like them. I don't understand them." He brushed a hand over his wet eyes.

"You ought to wear sunglasses," murmured Michel.

"Sure I ought." He grimaced with cracked lips. "But I don't. Kid defiance. This godforsaken country's like a stepmother, cross and hard and hateful, and no kin to me. Come back to the shed. You're stuck here now, so I'd better rustle up some supplies for you."

Zeke was in the shed, and he sprang up from his couch of sealskins when he saw Michel. His eyes looked sleepless.

"I thought you'd gone home," said Michel. "Didn't you want to watch the plane fly?"

"No. You might be on it."

"Touching," said Ide. "Now you can help us load the sleds."

"I'm glad you stayed, Zeke," said Michel, and the boy looked at him adoringly.

Soon the police sled and Nauligak's were piled high with lumber, coal, window glass, roofing asbestos, tools and canned foods. "Can you spare all this?" asked Michel as the junior constable brought out more armloads and he and Zeke loaded them.

"Sure can. We have enough to last until the ship comes. And I'm not planning to put in any windows or mend any roofs before that. Maybe never," he added with an uncharitable glance toward the police house.

[48]

The sleds were ready, fastened one behind the other, and Zeke was harnessing the dogs. "I'll go up to say good-by to Constable Davitt," said Michel. There was no one in the kitchen, but Nina was dabbing at the living room furniture with a feather duster. The curtains were pulled close over the windows and from the radio a murky adolescent voice sang to the throbbing of an electric guitar. It could have been any little house in any big development. It was not Davitt's style. Michel considered the puzzle momentarily, then dismissed it.

"Constable Davitt?" he asked.

"He is not here," she said carefully, the first words he had heard her speak in English and the first ever addressed to him. They were accompanied by her enticing smile. "You will go on the ship? Perhaps I go then also?" It was both question and invitation, and Michel backed toward the door.

"You wouldn't like where I'm going, young lady," he said severely. "It isn't your style of place at all."

Nina approached him, her hand outstretched, and Michel retreated before her into the kitchen. She opened her hand. In it lay the ivory cigarette holder. "For you," she said. "Remember me." He took it and fled.

"Couldn't find Davitt," he told Ide breathlessly. His face burned with embarrassment.

"I take it you found Nina, though." He crooked his mouth in amusement.

"Yes. For God's sake" — he glanced at Zeke, fixing a harness, and kept his voice low — "take this thing back and leave it around the house when she's not there. The girl's a menace." He thrust the cigarette holder into Ide's parka pocket.

Ide laughed. "She doesn't mean anything. All she yearns for is city lights. I get the treatment once a week."

"I don't care what she yearns for. I don't want to make an enemy of Jacques Davitt. Zeke," he called, "do you know where Constable Davitt is?"

[49]

"He went to Char Fork after the airplane was gone, to see if the water is open for fishing."

"It'll be another month," said Ide. "Jacques knows that better than I do."

"He didn't want to see me and change his mind." Michel shrugged. "That says I'm on my own. All right with me. Let's go, Zeke."

"Good luck," said Ide as they shook hands. "Bring our dogs back tomorrow, Zeke. Don't go on any hunting parties with them."

Zeke looked hurt. "Sure I bring them back. They are not mine. I have my own team."

"Half a dozen ill-mannered pups," said Ide to Michel, "that his father gave him to play with. Ten minutes out of Splaine's River and they'll all be under the sled. He ought to pull it himself and let the dogs ride."

"I train them," said Zeke with dignity. "They will be good dogs. All dogs are once upon a time pups."

"Just don't let him take you near any open seal holes." Ide gave a short nasal laugh. Zeke frowned, his face turned away.

"I'd like to go out with you when you train them, Zeke," said Michel, and the boy smiled gratefully. They sat down on bags of flour, Zeke swung the big whip and called to the dogs, and the heavy sleds bumped slowly over the shore ice, the dogs leaning into the leather and complaining with perfunctory howls. They leaped ahead when they reached the smooth ice, and Michel turned to wave to Ide. The junior constable raised his hand in a mock salute.

In a minute Michel had forgotten him and Davitt and Nina. He turned toward the dark mountain and the distant blue coves. The elusive vision had a name at last. He was going home.

5

THEY WENT straight to Splaine's house. Zeke helped unload, stacking the perishable goods in careful piles well out of the way of roof leaks and the open porch door. Sometimes, in passing, he ran his hand in a light caress over the books or looked fondly at the organ or touched the cold clean stove.

"You're not afraid any more," remarked Michel.

Zeke answered simply, "You are going to live here."

"I already live here. Will you have supper with me?"

"Some day . . ." His glance slid to the floor. "I think I must go now."

The evasiveness was unexpected, and Michel asked bluntly, "Why?" Zeke did not answer. "Oh well, I suppose you have to get back with the dogs. Ide will be biting his fingernails."

"He has none left to bite." The boy's unease had vanished. "Soon, tonight, I will go with my father seal hunting. We will take the two teams and hunt all the way to the police post."

Michel laughed. "That's because Constable Ide told you not to."

"I do only what my father says," said Zeke innocently, adding, "Sometimes I help him know what to say." He untangled the long leads and was off with a wave, a friendly troll dwarfed by the huge dogs and oversized sleds. He would make a mischievous enemy — he and his people. Ide's tortured discontent was a warning.

Alone, Michel heated a can of pork and beans over the primus.

[51]

Without Zeke's cheerful presence the damp dark house depressed him. He took his pan outside and sat on a rock by the muffled river. Fog had melted surface snow on the inlet, and still puddles reflected the topaz of the heatless evening sun. The twin peaks lifted into an immaculate sky, their heads in flame, their icy flanks shadowed blue. A gull swooped, then circled up, shrieking plaintively. Small land birds, larks and snow buntings and longspurs, soared upward and floated down toward flowered mud with showers of song.

His new land was beautiful in its immensity, beautiful in its subtle detail — and frighteningly lonesome.

He rinsed the pan and fork with snow, cupped a mouthful of melt-water into his mouth with his hands, and set off for the hilltop graveyard. It was silent as it had been when he first saw it. His offering was dying, the flowers brown, the willow drooping. Beside them lay tufts of down, black and white feathers and one broken eggshell. Small sharp paw-prints surrounded the grave and disappeared into the nest hole. The silence was suddenly terrible. Death had been here — not the orderly death of crosses and stones. He fled.

The house seemed withdrawn and unfriendly. He dragged the cot from the chilly study that opened off the kitchen, lighted a kerosene lamp and placed it on the table. There was no need for light, but the lamp dispelled the shadows in the corners and made the room look warmer. He unrolled his sleeping bag on the cot, took *Utopia* from the shelf and lay for a long time, trying to read. The reasoned, civilized sentences had no relation to the alien world beyond the lamp; in their place he saw savage little footprints in the snow. At last he fell asleep with the smoky light still in his eyes, the thin gleam of early morning sun probing the tarpaper at the windows.

The sound of bird song woke him. He seemed to have been hearing it in his sleep for hours and sat up with the guilty sense that it was past noon. His watch read eight o'clock and was ticking healthily. Eight in the morning or eight at night? The lamp told him — it was still half full of kerosene and burning dim in the drift of high sunlight that fell across the comfortably ugly golden oak table. Michel jumped out of bed and rummaged in his duffel with nervous haste. He uncovered a small calendar, touched it as if it were a talisman, then nailed it to the wall over the desk. He gazed at it, brows knotted in concentration, and finally crossed off the days that had flowed one into another since the plane had landed in the timeless fog. The calendar was realistic; it was not haunted by long-dead spirits, startled by new death, vulnerable to loneliness, beauty, hostility.

After breakfast he took stock of his new home. Streaks of mold discolored the pine walls, below holes in the roof the floorboards had buckled, the porch was a splintered ruin, tarpaper hung tattered at the paneless windows. The house breathed dissolution. But Splaine's few possessions were as carefully preserved as if a good housewife were lovingly tending them against the return of the long-absent master. The books stood upright in their shelves, the Victrola was dustless on the unwarped table, the organ's clean yellowed keys seemed waiting for someone to touch them, the easy chair displayed cretonne many times washed, faded but spotless. No sleet or snow or winter wind had touched the missionary's earthly belongings, though the ceiling oozed moisture and a fresh spring wind blew through the windows.

Outside he dragged two crates to the porch and climbed gingerly onto its weather-torn roof. The main house roof, at the level of his eyes, was patched with tarpaper in spots over the original red asbestos shingling. These were the spots beneath which lay bookshelves, organ, Victrola, chair. Descending, he circled the house and found other evidences of an attempt to keep it from collapse. The rotting corner posts had been propped with bits of old lumber; the derelict porch was supported by two large stones;

more stones upheld a corner that drooped perilously toward a slight hollow. Someone with few materials had labored with love to keep a forsaken house alive.

Suddenly cheerful, Michel got tools and weathered planks and climbed to the roof. He ripped off a section of the rotten shingling and set about reinforcing or replacing the warped boards. The earth, its northern axis tipped toward the sun, warmed under the high southern light of noon and turned until the sun gleamed in the low northwest and afternoon chill crept from the iced ocean. Still Michel was absorbed, unnoticing of cold hands and empty stomach.

The sound of a child's laughter made him lift his eyes in startlement. Children were sliding down the bank to the ice-covered pond, pushing one another and giggling. On the near side a group of adults approached the house, led by Nauligak, a small hooded figure wrapped in caribou skins. They stopped a few yards away and the children ran to join them. About forty people of all ages — apparently the entire village — stared and gossiped and pointed as if they were on a sight-seeing picnic. Nauligak alone was silent.

Michel descended and went to meet them. He and Nauligak stopped five feet from each other. The chief held an iron-tipped ivory spear bound with strips of leather; his solemn face was framed in wolf fur and he looked at Michel with an impassive, probing stare, all the authority of the North behind him. Michel smiled tentatively and held out his hand. Nauligak made no move, and Michel changed the gesture to a motion toward the box of tools and the new lumber on the roof.

"I'm fixing the house," he said unnecessarily. The chief uttered many words, still facing Michel, and Zeke stepped from the group of young hunters. His voice was formal.

"He has said that the house is already fixed."

"It is well fixed, and I only add a few unimportant things to make it better to live in. Please thank him for all the work he and his people have done to take care of it."

Zeke spoke happily, forgetting his responsible position by the side of his father. "It was only I, and I had nothing to make it beautiful. But I did not want to see the books and the organ lying under the snow. It is good that you are here."

"I knew it was you, Zeke. And you read his books, too, to make your English better, and played on the organ. I could not have stayed here if you hadn't loved his house. Why didn't you tell me?"

Zeke frowned confusedly. "Because — I did not know you — yet." His father interrupted with more guttural speech. "He wants to know if you are the new missionary."

Michel was jolted. "I am not a missionary. He must know that from you and Constable Davitt. I will be here only a few weeks, to see how your people live and write it down for my people."

"I have told him. He does not believe it. When the missionary came my father was already many times a father. The old ways were still believed when he was a grown man. Father Splaine changed everything, and this was his house, and now you are in it."

"Does he want me to be the new missionary?"

"I think — I am not sure — maybe he only wants to know how to act toward you." Zeke smiled appealingly, his eyes troubled, but the ambiguous, halting words were obscurely threatening.

Michel fixed Nauligak with a bright stare. "Do you want me to stay or go?"

Nauligak dropped his eyes then, for the first time, and turned to Zeke. Their slurred conversation held no human emotion; it was a sound of animals. Michel clenched his hands. The old fear haunted him. They weren't going to like him; he wasn't, after all, to be accepted. He was torn. He wanted to run away from the inimical old hunter and his uneasy, evasive son; and he wanted to stay and defend his little house and live in the wondrous isolation of mountains and sea and slow-unfolding spring.

Zeke spoke, carefully expressionless. "He says that it is not for him to say stay or go. It is not his house." Nauligak unexpectedly stepped forward to shake Michel's hand as if to render the armed truce palatable. Behind his father Zeke smiled and was instantly grave again. But his forehead was clear and the smile lingered in small lines around his eyes.

Most of the villagers followed Nauligak and his son back over the hills. A few stayed, a handful of children and three young men, watching while Michel climbed back to the roof. They stared up as if he were something in a cage. He turned his back on them wielded the hammer with impatient defiance and hit himself on the thumb. His jerk of pain upset the box of nails, which slithered down the roof and scattered in the snow. Michel glared at the Eskimos, daring them to laugh.

One man spoke quietly and the children ran to pick up the nails. They lifted their sealskin parkas and wiped the nails on their woolen shirts — each one separately until it shone. The box filled again, the man who had spoken climbed agilely up the porch and ran over the slanted roof to Michel, who still scowled, nursing his sore thumb. The Eskimo picked up a plank and smiled questioningly.

The rankling irritation dissolved. Michel placed a nail carefully while his companion held the plank steady against the roofbeam. The other two young men appeared, each carrying a stone. Grinning shyly, they took a handful of nails and squatted beside Michel, using the stones as hammers. The four worked together in wordless amity until the sun dropped behind the mountain and the sea ice burned sulphur.

The Eskimos swung themselves lightly down to the ground; Michel descended more carefully. He handed around cigarettes, then went inside to make coffee, gesturing them to follow. They stood uncertainly just outside the doorsill.

While the water was on the primus he dug out biscuits and cheese from his unpacked food boxes and looked for cups. Zeke's housewifely care had not extended to washing dishes. Michel surveyed the missionary's tableware, crusted with dirt and mold, and reached for his own tin cup. He waved at the Eskimos hovering at the entrance, the children peering wide-eyed around their legs. "Come in — you must be hungry." They moved from just outside the door to just inside it. Michel poured black coffee over sugar and powdered milk, which rose to the top in a rich fluff. He handed the cup to the nearest man, who gave an embarrassed smile but made no move to take it.

Was it their own idea, or had Nauligak told them not to accept anything?

"I haven't got leprosy," said Michel impatiently. He broke a bar of chocolate in pieces and held them on the palm of his hand, beckoning to the children. In seconds they had downed it and were holding out their hands for more. Michel gave them another bar, watching the young men. Their eyes moved anxiously from him to the children.

He laughed. "Are you afraid I'm going to put them in the cooking pot?" He sipped the coffee and again held out the cup. This time it was accepted gingerly. The young man took a small swallow, his bright eyes on Michel, who nodded encouragingly. He swallowed again and passed the cup on. Michel refilled it and handed out cheese and crackers and more chocolate. The cloud of shyness began to lift. The Eskimos murmured to one another, laughed a little, wandered around the room touching books and organ with careful fingertips, gazed with appreciative wonder at Michel's climbing equipment, ice axe and crampons and smooth coil of nylon rope, marveled at his typewriter open on the table. After a few minutes they approached him one by one, shook hands, spoke soft courteous words, and departed.

They came back the next morning and Zeke was with them. Michel welcomed him warmly, but the boy was elusive, retreating into his Eskimo personality and talking only with his companions.

"Will you help me with the roofing paper, Zeke? The others

can start with the lumber on the other side." Zeke acquiesced but seemed listless as he nailed the asbestos shingling, using a stone as hammer. His head was downcast, his eyes fixed earnestly on his skillful hands.

"Does your father think you are seal hunting today?" asked Michel casually. The boy was absorbed in his stone, examining it on all sides, feeling for the best hold.

"I did not ask my father what he thinks. I am a man." Setting to work with his stone, he hammered a nail with such violence that it flew out of his fingers. Suddenly he laughed. "The nail is alive. It does not like to be hit like a dog but patted like a woman."

"I'm glad you're here."

Zeke looked up then, his eyes alive with happiness, and they set to work again in companionable silence. The muted voices of the others came to them from the far side of the roof. The high sun was hot on their heads and the snow cold fire on their eyes.

"I'm hungry," said Michel. "Come down, let's eat. I've even washed a few cups."

The men showed no hesitancy when he passed the soup. "Yesterday they were afraid to drink coffee with me," said Michel. "Why? Has your father warned them against me?"

Zeke's forehead tensed. "He does not tell them what to do. They are men too. Only he tells them when they must go hunting." He relaxed as he spoke rapidly to the others, and they all laughed. "My father is a great hunter," Zeke explained. "He always knows where the seals are, so we can eat. But it is much work in the winter when it is cold and dark and we stand many hours over a seal hole. Sometimes we would rather be a little hungry and sit in our warm houses and make harpoons. The harpoons are to catch the seals, are they not, so it is important work. But my father says we waste time."

Michel laughed obediently. Some day he might get used to

Zeke's ruse of changing the subject to avoid making a definite statement. "Why wouldn't they drink with me, Zeke?"

Zeke's face was shadowed again. "Sometimes they are not sure of one from outside. Maybe he will not drink from the same cup with our people."

"They know better than that. Look at Davitt . . ." Comprehension hit him. "It was Father Splaine, wasn't it? And because I am living in his house."

Zeke answered reluctantly. "He taught us rules of health. He was a kind man but maybe some thought he was strange . . ."

Michel's thoughts fled to the lonely grave on the hill, and he shivered.

The young men came regularly, two or three, not always the same ones, to help him. They stayed a few hours, accepting coffee and biscuits now with ease before they left. On his sixth day in Splaine's house — he hadn't yet been able to think of it as his own — Michel was working inside, boarding the gaping windows of the little study. He had no use for it, and there was only enough glass for the other two rooms. There were voices outside and he called, "Come in." Nothing happened. Secret sounds came through the wall, whispering, shuffling of feet on rough-grained snow. He felt like overgrown Alice in the rabbit's house. Were they going to send a reluctant Bill in after him?

The porch door, which he had fastened roughly with a piece of wire, opened a crack, and a child stood outlined in the sliver of brightness. His eyes were large and apprehensive through a ragged fringe of black hair. "Hello, Bill," said Michel heartily. The alarmed child disappeared.

Michel strode to the porch and threw the door open. It crashed against the wall and swung crookedly, its rusty hinges creaking. A group of young men and children backed away, smiling uncertainly, looking in every direction but at him. Hands on hips, face red, Michel stood over the polite-faced little crowd.

"What is it?" He tried not to sound belligerent.

Zeke stepped forward uneasily. "I told them not to," he stammered. "I said you were not the new missionary . . . It is Sunday . . . They used to come here."

Michel breathed slowly and deeply, remembering Ide, willing the flush to leave his cheeks and the anger to leave his voice and Nauligak to leave his mind. "Tell them, Zeke, that no matter what *anyone* says I am not a missionary. I will not read the service because I am not an ordained minister and I am not religious in a minister's way. God is not in a book or a hymn, or a mountain or a cloud, he is only in our minds."

Zeke spoke haltingly to the others, evidently floundering. Puzzled faces turned from Zeke to Michel. No one spoke as they slowly turned to leave, drooping a little as if they had been scolded.

"Wait!" called Michel. "Please all come in. You won't get the service, but I can tell stories and sing and play the organ. I am sure God would like us to be happy on Sunday." Zeke translated rapidly and the bent heads lifted. They followed Michel into the house, still diffident but smiling, sat on the floor and looked up with expectancy at the tall man at the organ. Michel pumped vigorously, the bellows rasped, chords shuddered and died beneath his fingers, then unexpectedly took new life with a squealing roar. Over the racket he bellowed in a strong, untrained bass all the livelier folksongs and ballads he could remember. Before each song he turned to his audience and slowly recited the words. Zeke translated, then repeated them in English, and the Eskimos, now entirely at ease, laughed as they stumbled over the unfamiliar syllables. Within an hour they knew most of the choruses and tunes of the gaudy old favorites, and the shaky house trembled with their voices — basses, high young tenors, piping child tones.

At the end Michel opened the volume of Bach chorales. The voices slowly died away, and the quiet noble hymns filled the room.

Michel's heart lifted with the sound, as he knew would the others'. His ingrained reticence found a temporary outlet. Music had always made friends. At last he slid his feet from the pumps and let his arms drop. The people sat unmoving in reverent silence.

"I feel as if I'd been climbing the Matterhorn hog-calling all the way up," said Michel into the churchlike stillness. "Let's have coffee."

"I'll get it," said Zeke and quickly slipped into the kitchen, followed by his three little brothers. The young men talked and smoked black pipes while the children flocked to the typewriter like filings to a magnet. Michel rolled in a sheet of paper, took the hand of the nearest child and guided the small index finger over the keys, spelling out one slow sentence. He pulled the paper out and handed it to the child. It disappeared beneath a huddle of smooth black heads, and in a few seconds eight index fingers were extended toward the machine, eight pairs of shining eyes begged him. A short time later eight more typed sheets were happily clutched.

"Bless you, Zeke," said Michel as the boy appeared with a length of board covered with cups, plates, biscuits, jam and honey. "You've done the rest of my dishes!"

The boy grinned widely as he passed the rude tray. "Only one time. It is for a woman, not a hunter, to clean dishes."

"Don't find me any woman," said Michel hastily. "I'll do my own."

One of the children handed his typed paper to Zeke with a soft-voiced question. "Michel is not a missionary," he read out loud. The others crowded around him with theirs.

"They're all the same," said Michel. "My propaganda leaflets. You promised to help me, Zeke. Will you tell everyone what the papers say?"

Zeke frowned uncomfortably and his "Yes" came low, after a short silence.

"You think I'm pushing it too hard. I intend to. Everything

is to be clearly understood." He looked straight at Zeke and the boy's eyes slid away. "Your father, I think, doesn't like missionaries, and I don't want to be classed with the people your father doesn't like." His tone was cold and the boy looked up again, troubled.

"It's only me from over the sea!" a hoarse voice called from a corner, and Zeke's face cleared as he joined the raucous chorus.

6

HUNTING claimed Michel's helpers. He worked mostly alone, and when the young hunters came they looked tired.

"Your father makes them work too hard," he told Zeke.

"They must. We need skins to trade and the ship will be here soon."

"You have fox and ermine."

"The silverjar is good now — the young ringed seal that were born in early spring. We must have many skins, to make up for next year."

"What's the matter with next year?"

"There will be nothing," said Zeke bleakly. "We caught too many foxes and weasels in our traps. We caught owls and ravens too. They all came because they could not find food." He pointed to the ground, where last year's dead grass did not quite cover the pitted remains of lemming burrows. "They are old holes. When the mice go away the other animals have nothing to eat. First they come to our traps, and then the ones who are left starve or go somewhere else."

"But you'll eat," said Michel, remembering the furs shimmering in the darkness of Nauligak's storeroom. "You can buy the whole ship. You'll need a storekeeper . . ." He stopped, astonished at the idea that had appeared full-blown, unannounced. In momentary silence he looked out over the ice as if he could find there the origin of his thought. The weather had been still and cloudless for a week, with the spicy chill of spring, and under the high sun the melting sea ice was a geometric abstract in blues: cold star sapphire, glowing turquoise, rich amethyst in sharp-etched polygons. The horizon trembled, and at the rocky gateway to the open ocean stood two tall Gothic mirage-towers slightly lifted off the surface. The heavy mass of the guardian mountain thrust out of the sea, its folds of cliff shining with new water, its twin peaks bearing drifts of cloud. A snow bunting sang on the new red roof as if he owned it. "Said Barnacle Bill the Sailor" floated recurrently on the ice-pure air, spaced with throaty Eskimo words and loud laughter and punctuated by hammer taps.

Six weeks was not going to be long enough. If the writing did not go well — so far it was hardly going at all — perhaps he had found another way to stay on.

Michel sighed. "Do you ever think it's beautiful, Zeke?"

Zeke had been looking out to sea too, eyes narrowed in concentration. "Seal out there — three, maybe four. I run back and get my gun quick." He added, gently serious, "I do not know any other place, Michel." It was the first time he had addressed his friend by name. He was gone before Michel could remind him that he had been to school in a big city.

The windowpanes were in and now, at last, it was a real house and it belonged to Michel, not to the dead man on the hill. When the sun lowered toward the mountain, Michel walked all over his house. The weathered pine boards of the floor and walls, repaired with old lumber, shone pale gray with sanding and scrubbing. The reinforced rafters were thick, to withstand the Arctic wind. The little black pot-bellied stove had a shining new stovepipe. A faint sweet-acrid smell of coal smoke escaped from the draft of the softly hissing kitchen range; pots and dishes shone. The house was bare except for Splaine's few belongings, Michel's typewriter and his only picture, the little calendar on the wall. He had no need for pictures. His front windows gave on the seaward promontory, now painted with flowers — purple lupine, cinquefoil yellow as sunlight, pale dryas open-eyed to the sky, downcast waxy heads of bell heather, miniature daisies — and willow dusty green against sparse new grass; beyond it the sea ice was gilded by slanting sunlight. On the west side the colors of spring gave way to snow as the hills rose to the mountain, still holding its fire-touched collar of vapor. On the east, through the broken porch, he could see the hollowed cover of ice on the river and hear the experimental purling of water, a whispered undertone to cascading bird song.

Michel went to his typewriter unwillingly. A thin pile of paper lay beside it, but the words were lifeless against the radiant vitality outside. Writing, he found, was increasingly difficult. Unaccountably this did not disturb him.

"Today I saw twenty-five snow geese," he wrote inconsequentially, "courting on the other side of the river." His hands dropped and he looked out the window, finishing the thought silently. By the time the geese have made their nests my house will be finished. When they have raised their young and molted and grown shining white again they will gather and fly south, ten thousand of them in proud arrow-shaped flocks, filling the air with wild clear calls. And I? — when my house is done who will live in it? Will I fly south too? These windows should have curtains to tame the savage view — curtains of silverjar seal shadowed and faintly yellow like the evening sea ice.

He stood aside for a moment and looked at himself. I'm beginning to forget the world I knew, he said to the strange image. I never felt this way before; no place has claimed me as this one has.

He closed the typewriter, sat down at the organ and wheezed through a dozen chorales, pumping vigorously, still thinking. Have to mend these bellows. Have to rebuild the porch for food and ice. Have to climb the mountain. Have to paint the kitchen walls. Have to . . . He dreamed on happily while the nighttime sun moved imperceptibly along the horizon, not quite touching, from the northwest to northeast.

Next morning he slept late, and the smell of fire woke him. He sat up, his mind awash with horror, still half asleep. The sunny room was blue with smoke, and at the far side crouched a dim figure, fat and featureless. At his shocked outcry the figure straightened and turned and he saw Mauyak, the chief's diminutive daughter, swathed amorphously in caribou, her wide face impish in the orange light of the stove fire. She spoke briefly, lifted her hand to adjust something on the chimney, and closed the stove door. The smoke drifted out the open doorway and the fire settled to a hushed crackle.

Michel swore, pulled his trousers over the long wool underwear that served as pajamas, grabbed a towel and soap and brushed past her out the door. Damn the girl, he muttered, splashing icy water on his chest and arms and face. Could have set the house on fire. Could have caught me without my pajamas. He raised his numbed face and hands to the clear high sun. A light wind wafted an aroma of bacon and coffee. Damn the kid, she doesn't know how I like my bacon fried. Still growling, he went back to the house. She was frying a slice of seal liver in the bacon grease. He turned his back on her and frowned furiously while he finished dressing.

Breakfast was on the table, irresistible. He sat down to eat it, deliberately looking out the window. Mauyak rustled softly behind him, shaking out his sleeping bag, hanging it over the porch railing to air, sweeping the floor with a brush of sedge grass, fetching water. Then there was a brief silence. Michel turned suspiciously, to see her half disappeared into his duffel, her shapeless little rump in the air.

"Here, you . . ." he exclaimed. But she was already out, smiling at him, holding several pairs of dirty socks. Before he could say anything she dove in again for more. Michel grunted and stamped to the porch. He knelt and ripped at decayed floorboards as if he were punishing them, while Mauyak went back and forth past him, her hands full of wet clothing, her eyes brushing his with a merry sidelong glance.

The washed clothes lay on a patch of grass, anchored with stones, and there was silence again in the house. Michel peered around the corner and saw her sitting in the big easy chair darning an old gray work shirt with green wool. Her eyes were demurely downcast, her black braids shone against wide flat ivory cheeks.

He walked over and confronted her. "Ma — Maggie — whatever they call you," he began severely. She looked up at him, the planes of her face rounded and softened by her very young shy smile. "Little one," he went on, his voice less sharp, "it's time to go home to Mother. Thank you for the breakfast and all."

She spoke, her low sweet voice rising at the end in a question. Taking her hand, he pulled her up and propelled her gently toward the door. When he tried to take his shirt from her she murmured melodiously and pointed to the half-done mending. He waved in the direction of the village. "All right, take it with you. I'll pick it up sometime." Mercifully she was gone. He would speak sternly to Zeke.

But Zeke did not come that day, nor did his friends. Michel counted back; it had been four days since he had heard the chattering singing voices. He worked hard, fighting loneliness and unease, and went to bed before the sun touched the mountain. In the morning he was up early, racing through the chores to forestall the girl. His fire, built too hastily with damp splintered wood from the porch floor, smoldered sullenly and went out just as he had the water on. Impatiently he lit the primus and made an inadequate breakfast. He was still gulping the meager meal, standing up, when cool air touched him and Mauyak was inside, her feet noiseless in the supple sealskin boots. He reddened, started to speak, choked on a biscuit crumb, spluttered and glared down at her, his blue eyes fierce.

She backed away, then, with a placating childlike smile, held out the shirt. It was finely mended in five places with many colors of bright wool, and a square of red plaid covered the pocket. In spite of himself he laughed and her soft voice echoed. Reaching into a fold of her garment, she pulled out a small leather bag and showed him its contents. Among the skeins of wool was one strand of dull gray, a match for his old shirt. She picked it out, wrinkling her small nose and shaking her head, then held the harlequin shirt wide, nodding enthusiastically. Michel looked down at the drab little creature lost in her hairless caribou robe; and understood.

"Maggie, have coffee with me." He brought a cup, poured and handed it to her. She sat sideways to him, on the edge of her chair, not looking up while she drank. Quickly finished, she gathered the breakfast dishes and went out for water, face still carefully averted. When the bit of housework was done she left, small feet quick on the snow, one swift look back at him standing in the doorway. "Thank you, Maggie," he called. She waved and was gone.

Even the birds were quiet during the long hot midday. No breeze stirred the grass, and wide-petaled flowers, close to the ground, stared motionless at the sun. The river whispered hypnotically against its ice cover. Sawing and hammering, Michel broke the stillness, but whenever he stopped it enveloped him as if he were becalmed on a limitless ocean. Later, when the sun was low and the cold night wind came off the inlet and the birds sang again, he put away his tools and sat by the window, gazing at the moon-colored landscape and scooping lukewarm beans from a tin.

The forlorn supper done, he set a cracked record of Strauss waltzes on the wind-up Victrola, uncovered his typewriter and poised his fingers resolutely over the keys. Nothing happened. The large loneliness outside reduced his thoughts to impotent littleness, and the warped music vied unsuccessfully with the cries and songs of the wild birds.

The North couldn't be confined on paper. Michel's purpose in coming here was negatived. I should have left the first day, he thought; it's a fine place to live but you wouldn't want to visit.

Footsteps sounded and Michel jumped up eagerly, overturning the chair. "Zeke!" he cried. The boy grinned tiredly. His eyes were large, blue-circled, and his cheeks drawn. "Zeke, it's good to see you again. Where were you?"

"At the floe edge, where the ocean meets our ice, looking for walrus. Two sleeps away."

"But no sleeps for you."

"No walrus either. Too much ice, moving fast all the time, far out in the ocean. The walrus do not like that, and they have gone somewhere else."

"But they'll come back when the ice melts?"

"Not here. They want big floes like islands, or flat rocks. There are no good rocks here, and this year no good ice." His face was old with fatigue and worry. "Walrus is our summer meat. Seals are hard to catch after the ice goes, and have not much meat."

"You have plenty of furs to trade. Don't you get enough food when the ship comes to last all winter?"

"We hunt all winter," said Zeke simply.

"You need a trader," said Michel, half to himself. The idea slowly taking shape no longer surprised him. "Zeke, I want silver-jar seal. Can you sell me a few skins? I'll pay you money and you can buy more food from the ship than if you traded directly."

The weariness lifted momentarily. "I will bring many skins and you take only the best. You are kind to help us. I will get them now. After a short sleep, maybe two days," he added with a faint grin as he turned to go.

"Oh, one more thing . . ." Michel tried to sound offhand but he felt his face flushing. "Your little sister . . . she's been coming here, cleaning up and so forth. It's good of her, but . . . well, I guess she has a lot to do at home, helping her mother . . ."

Zeke chuckled. "She is a woman, my little sister, ready to be married."

Michel, startled, turned redder. "Did you tell her to come here?"

"No. I do not tell her anything." His voice was contemptuous. "She is good with needles and stoves. You do not have to speak to her. She is only a woman."

Unexpectedly, Michel defended her. "Your women are just as important as your men and I bet they're cleverer."

"Yes. It is not that. It is . . . I have learned from Father Splaine, and I am your friend." His glance at Michel held shy pride. "Mauyak is just Mauyak and will never be anything else."

"She can learn too."

"She did not," said Zeke shortly, "and she will not. She wants to be the way she is, the old way." His expression held confused annoyance, and Michel had a glimmer of understanding. Zeke's way had many paths, and often he paused at blind forks wondering which way led to the cliff and which to the valley — which was his father's way and which the white man's. But Mauyak's softly shod feet took her unhesitatingly down a straight road. Michel did not ponder what lay at the end of Mauyak's road.

"Ease up, Zeke," he said with the voice of an indulgent uncle. "It doesn't matter to me what Mauyak thinks or does. If she wants to clean and cook here I'll pay her."

"What would *she* do with money? She would make earrings out of pennies and fold dollars into toy boats for the little ones."

"There are worse things to do with money." Obscurely, they were quarreling. Michel gave a quick laugh and patted the boy's shoulder. "I do believe you're jealous. As you say, your sister is just a girl." Zeke smiled uncertainly. "By the way, why doesn't your mother give her anything to wear?"

"No need for a girl," said Zeke scornfully, "until she marries."

"She won't get a husband the way she looks."

Zeke, looking out the window, pointedly shifted the conversation. "The ice will not last much longer. When I wake up, when I bring the skins, we will go out and train the young dogs."

Michel gazed at him appreciatively. "Talking to you is some-times like handling an eel," he said. "Yes, I would like to go out with you, when you've finished sleeping."

Zeke came late in the morning two days later, driving his inex-pert team, his small sled piled high. Mauyak ran out of the house, her bare arms glistening with soapsuds, and jumped on the lead dog, who seemed about to enter the house. The others piled up behind, squealing and barking, in a tangle of traces. As the trapped puppies fell on their backs, oversized paws waving helplessly, Zeke and Mauyak waded into the heap with shrieks of merriment and set about extricating them. All children playing together, thought Michel, smiling his uncle smile. He approached a large puppy. It lifted black lips over long white teeth and backed away, snarling, until its trace brought it up short and it fell suddenly backward. Zeke picked it up with one hand, loosed the harness and threw the dog into a willow clump. It landed on its back again, stood up with a surprised expression, shook itself thoroughly and trotted down to the beach, curling plume high. Zeke laughed and Michel's face turned red.

They brought the skins into the house and spread them over the floor, a carpet of sleek shining fur, shadow-ringed and tinged with yellow as if the daybreak sun touched them. Their smell filled the room, pungent and oily, sensuously animal.

"I'll take them all," said Michel instantly.

Zeke was doubtful. "Some are better than others — you must choose."

"No, Zeke, I can't choose. I want them all . . ." He paused. "Unless . . . Zeke, how did you get so many? Did your father give them to you?"

"I caught them. And Kooluk and Itarvak and Lalinga — those who help you with the house."

"Does your father know?"

"He knows that we caught them." Zeke's eyes were blank and his words toneless. Unexplained fear touched Michel. He quelled it.

"Tell him I'll pay you well for them."

It was a short while before Zeke said "Yes" noncommittally, his expression guarded.

"Come, Zeke, take me out on the ice. I want to subdue those wild animals of yours."

The boy came alive again. "Sure, Michel. You teach them, they teach you. Everybody goes to school at once. Bring your gun."

"For the dogs?"

Zeke laughed as he went out. "For the seals. We will teach them too."

7

THE YOUNG DOGS scrambled over the rotting beach ice and set their noses toward the far hills across the inlet. The ice was a sea of long furrows and waves pointing east toward the open ocean. They crossed these, the sled pitching, to look, Zeke said, for tidal open-water leads in the center of the inlet where there might be seal. The dogs scrambled back and forth across their fan-shaped harnessing, weaving a mesh of long traces. They bumped into one another straining up the sides of ridges, then tripped over the lines as the sled careened downward. There was a continual chorus of short howls as one dog after another was dragged along by its harness. Righting themselves, they briskly shook off the snow and the fringed tails went up. Zeke sat on the front of the sled flicking his whip lightly among the tangled pups. Michel, at the back, the sled box he had packed with tea, sugar, jam and pilot biscuits held firmly between his knees, looked at sky, ice and mountains and tasted salt on the wind from the ocean. Behind was a child's picture: two wavering lines led back over wrinkled white paper to a paint-splotched hill. A square toy red-roofed house sat on the hill with a straight line of smoke pointing into sky improbably blue.

He was suddenly glad to be away from that tidy house. "Thanks for bringing me out, Zeke," he called. "I've seen nothing but the house for days — weeks."

Zeke turned and grinned. "When you see only the house you get house sickness. Also I like help on a seal trip."

"I won't be much help. I've never hunted. And they" — he pointed to the dogs — "don't like me."

Zeke started to speak, but one of his dogs caught a front paw in another's trace and fell on his back. The others trampled over him and the sled plunged downhill and turned on its side among the dogs. Without thinking, Michel picked up the squirming dog that had landed on his arm, unfastened its harness and tossed it ungently on the snow. Zeke gave a brief smiling nod through the howling turmoil and Michel, all at once confident, went after another big snarling puppy.

"Time for tea," said Zeke finally.

"But we haven't even been out an hour."

"What is an hour? When the traces are mixed up, then it is time for tea."

Michel laughed. "We'll be having tea all day."

"That is all right. The seals are not going anywhere. They wait for us." Reaching into the sled box, he brought out a pilot biscuit and a jar of jam. He spread the jam with his long hunting knife and put the whole dripping biscuit in his mouth, eyes roving continuously over the ice. Suddenly he jumped up, rummaged in the box and came out with two sticks nailed in a cross and a square of white cloth looped with leather at the corners. He slid the loops over the ends of the cross to make a shield, seized his rifle and ran off.

Michel strained his eyes and saw a seal, a dark shape far away on the sea of ice waves. Another took form and still another — a whole family of seals, sound asleep. He reached for his binoculars and focused. The seals had no heads, no bodies, no flippers. Flotsam ice . . . Michel grinned painfully and turned the glasses on Zeke, who was now creeping behind his shield. Then Michel saw the seal, a moving grayness among pale snow shadows. Its head went up and down in mechanical rhythm as it scented the air in half-sleep. Zeke's crawl slowed, then stopped. A light clear whistle sounded and the seal's head lifted high, alert. It dropped suddenly to the snow, and seconds later the report of the rifle reached Michel. It reached the dogs too. They had been sitting vigilant, wolf ears pointed toward their master. At the sharp sound they stood up and Michel swung the heavy whip through the air in front of them. It snapped back and coiled itself around him like a wet python. The dogs bounded away, trailing traces and loosened harnesses, the sled lurching behind them. Michel unwound the dank spiral and set off at a run, shouting at the dogs, tripping over hummocks, splashing through icy puddles.

Zeke, standing beside his dead seal with a ring of suddenly obedient dogs around him, laughed as Michel stumbled toward him dragging the whip. Michel flushed, glared, then laughed too.

The boy drew his long knife from its leather sheath, touched the seal's belly with the feather-edged point and swiftly drew a long deep gash. A fetid stench gushed into the fresh sea air and the two involuntarily stepped back.

"Tiggak — old male," said Zeke wrinkling his nose. "His skin is no good, his meat is no good. We will feed him to the dogs." He went back to the bloody slit and began stripping the flesh from the hide. Michel forced himself to watch until the dogs had finished eating and were quarreling over bones and flippers.

"I wouldn't eat that if I were starving," he remarked as Zeke cleaned his dark-dripping knife in the snow and dried it carefully.

"No, you would not. No one from outside can eat it."

"Could you?"

"Yes, to stay alive. I would close my eyes and nose. A bad smell is not so bad as dying."

"Have you ever been that hungry?"

"No. My father was, on a winter hunt long ago, when I was young. It was a very bad time, with nothing to eat." Zeke fell

[75]

silent and stared grimly over the ice, past Michel's shoulder. "There is another seal," he said finally.

"Tell me about your father's winter hunt."

"I was not there." He handed the shield to Michel. "You take that seal, Michel." Michel turned and looked at the blackness that lay on the ice too far away to distinguish form. "Here is your gun. Go quickly before he wakes up."

"You are changing the subject," said Michel, but he went. Cautiously he crawled over the ice waves, now losing his quarry, now for an instant seeing it again. The thing appeared to change shape continuously — at least it was alive. Judging thirty yards, he stopped, whistled once, then fired. The sooty mass dissolved into a flock of ravens flapping heavily off the ice with angry calls. Michel was not surprised. One was left behind dragging a broken wing, and he killed it gently, pinching the area around its heart.

There was a smothered laugh; Zeke was right behind him doubled up with mirth. "Your seal flew away!" he gasped.

"It was a sky seal," said Michel lightly. He swung the dead bird by the feet in a wide arc and let go. It riffled past Zeke's ear and landed among the dogs. In a few seconds there was only a handful of feathers on the scuffed snow.

"I don't think you meant to teach me, Zeke, but I'm learning. Now I know what a seal doesn't look like."

They had tea again, Zeke still chuckling, Michel quiet, wondering why the boy had needed his joke. After eating, Zeke stood up and scanned the ice thoroughly with Michel's binoculars. "There are no seals out here now. We will go in to the mountain where a river comes down and opens a hole in the ice. Good place for young seal."

The dogs ran towards shore as if winged, but Zeke turned them off, with difficulty, where the lowest ramparts of the mountain touched the sea, and headed west, away from home. There were small water-filled cracks in the ice here where tides had crushed it against the rocks. The dogs hesitated and jumped, ears flattened, tails down. Before a wider gulf the lead dog slowed, sniffed at the water, then sat down, looking miserably back at his master. Zeke flicked the whip, raising a plume of snow beside him, but the dog refused to move.

He laughed. "They are still babies, afraid of water." He jumped off the sled and unfastened the main trace. "Please hold this. I will make a bridge for the frightened little ones."

Michel held the trace uneasily, digging his heels into the rough snow, but the dogs stood still, dejected and trembling, while their master bridged the gap with his sled. He ran back across it, took the trace from Michel and dragged at his dogs, shouting gutturally. They crossed sheepishly, one by one, and paused on the other side, humiliated, noses nearly touching the snow, while Zeke put the outfit back together again.

"They will not be afraid now."

"They won't dare to be," said Michel.

The mountain loomed over them, sheer cliffs dropping to the tide-ravaged ice. They turned into a hidden inlet, a fold in the cliffs. A ravine held a twisted gray glacier unraveling into a narrow cataract. At its foot was a lightless pool. Above the deep bubbling murmur of the waterfall was another sound, thin and high, doleful as a lost child.

Zeke studied the ragged ice of the lake shore. "There is a seal pup. His mother is away and he is hungry. I cannot see him but I can see where he is. The hill of snow near the far rocks — that is his house. He is afraid to leave and hides there, maybe inside, maybe behind. Go for him."

"No jokes, Zeke?"

"Not this time." He grinned. "Maybe tomorrow."

Michel headed away from the querulous barking cries, far out on the ice, and came in upwind, keeping the west wall of the inlet between himself and the snow mound. Reaching the rocks that guarded the harbor, he climbed the nearest and peered over the edge.

A very young, downy-furred seal lay by its snow den just below him, complaining incessantly, big tears falling from its round dark eyes. Fifty yards away, across the roiled black pond, Zeke stood watching him. Behind the seal, in the cliff, was a cave where trapped water growled against the ice. The falling river muttered and a cold wet breath touched Michel's face like a warning from the mountain.

He raised his rifle, sighted one foggy eye, then lowered it again. "You're safe from me, little one," he whispered, and started to back down the rock. There was a cry and the seal lifted its head. Zeke had his rifle at his shoulder.

"Damn you, Zeke, with your jokes!" Michel raised his gun and shot in the moment of sighting, then dropped it as if it had burned him. The absurd bewhiskered head fell, and Michel, already running toward it, saw blood from the pierced eye mingle with the tears. A huge blurred form erupted from the cave behind it. There was a second cry, and Michel drew up abruptly, too late.

Over the body of the seal he and the polar bear from the cave stared at each other an instant in total disbelief. Michel slowly backed away, feeling for his knife. The bear shambled toward him, then charged, rearing on its hind legs. Small red eyes far above him, long yellow fangs and giant claws were all Michel saw as he turned his right shoulder and drove the blade home. He was hardly aware of a small thud overhead like stone hitting rubber. A claw raked down his sleeve and they fell together.

Gently Zeke drew them apart. Michel's knife was still in the bear's body, its hilt convulsively clutched in his fist. Blood streamed from his torn shoulder, and when Zeke tugged at the clenched hand the bear's blood fountained over his own. Michel stared at it without understanding, then turned his head slowly to the leaning cliffs, to the sharp-shadowed sea ice, to the far snow-pale horizon, to the blue and white spring sky. Only the monotonous plashing of the cataract broke the intense pristine silence of snow and ice and rock.

[78]

"It has just been created," he said. "Just now, for me. I should be dead." He gazed at the sprawling carcass of the bear and the pitiful soft-furred seal. Tears came, and he shivered violently. He shook the tears away and smiled apologetically. "Death is still too close."

"I know," said Zeke. He had taken off his fur parka and laid it over Michel's shoulders. "It makes you cold. Sit still. I will look at this bear." He took the white cloth of his seal shield from the sled and laid it over the bear's head, then examined the body, lifting each heavy paw.

"He was crazy," he said finally, "or he would not have tried to kill you. Look." He pointed to a raw tear exposing the tendons of a hind leg and still suppurating. "He could not go where the hunting was good — he could not hunt at all. When he saw your seal he was hungry and you were in his way. He came out of the cave quickly. I called and tried to shoot, but you were both behind the seal's house . . ." The words kept pouring out, too fast.

Michel was not listening. He was staring at the baby seal. "I thought you were after it. I was not going to kill it. It should not have died," he said tonelessly.

Zeke lifted the seal, weighing it in his hands. It hung limp, seemingly fleshless under the thick white fur. "Michel, listen to me." Michel forced his tranced gaze up and found Zeke's eyes on him, warm with compassion. "This one was starving too. His mother must have been killed and he was too young to find his own food. He could not swim. He could not even fly." He laughed, and Michel, awake at last, laughed too.

Zeke helped him to the sled, made him lie down and tucked a caribou skin around him. He tied the seal on the end of the sled, started it with a smart push, and jumped on, calling the dogs. Michel closed his eyes wearily on the gloomy cove and its corpse. Then they flew open again and he raised himself, turning to Zeke. "Did you cover the dead?" he asked, astounded. "I don't think even Father Splaine would have gone that far."

[79]

The back of Zeke's head was to him. "The ravens must not get his eyes," he said carefully to the dogs. "It is a good skin and must not be spoiled."

"But a cloth . . ." Michel was incredulous. "That's not going to stop any raven. Now a scarecrow . . ." His mind began to wander. A snowman in Maggie's flapping caribou robe . . . He succumbed to the swaying of the sled. The ice rippled under them, the pups raced toward home, easily leaping the water crevasses, and Michel was rocked to sleep.

They did not go to Michel's house but sped past, only slowing when they came to the ice debris at Nauligak's beach. Dazed from loss of blood and the hypnotic motion of the sled, Michel asked no questions as Zeke helped him over the beach and into his father's house. Half fainting, he saw Mauyak's tranquil face and eyes, for once not gay but unfathomable as she knelt before him to pull off his boots. He felt Aitu's gentle, experienced fingers cutting away the ragged sleeve and rubbing soothing ointment into the long gash. Then he closed his eyes and knew no more.

When he awoke the house was filling. Children, young men, old women crowded in until it seemed the walls must give way, and still more came, smiling and questioning, staring at Michel with admiring curiosity. Aitu sat beside him to keep a quiet space in the bursting room, but it was not necessary. The visitors kept apart with instinctive courtesy, respecting his wound.

This was Zeke's hour, and he held his audience bewitched. He talked histrionically, acting as the drama unfolded. First he was Michel shooting the seal; now he was the bear, grotesque, clawing the air and grimacing with teeth bared as the knife entered its ribs. Once Nauligak interrupted with a question. The boy answered boldly and repeated the stabbing and falling pantomine to the shocked delight of the company. Only Michel noticed the old hunter frown and shake his head. The others were repeating the story to one another, turning again and again to the wounded man with marveling smiles. Several spoke to him.

"They want to bring the bear home for you," said Zeke, "and their women will cure the skin. But it is not necessary."

"It is very kind." He turned to the young men. "Thank you. As soon as I am strong again we will all go out."

Zeke intervened, speaking rapidly to his friends. "I will do it," he told Michel, "and Mauyak knows well how to cure a skin." The girl, quiet in the corner by the cooking lamp, looked over at him with a flicker of a smile.

"Zeke, don't go without me," he said firmly. "I will help to skin my own bear." Zeke looked dismayed, and Michel quickly added, "But they shall have all the meat. And please tell them that I'm not all that good. You were there — you know I was reckless, and no hunter."

Zeke spoke briefly to the crowd. "I told them about the meat. Let them think as they wish. It is a new story for the long winter night."

"And their grandchildren's grandchildren will tell a legend of a saint killing a dragon. Who will ever know the truth?" Zeke looked at him with alarm, but Michel, faint again, lay back on the piled furs and smiled ruefully as one by one the young men came to shake his hand.

It was three days before Michel could walk without dizziness; then he told Zeke they would go back to the inlet.

"You need not," said Zeke. "I will go with Mauyak."

"It isn't a woman's work," said Michel stubbornly. "She can come if she wants. But I will be there. After all, it's my bear."

Zeke hesitated, doubt in his eyes. "Come on, Zeke. I won't do anything foolish again." He walked firmly down the beach to the sled, careful not to show the weakness in his legs. Zeke followed unwillingly. Mauyak was already there, folding skins against the sled box for Michel to lean against. With shy tenderness, eyes averted, she tucked a robe around his knees, then seated herself in the front, near her brother. Every now and then she glanced back.

When the chill breath of the inlet hit Michel he shivered, and Mauyak looked at him with concern. "It's all right, Maggie," he said, consciously squaring his shoulders. But when the carcass seemed to disintegrate into a flock of croaking ravens, Michel stepped back abruptly.

"Tell Maggie to stay with the sled," he ordered.

"It is safe now," said Zeke. "But you should stay back. You are still sick."

"I am fine. Don't treat me like a child."

Zeke spoke to Mauyak, his voice uncertain, but she smiled and obediently sat on the sled. The two men advanced with caution, rifles ready, eyes on the black cave mouth. They stared down at the huge corpse.

"I didn't think there would be any bear left by now," remarked Michel. "Cloth or no cloth."

"No, there would not. But I was here to guard it."

Michel glanced at him curiously. "All the time?"

"Yes, until today."

They rolled the heavy body on its back. Zeke slit it up the belly to the throat, and together they flensed, slipping their knives carefully between skin and flesh, cutting the meat out chunk by chunk. Michel lifted the large heart. It was intact. A flicker of doubt touched him.

"I will do the head," said Zeke, moving quickly to stoop over the great head, hiding it. But Michel was faster. He knelt by the once fierce red eye and tearing teeth and turned the head toward him. The other eye socket was clotted with blood, the fur around it blasted, the flesh raw.

He straightened and stared at Zeke. "You killed him. Not I."

Zeke turned away and spoke low. "I was only watching. He came out of the cave quickly and then you were both behind the snow hill. When I saw him again he was on you and my rifle went off. You killed him."

"My knife did not even reach his heart. Why did you lie for me?"

"Because you are a brave man. You stood to the bear. If I had been there I would have run."

Michel shook his head sadly. "You hid the head so I wouldn't see it and guarded it alone so no one else would find out. But they will."

"Please do not tell them. They love you."

"They love the story," said Michel, "and your father already knows."

"He cannot know," said Zeke uneasily. "No one has been here. No one will ever know. Mauyak is clever with skins." Michel turned to the girl. She had left the sled and was working on the skin, scraping off the fat with a wide curved blade. Her face, bent over the bloody work, was innocent and soft and she lifted dancing eyes in a quick glance at him. "She is proud of you too," added Zeke.

"As you said, she is only a girl. But you, my good friend — my only friend — have made me either a liar or a fool. How can I change you?"

Zeke frowned in worried puzzlement. "I do not understand you."

"I don't understand you, Zeke."

8

IT WOULD BE an Arctic house, with windows framed in silverjar, wide to the gold-white nights. The stone carver Saloositak Tana would make him soapstone and ivory sculptures. Caribou would cover his chair. There would be no chintz and cretonne in this house, no curtains suburbanly closed against the night sunlight. No Nina either.

He picked up one of the sealskins and held it lengthwise beside the window. Measuring quickly, fingers to elbow, he calculated eighteen skins, three on each side of the three windows. Zeke had brought him twenty-one. The remaining three would make mittens and boot tops, and he would buy more for a jacket, and later on a warm lined parka. Later on . . . he downed the instant pang of sorrow that there might be no later on.

With a tent-mending kit he tried clumsily to stitch two skins end to end. They didn't fit together; the thin, brittle leather tore at the edges; the heavy needle pierced his finger.

"Hell," said Michel, and heard a soft laugh. Mauyak stood in the kitchen doorway. He had forgotten she was there and he scowled, embarrassed. She approached shyly and took the skins from his inexpert fingers. Out of a fold in her large garment she produced her curved scraping knife and neatly trimmed the two skins. Taking the edge of one in her mouth, she worked across it with her white teeth, then did the same with the other. She laid the edges together, threaded her own needle with caribou thong, and plied it in and out with swift small stitches. She had settled in the easy chair and looked as if she were there for the day.

Michel watched her for a while, then got a can of white paint and started on the kitchen walls. But her presence prickled: she was too domestic. He worked himself up to exasperation and finally slapped the lid on the paint can and strode back into the living room.

"I know how to do it now; you can go. There is nothing more to do." She looked up questioningly, needle still poised over the empty hands, then lifted them palms up with a low-voiced musical phrase.

"No, Maggie," he said, slow and coldly definite. "Whatever it is, no. I am very good at living alone. No one needs to manage my life. *Go now.*" He shook his head and frowned at her and pointed to the door. With a sad glance at the skins he had dropped on the floor, she rose and went on noiseless feet. At the door she looked back for an instant.

The edges she had chewed were pliable as silk. Michel took another skin and clamped his molars firmly on it. It tasted long dead; hairs got into his throat and the wet leather slid oilily away from his teeth. He threw it down in disgust. There would be no Arctic house — it had been a frivolous conceit. He stooped and gathered all the unyielding skins in his arms, carried them to the empty study and tossed them in a corner.

Feeding snow geese padded flatfooted across the river, plump and complacent. When he went out the porch door they scattered and flew honking back into the hills. He stumped up toward the graveyard, startling small birds which fluttered high in the air and hung there, scolding. Maggie had been frightened away too. Her last look had been neither merry nor shy. It had simply been a last look. He had told her to go and she had gone.

He stood before Splaine's stark grave and wondered why he was there. It was only a stone and the missionary a foolish, interfering man, soon forgotten, his spirit kept briefly alive by a confused boy. He could die here too and his memory be obliterated. The countryside stretching out before him, mile on mile, brown and white forever, was harsh, impersonal and unproductive. The sea was a motionless desert of ice. Why didn't it melt? When would the ship come and take him back to trees and conversation? A vision of silverjar-bordered windows and Maggie's flat sweet face framed in caribou in the deep chair appeared in his mind like a past sorrow.

He erased it and strode up the river valley. The channel narrowed and deepened as he climbed the foothills of the mountain. Undercut snowbanks revealed translucent blue-green caves. Silt-laden water raced between them, gobbling and sucking. The mountain, now close, had lost its contours and was a desolation of gnarled glaciers, black-grooved cliffs and abrupt snowfields.

Imperceptibly his gloom lightened as he studied the wastelands above him with a practiced eye. Two glaciers led to the twin peaks. The one nearest the sea rose like a ladder, its top a cascade of seamed ice with a crown of rock. The other, source of Splaine's River, circled the mountain and flattened where it met the milder rocks of the inland peak. The seaward glacier, shining with snow, held almost certain death. One false step, one day of too much sun, would loose avalanches. The Splaine's River glacier was a broad wrinkled wilderness. Broken ice and rocks spilled down it, jammed in their slow fall and locked upright by the fierce winter freeze. Blue crevasses wider than a man's height and thinly snow-covered traversed the discolored ice. It was a brittle, hollow-crusted glacier — but negotiable. Framing both glaciers were deeply eroded rock ridges, crumbling and dangerous.

The challenge of the mountain had dissipated his melancholy. He looked down over the long terraces to the sea ice, now gleaming under low sunlight. Deep purple open-water leads threaded the clear turquoise of surface water. Beauty had come back to the cold northern world and the sunny timelessness was peace. It could be six o'clock or midnight. Tired and hungry, he ran and slid down the round hills along Splaine's River, his guideline to home. His long shadow reached ahead to touch the waiting house. All the way down he rehearsed a word. The word was "Please," and it came hard. He ate supper by the bare window, looking out at the empty ice. "Please," he said to himself. "Please, Maggie, make curtains for me."

Aching loneliness crept through him. He put his head in his hands and said aloud, "Please, Maggie, come back."

A day passed, and he finished painting the kitchen walls. When the sun touched the mountain he went out, supperless, and followed the river until it narrowed enough to jump across. He stood irresolute on the edge, his eyes tracing the faint track that disappeared over the far hill in the direction of Nauligak's village. The track had been a regular route, trodden into a narrow depression over the years. Now only Maggie's light step had touched its early flowers and moss and new grass. They still flourished, barely crushed by her soft-soled feet. Yellow poppies bloomed by the imprint of a small boot just across the river.

He stepped across, careful of Maggie's poppies. Over the hill above him appeared a small figure carrying a bulky bundle. He ran to meet her. "Maggie! I was going to find you. Please . . ." She looked up at him quickly, then dropped her gaze and handed him the bundle. It fell open as he took it, and silverjar streamed silkily from his hands. He stared at it.

"The curtain — Maggie, how did you know?" She had already turned back toward the village. He overtook her in two strides, took her hand and brought her around to face him. "Thank you, Maggie," he said seriously, looking down into eyes now unveiled and luminous. "Please come back with me." She went willingly, her small square hand warm in his.

They made supper together and ate together silently, Maggie with eyes downcast, Michel carefully looking out the window. The

moment they were through she carried the dishes out, and soon
came the gentle clatter of washing. He tacked the curtain to the
west window and stood back to look. Dark rings melted into silver.
Along the sides ran a paler border cut from the belly and sewed
with tiny stitches of caribou thong. The lower edge was finely
fringed. The skins had been kneaded supple between her strong
fingers, and they hung in rich folds. Beyond the gleaming fur the
mountain lifted from ice high into fire-streaked sky.

"Maggie, come and look at what you've done." She stepped
softly beside him. His eyes were still on the mountain as he laid
his hand on her shoulder.

"You've made the mountain even more beautiful." He looked
down at her. "I wish we could talk, little one."

Her face lifted, her eyes full on his, she spoke. The low voice
rose and fell sweetly with hardly a breath to mar it. It died off at
last in a lulling downward cadence, and Michel, deeply moved,
leaned to kiss her forehead.

Startled at his feelings, he stepped back. "Maggie — little sister
— it's time to go home. It's late." He turned quickly and went to
the porch. Unfastening the makeshift wire latch, he let the door
fall open to the bright summer night. Birds sang, an echo of Maggie's voice, and the air smelled of thawed earth and young grass.

"Come, Maggie. You must not stay here." She stood where he
had left her, slim eyebrows raised in a question over the fathom-
less eyes. They moved toward each other at the same time, and
Michel took her hand to lead her out.

Instead he drew her toward him and she came into his arms.
Her head lay in the curve of his neck, her small body arched
against his, touching him along its whole length. Slowly he caressed her then, his hand on her hair, pulled almost violently so
that her head fell back, eyes closed, young smooth neck exposed
and pulsating faintly. He kissed the hollow of her throat and lifted
her. She was light as a child. Her eyes opened wide in wonder

and fear as he gently undressed her and revealed the perfect small-scale ivory body that the shapeless robe had denied.

"Don't be afraid, Maggie." She smiled then, her mouth soft as he drew her to him. They came together with quickly rising ecstasy. At the climax she cried out and pressed him closer, trembling, then relaxed with a dulcet sigh and curled against him, her heavy hair caressing his chest.

"Little animal," he whispered. "Lovely graceful little animal — how do you know so much? I was the first one." She raised her head and her smile was a woman's, wise and tender. A first doubt chilled him. He saw Nina, pretty and calculating, and Davitt, obsessed. "Oh hell," he said out loud. "She's no Nina and I'm the original independent male." His tone was rough, and Maggie's smile died.

"I'm sorry, little one." He teased the smile back again with two fingers on her lips, until she laughed. "Go to sleep, Maggie." He stroked her lids down over her eyes and she slept as quickly as a pup, her head on his shoulder. But the doubt grew, and he lay wakeful under the light burden. When sleep finally came, he dreamed uneasily.

Later she moved closer to him, still asleep. At his touch she was awake in an instant, sweetly ready, and their union was enchantment that, for Michel, faded the moment they separated. They lay, barely touching, her face beautiful with happiness, his tortured with the remnants of his dreams, while through the still open doorway came the heady scent of summer earth. Early morning sunlight was a pathway to their bed and birds sang of love, but the thoughts of the two lying close together were as far apart as moon and stars.

Maggie sat up and looked down at the lean body of her lover. She traced his ribs with one finger like a wondering child, smoothed his creased forehead, laid her cheek against his for a moment, then slipped out of bed. He did not try to stop her. Heavy drowsiness overcame him, and he slept soon as if drugged.

At noon he awoke, distressed. He tried to force his thoughts into a semblance of discipline: he had taken the girl, who was not his to take, with whom equality and understanding on any level was inconceivable. His attraction to the North and his Arctic house had momentarily enveloped an innocent native; their union was an evanescent symbol. He had always avoided lasting, close relationships, and she might be hurt. The indiscreet night must be erased — for her sake. Thus he argued disingenuously, while the memory of Maggie lingered in his body, the touch of her small breasts, the cool brush of her hair over his shoulder, the entrancing song of her voice.

Shaking off the miasma of disordered images, he strode down to the river. He must think, he told himself, kicking a stone out of his path, dispassionately. He must think — deliberately he stepped on a clump of fragile, pale-petaled dryas — without Maggie in the house.

The sting of glacier water quenched lingering desire; the straight hard sunlight of noon denied the voluptuous night. A longspur, painted in motley, perched on a rock and whistled, a scornful echo of the sensuous voices of evening. Michel threw a rock at it. The bird was gone in a swift dart but landed a few yards away and trilled again. A chilly sense of loss crept over him. He shook the water from his shoulders violently and toweled himself until his skin was raw. Then he went back to the lukewarm stove, where he sat shivering, drinking tepid coffee and chewing a dry pilot biscuit. The dying embers mocked him.

He spent the afternoon typing, piling up words, page after page, finally shuffling together the results of his emotionless labor. Maggie's light footsteps sounded on the porch and he leaned again over the typewriter, frowning, to adjust the ribbon.

"Michel," she said softly, the strange syllables slow and sweet. He half turned and nodded brusquely, still scowling, saw the smile fade and pain widen the lustrous eyes, turned quickly back to the machine. No tears, he implored silently, no dramatics. Her foot-steps retreated to the kitchen, and there came the quiet sounds of supper preparation. Soon she came back and put a plate on the table — one plate — and he ate alone, feeling as if his heart had shriveled.

"Maggie," he wanted to say, "don't be so hurt, I only want to think, nothing is your fault — Maggie." He said nothing, and she walked noiselessly from the kitchen to table and back again, her eyes on the floor.

Zeke came with his sled and team as she was ready to leave, and his friend welcomed him with unrestrained relief. "Sit down, Zeke, have coffee, stay awhile. I am lonely. If Maggie could talk . . ."

"No good to teach her. Michel, there are whales in the leads. Many hunters will go to catch them. Will you come with me?"

"I'd like it more than anything. First you must do something for me. Ask Maggie what she wants most. She's to make the rest of the curtains for the windows, and she must know she is not doing it for love." He crimsoned.

"I know what she wants most, but it does not matter if it is now or next year. She wants new clothes. Now we go after whale."

"Yes it does matter," insisted Michel. "I want her to do the curtains now, to take the skins and do them at home, right now. You have to ask her, then tell her she will be paid."

Zeke's eyes, fixed on Michel's, were as childishly trusting as Maggie's. "I will tell her. But we must go to the police post. There will be white cloth and colored wool. That is what she wants. We have skins here, but not enough for just a girl."

"She is to have whatever skins she wants and the white cloth from the police post." He got his wallet and handed money to Zeke.

"You keep the money. We will all go tonight, you and I and Mauyak, and hunt whales on the way."

"No," said Michel hastily. "You go with her. I must stay and work." He waved vaguely toward his typewriter. "Take the skins with you, and she can do them when she gets back, at your house. Her mother can help her."

Zeke looked at him curiously, then spoke to his sister. She answered in a whisper, not looking up. "Yes, we will go tonight. It must be quick because soon the ice will be bad for sleds. She says thank you, and she will not come back here."

They brought the skins from the back room and lashed them on the sled. Michel went inside before they had finished. He heard the crack of the whip and the rough voice Zeke reserved for the dogs, then the short howls and the creaking of the sled, and then nothing.

Standing at the window, he looked out on untenanted sea ice. The calendar hung beside him, long forgotten. Painstakingly he went backward. There was a time he had seen the moon in the third quarter. He had lain on the sled sore and dazed and triumphant, the little seal at his feet, the vanquished bear dead behind him. The moon hung over the sunny hills like a wraith from another world. It didn't belong — but he did. Michel winced and crossed off that day with a heavy black line. He had stayed in Nauligak's house three days while Aitu treated the wound and Maggie waited on him, quietly loving. He drew a line through those three days, an ache at the pit of his chest. Then there were the days of writing, of repairing the insulation with moss, of painting the kitchen walls. He crossed them off quickly and stared again at the ice. The emptiness out there was appalling. The sun was a dim disk behind an unmoving film of cloud, and there were no shadows. One ghost-white gull floated low over a lead, its slender wings reflected darkly. It touched the water, shattering the reflection, then flew up and away.

Michel followed it with his eyes until it disappeared into the haze that blended pale horizon with watered ice. When the ice was gone the ship would be here. How can I leave? he cried silently. How can I stay? He shivered and turned to the pot-bellied stove.

Its fire had long since gone out, and the ashes smelled bitter. Without warning, desire for Maggie swept through him. He knelt and leaned his forehead on the chill iron. It had been hers; she had kept it alively warm and would not again.

He had banished himself to a cold world.

9

MICHEL meticulously filled the days, closing his eyes firmly on the shining nights, scrupulously marking crosses on the calendar, mind and heart blank against the waiting. Fog came over the house, blotting sea and earth, then straight, heavy rain invisible and silent in the inert mass of cloud. Days and nights were twilit. He hardly noticed.

After ten empty days Zeke came back, a mound of sealskin on his sled. "The ice was bad," he said apologetically. "It was long to come home. Now the dogs can swim." He grinned.

"And I made you miss the whale hunting. I'm sorry, Zeke."

"No, it is better now, and we will hunt them with kayaks. The last days, when Mauyak worked the skins at my father's house, all the ice melted. Will you come back with me?"

"Your father won't mind?" Or Maggie?

"My father likes another hunter. There is more to eat." His smile was guilelessly friendly, and suddenly Michel smiled too, for the first time in many days. Like a newly released prisoner he tasted fresh air and sunlight, though the windows were still opaque with rain. But the world was larger and more vivid than he remembered. Maggie, even in her absence, had made a puzzling change in him. The new way she had opened before him had no signposts, and he no longer knew in which direction to go.

"Whale hunting will be fine, Zeke. You go now, with your friends, and I will come alone, later. And please tell Maggie . . . No, don't tell her . . ."

Zeke ignored his discomposure. "If you do not see me at home you will see me in the water. They are close to shore now. It is good hunting. Perhaps we will have enough to eat for the summer."

"Don't you keep some for the winter?"

"We try, but we get hungry." He laughed.

"Well, we'll see about the winter," said Michel. His own words gave him an unexpected lift of the heart. Perhaps — with Maggie . . . he hushed the thought. Later, he said to himself, I will go over it inch by inch.

Alone, he hung the curtains and stood back to fill his eyes with their barbarous magnificence. The rest of the room now seemed severe. Maggie had brought the bear hide, cured and softened, and the stretched skin of the seal pup in the days (so long ago) when this had been her house too. She had taken one look at his shocked face and hastened them into the unused study. He had not looked at them since, shrinking from the unnecessary deaths and the fungus-like lies that grew on them. Now he plucked the skins resolutely from their cold corner. The bear would lie on the floor by the stove and the seal beside his bed, warm to his feet. The room needed them.

The bear was a flattened giant, belly hairs coarse against the scrubbed pine floor, murderous claws helplessly splayed, head a grin-toothed mask with blind eyes. Maggie had stitched them shut, and Michel, who knew, could not find the fur-buried gap where the bullet had entered. The seal had large round eyes of polished soapstone, shining as if the tears were still there. Its black claws, never used, were pathetic on the thin flippers and its fur was the thick pile of the newly born. He would never step on it. It lay on the organ, eyes facing its native ocean.

Michel looked once around his room. It was all he had wished, an Arctic house, but it was still empty. It was a dream of a house, not yet waked up to — perhaps never to be made — reality. The passages of his mind were darkly silent. He could not decide; he could not even think.

With a sigh he sat down at the organ and opened the volume of Bach chorales. The soaring prayers filled the lonely house, drifted out over the bleak earth and the steely ocean, mingling with the cries of terns and the warble of flocking songbirds. Peace entered him with the music. Coming to no decision, perhaps, was a condition of living in the North. The days took care of themselves.

A voice spoke into the ringing silence of an Amen. "Outer suburbia," it remarked coolly. "Next you'll be growing hybrid chrysanthemums." Michel was shocked. He sat motionless, his hands still on the keys, his head full of music. "Is there any coffee?" said the voice with a hint of impatience. "It's cold outside."

Michel turned stiffly. Jacques Davitt leaned against the door frame, hand on hip, slow smoky eyes moving from silverjar to bear to Michel. "Why didn't you knock?"

"I did, but you were too involved — working." His glance rested for a moment on the closed typewriter. "This is a nice job of interior decorating. Pity you have to leave it."

"I wanted to make it comfortable," said Michel lightly. "No sense living six weeks in a broken-down shack."

"Six weeks ago you were all for living in a tent."

"I've changed." Abruptly he got up from the organ and went to the kitchen. When he returned with coffee, Davitt was studying the head of the bear.

"Interesting," he murmured. Michel set the cups on the table. The policeman joined him and they sat opposite each other, wary, silently sipping coffee.

"I've come to take you back," said Davitt finally. "The ship will be here in two days."

"I haven't decided I'm going back. This is a good house and the landlord hasn't given me notice."

"Nauligak?"

"No." He added under his breath, "An uneasy ghost in a hill-top grave."

Davitt looked up sharply. "Ghost? You're going bush. Good thing I came. It's unhealthy, harping on old Splaine. He was only an incident, of no matter in the long run. Except to himself, of course, poor fellow."

"No doubt," said Michel. "I came here, Davitt, to see how the Eskimos managed. You're right; in spite of a small dose of Christianity they're still living in the old way — at least Nauligak is. I have a lot to learn."

"You've had six weeks to see how the people live." Davitt rose, put both hands on the table and looked squarely down at Michel. "I'm not sure this country's good for you. It has strange effects on outsiders. You have to know how to take solitude and like it. This isn't like going down to the farm to retire for a season. I'm responsible for you and it's better if I take you back with me now."

Michel stood up, returning the policeman's look at the level. He smiled, blue eyes widening disarmingly. "I haven't been exactly solitary. They've all been extremely friendly. I'll be at the post in two days, when the ship comes. You don't have to nursemaid me, but thanks anyway."

"I'll expect you." Davitt turned toward the door, saying casually over his shoulder, "Where did you get the bear? Nauligak?"

"No, a bit of luck. It nearly killed me."

"They were eating fresh bear meat when I came through. That's why I wondered."

"Then you must also know that I gave them the meat." He went ahead to prop open the sagging porch door. "It was good of you to come."

"My job," said Davitt noncommittally. "Don't get in the way of any more bears." He moved down the beach with his leisured swing. Michel watched as he pushed his heavy rowboat off the rotting pressure ice, rowed carefully between floating ice pans, and started the outboard motor in the silt-laden delta of Splaine's River.

When the boat had grown small in the distant gray water, Michel, decided at last, left his house.

Aitu sat outside her house scraping a sealskin. The effluvium of decaying seal fat surrounded her and Michel stood well away. She smiled at him, her eyes narrowing and brightening like her daughter's, and gestured with one greasy hand toward the water. Michel saw blurred figures on the misty inlet. He walked down to the edge of the beach. Aitu's three little children followed him, eyes round, more interested in the big man than the performance in the water.

Two kayaks, far out, seemed to be executing a dance. One sped forward, then turned in mid-flight, stopping short, while the other glided toward it from an angle. Just short of hitting, it veered off and they fanned outward from one another, then shot in again. A dark head showed between them and the shore and vanished. The two kayaks spun toward the eddy and separated again. Gradually they worked toward shore and the head appeared, much nearer. This time the back arched hugely out of the water and disappeared with a hard splash of hind flippers. Now the kayaks danced back and forth in a straight line parallel with the shore, pushing the creature into shallow water. The animal broke surface more frequently and Michel heard its desperate snort. The children beside him laughed.

The back broke water helplessly, and one kayak spun swiftly between it and the shore, driving it toward the other. Kayak still, harpoon lifted against the dim sky, the second figure was a stone image on the disturbed water for a long instant, then the raised spear thrust down powerfully. The kayak dipped and rocked in the waves as the wounded animal dove for deeper water. An inflated seal bladder bobbed erratically in its wake and the two light boats streaked after it. In a moment they were small in the distance. A diminutive arm lifted a toy harpoon and a geyser whitened the dark sea like a miniature flash of lightning.

Slowly and decorously the kayaks returned to shore paddling in unison, a monstrous shadow following them. Nauligak and Zeke stepped into the shallow water, holding their kayaks off the beach, and pulled on the harpoon lines. The animal, gray and flaccid, lolled in the shallows, spears projecting from neck and eye. Blood streamed from the wounds and disintegrated palely in the water. Zeke secured the harpoon lines to a rock, then the two men lifted their slim hunting boats lightly and came up the beach. Nauligak's grin sat incongruously on his carved-wood face.

"Bearded seal," Zeke told Michel. "Meat for a week and new boot soles for everyone." He laid his boat gently, bottom up, on the sand and went back to the dead animal. Within a few minutes he held aloft a huge dark red liver. "Now we will have a feast."

Nauligak spoke to his children and they scattered up the beach to the terraced village. People crawled out of their low stone houses. From Nauligak's house a white figure emerged. Michel's eyes focused suddenly on it, but it fled over the pebbled earth and disappeared into a distant stone hut before the first guests had reached the door.

Lilting conversation filled Nauligak's house, rising and falling like water over rocks. The sharp smell of fried liver hovered, mingled with the seal-oil odor of the people. Contentment was in the air along with the animal smells and the low laughter.

Nauligak spoke quietly, and at the sound of his hoarse voice the conversation died. Everyone watched him. The throaty monotone lacked the musical cadence of the others but it carried authority and a touch of political oratory. At the end of his speech Aitu and the children handed the meat around and the busy voices rose again.

"What did he say?" asked Michel.

"He said the meat was poor and his wife's cooking was terrible. And as soon as they finished eating they must all go out and catch more bearded seal and whales."

"Is that all?"

"Yes." Zeke smiled. "It is better if it takes long to say. They listen to a lot of words. Our people like talk."

"Will they listen to me then? I have a speech to say." He made it long and florid, and Zeke struggled with the translation. The conclusion was somewhat pompous: "And since you have all been so good to me, a stranger to your ways, I would like to give you something in return. Not just a gift which would amuse you for a few days, but a gift of myself, of my services, to buy your furs and bring you all the food and tools and clothing you need, for as long as you will let me live among you." The speech had lasted fifteen minutes and the people were pleased. A happy buzz followed his words. Only Nauligak was silent, withdrawn behind the shell of his impassive face.

Michel faced him across the room. "Nauligak, it is for you to say. Shall I stay?"

The old hunter looked slowly around at his people, and the voices diminished under his brooding gaze. His appeal, when it came, had a strained urgency. "Have I not led you to the walrus and the white whale? Have I not shown you where the mother seal feeds her pup, so that you might take both together? Have I not taken you where the wild goose nests and the bear has his winter sleep? You have not died of hunger and your sons are growing up to be new hunters and keep you safe forever. Is this not enough?" There was an uncomfortable pause when he finished. Eyes sought other eyes but did not turn to Nauligak, and when the voices started again they were grumbling murmurs.

"My father has said this before," whispered Zeke unhappily. "It was a long time ago, when I was young. But Father Splaine stayed anyway, and everyone went to learn the new religion, even my father."

And Father Splaine died, thought Michel. His pulse tapped against his wrist, too fast. The chief clearly did not want traders any more than missionaries. Money as well as prayers might interfere with the old, safe ways.

[100]

Nauligak stood up and walked to Michel. Small, thin, dark of face, the man still dominated the room, and Michel had to force himself to look at the flat black eyes. Slowly Nauligak raised his hand and Michel took it. They shook hands solemnly.

"They wish you to stay," said Nauligak. Relief was tangible. Everyone laughed and clapped, young hunters stumbled over one another to shake Michel's hand, young wives smiled demurely, eyes quick on him and quick away. Slowly, in pairs and families and singly, they drifted out of the house until only Michel was left.

"This is going to be harder," he said to Zeke. "I would like your sister to come back."

Zeke was startled and confused. "Please, Michel, no, I cannot ask that."

"Is she so set against me then? Poor little Maggie, I can't blame her."

"No, not Mauyak. She is never against you. But he has said she must not go back. He has sent her away to another village."

"Zeke, you are not telling the truth," said Michel severely. "She is in this village."

"Please do not try to find her. It would be very bad."

"Just tell me one thing: did she want to be sent away?"

"It did not matter what she wanted."

He stood up. His head touched the roof and he looked sternly down on the little family. "Thank you, Zeke and Nauligak, for allowing me to stay here. I will do my best for you and your people." He bowed toward Aitu. "The meat was delicious. Now I am going to find your daughter. I think you will understand, Aitu." He gestured to Zeke to translate, and went out of the house without waiting.

There were eleven houses in the village. Two were set apart from the others high on the hillside, and Michel went to them. It was in one of these that the white figure had vanished. They were in ruins. Stones had fallen from their walls, the roofs had partly caved in and were carelessly covered with ancient hides; the huts were slipping back gracelessly into their native earth. Only one showed a sign of life: a thin shred of smoke seeped unevenly from a hole in the roof.

Michel crawled through the narrow opening and was assailed by the stench of decayed meat. He recoiled. What had happened to his fastidious girl? Unwillingly he inched into the house around a fallen boulder that blocked the passage. Inside, the smell was almost unbearable. The room was dim and smoky. The gut covering the small back window was black with years of grime. By a flickering lamp flame sat an unkempt man fumbling with a knife at a piece of soapstone. He looked up at the intruder, his small eyes glittering.

"Saloositak Tana?" asked Michel, staring past him, trying to pierce the fetid gloom. The old man nodded, reached behind him and held out a small carved seal. Michel glanced carelessly at the exquisite workmanship. "Where is Mauyak?" he demanded. The sly eyes slid away. "Damn you, I'll find her."

A slovenly heap lay on the broken sleeping platform. Trying not to breathe, he touched it. No living thing was there; this was the old man's worldly possessions, all in a tangle, dirt-colored, ill-smelling and disreputable as the man himself.

He backed out of the house quickly and breathed again, vaguely wondering what offal the man ate — and glimpsed a flick of white at the door of the second hut.

"Maggie!" he called, and ran. She flew ahead of him over the hills and he could not have caught her. But suddenly she stopped and turned, one hand raised palm out against him. Surprised, he stood a yard away and regarded the slight, aloof figure. A graceful white parka embroidered with many-colored wool fell to her knees in front and was cut in a curve high on the sides, revealing full-cut silverjar trousers. On her feet were new sealskin boots with heavy black soles and wide cuffs of embroidered flannel. Her hood, full around her shoulders, framed the black hair with white fox fur. Her slim waist was cinched with a braided belt of bright-hued wool.

The sweet flat face was sad and tears gleamed in the wide-spaced eyes. He held a hand toward her, but she shook her head slowly and walked around him, back toward the village, a white shape small and elegant and doomed against the terrible brown earth. Michel watched until she reached her ruined hut, then went back to his house.

Wind had risen, clearing the weather, and he sat long over supper, gazing at tinted clouds flying across the washed blue sky. A carpet of low willow spread over the promontory, short and thick as an English lawn, and clumps of sun-yellow poppies swayed above it, bent to the ground and rising between gusts. They were dying. The petals were dark green at the edges and curled inward. The sea beyond was lively dark blue flecked with the white of insubstantial ice pans — a summer sea. Westward, toward the mountain, the ground was free of snow and painted with a subdued pattern of lichens and mosses, brown and gray, with random splashes of orange and traceries of black. Birds flocked, just-fledged young with adults, scudding before the wind like leaves, circling and landing, circling again, calling sweetly. In a few days they would be gone.

He wanted no other world but this, subtle-colored and small-lived, its white horizons and etched mountains endlessly beckoning. But it was too lonely for him. Davitt was right. With a gentle and undemanding companion — with Maggie — he could defeat solitude. And she had denied him.

Early the next morning he was back in the village. Nauligak was directing the young hunters gathered on the beach with kayaks and harpoons, and Michel went straight to him. "I cannot stay," he said. "Today I will go, if you can take me."

Zeke looked at him once and spoke to his father, his voice hopeless. The old hunter nodded abstractedly and turned immediately back to his instruction. Clearly Michel was of less importance, staying or going, than the never-ending hunt for food.

"I will go and say good-by to your mother. She has been kind."
Zeke went with him and they found Aitu among her sealskins,
cross-legged and calm like a benign household deity. Her face
lighted when she saw Michel and she gave a gentle welcome, in
Maggie's voice.

"The ship is coming," said Michel, "and I must go away on it.
I am sad to leave and will remember you." The careful politeness
hid sorrow. Aitu gazed at him searchingly. She spoke briefly to
her son, then rose, dipped her head incomprehensibly to Michel,
and left the house.

"Has she said good-by? I thought it would take longer."

"No, she has said nothing. She only asked what you said." The
worried wrinkles were on Zeke's forehead. "Michel, must you go?"

"I am not wanted. You all got along very well before I came.
This is not my country." He was brusque, disappointed by Aitu's
casual dismissal. "I will be back here in an hour. There is not
much to take with me," he said over his shoulder, already in the
passageway.

The hunters were on the sea, and the fresh wind blew the points
of their kayaks clear of the water so they seemed to fly over the
whitecaps. Nauligak walked up the beach toward his own kayak
and suddenly stopped, frozen, staring beyond Michel. Turning,
Michel saw Aitu with Maggie behind her. They came to him, and
Aitu took her daughter's hand and put it into Michel's. He looked
down at the still, withdrawn face and eyes distant as well pools.
No one spoke.

She was dressed like a bride, he thought, and winced.

"Maggie, you look beautiful," he said stiltedly, still holding the
small hand that lay inert in his palm. Zeke murmured to his sister
and the ivory face came vividly alive. "You really are lovely, little
one, and right now you are as embarrassed as I am. I think we
had better go home." He turned to the family. Aitu was smiling
maternally and for a moment he was afraid of her. Nauligak, vanquished, looked at the ground, his dark countenance devoid of

expression. Zeke was a study in contradictory emotions. Why didn't they say something?

He spoke decisively to Zeke. "Now I can stay. We'll take all your best skins and go to the post tomorrow. The decision is not precisely in my hands but neither is it in Davitt's. Who comes on the ship?"

"There is a man who comes to talk to Constable Davitt. He has to know if we brush our teeth and don't kill each other with knives." He smiled artlessly, his eyes glinting. "He is always the same. His name is Hodge. There is another man from the big trading company in Hudsonton. It is always a new one. I think they do not like to come here."

"Why?"

Zeke hesitated, his gaze avoiding Michel's. "Maybe we are not rich enough."

"If someone comes every year the company must expect a profit. There has to be another reason."

"I do not know," said Zeke, face averted. Silence yawned between them. Aitu's goddess-like benignity had not changed, and Nauligak was still solemnly absorbed in the pebbles at his feet. Michel looked from one to another doubtfully.

"We want you to stay," said Zeke in a small boy's voice, and turned his eyes again to Michel.

"Thank you, Zeke. Till tomorrow then."

Maggie's trim-shod feet tripped quickly beside his long stride as they crossed the round hills, and the grasses sprang up behind her.

10

THE LARGE skin boat entered the harbor at Aurora Sound to the tumultuous music of hundreds of dogs. Two young men and two girls were rowing. The forepart was loaded with a covered mound high as the gunwales, and in the stern sat Michel and Maggie. From the massed tents on the higher terrace poured streams of people, and by the time the bow touched sand the beach was a sea of curious grinning faces. At the door of the police house an unmoving figure watched. The two in the stern looked at each other, then turned away. He flushed to the roots of his sand-colored hair and she contemplated her quiet folded hands, face lowered against inquisitive stares.

A few of the onlookers waded into the water and pulled the boat close to shore. Michel gave his hand to Maggie and she stepped lightly onto the beach. Immediately she was surrounded by women and girls, examining every detail of her new clothes, smiling and touching and murmuring. She slipped away from them and hovered close to Michel as he helped lift out the bales and beach the boat.

Michel walked up to the police house, and the flush was gone when he faced Davitt. "I came, you see."

"With your retinue." Davitt's iron-gray eyes moved from Michel to the small white shadow half hidden behind him, then to the men on the beach with bales on their shoulders. "What's all that for?"

"Fox and seal and ermine that they brought in to trade. They have asked me to be their representative and to stay on at Splaine's River as trader."

"The ship arrives in the morning. Discussion will wait until then," said Davitt with no expression. "Will you come in for coffee?"

"No, thank you. There are too many of us."

"I only asked you."

"They are with me. If you permit, we will pitch our tent on the beach."

Davitt nodded and went into the house without another word.

Michel's friends set up the tent and departed, gossiping. "We will visit everyone," said Zeke on his way out.

"There must be two hundred people here."

Zeke grinned. "They all like visits."

Soon afterward Ide came with tea and chocolate and canned beef and vegetables. "I thought you might be tired of seal meat."

"Thanks. Stay and help us eat." Ide glanced uncomfortably at Maggie, demure over the primus stove, and sat well away from her. Michel laughed. "She's no Nina. She doesn't want to be anywhere but here."

"Be careful anyway. They change."

"Not Maggie." She looked up, her sunny smile like her mother's, her eyes vivacious.

"At least she's not pretty," said Ide.

"Do you know," retorted Michel sharply, "some of them speak English?"

Ide shrugged and sipped tea. "Jacques says you want to be a trader."

"I plan to. Why is he set against it?"

"Himself is the only one who can understand the natives." Ide's lip curled.

"There's more to it than that."

"Nothing more than conceit. Unless you count theories."

"What theories?"

"The dear little people aren't to be exposed to the corrupting influence of outsiders."

"How did he react to the missionary — was he a corrupt outsider?"

"I couldn't be less interested. If the man wants the place to himself he's welcome to it. He claims he loves solitude. I don't. And the company of the natives is worse than solitude. They're tricky — you never know what's behind those nice big smiles, except that it's nothing to do with what they tell you."

"They've been kind to me, mostly."

"They make a practice of being kind," said Ide shortly. "You don't know what they really mean." He added with a grimace, "To be frank, neither do I. They don't confide in me; they don't like me. I've been here half a year and that's six months too long. Every night I get down on my knees by the bed and pray for the transfer to come through." He lifted his cup. "Here's to the superette on Aurora Sound. And to the fourteenth-floor apartment on the main street of the noisiest, busiest city in the country." His watery red-rimmed eyes protruded at Michel and his small mouth twisted. It seemed he was smiling.

"Good luck to both of us," Michel responded dutifully. When Ide had left he turned fondly to Maggie. "I'm glad you don't speak English, little one." He twisted his fingers in her thick hair and bent her head back. "Beautiful Maggie," he whispered, and kissed her lips.

Early in the morning the dog chorus announced the arrival of the ship. Michel and Maggie went out hand in hand. The sun was still touching the northeastern horizon, and in the golden water, against a background of glistening mountains, lay a reinforced freighter, clumsy and homely and out of place as a milk truck on the moon. A squat boat was chugging toward shore. The Eskimos crowded to the water to pull it in, and two men in business suits stepped gingerly onto the wet pebbles. The sailor at the tiller waved and backed off again.

Mr. Pryde, the representative of the Northern Trading Company, was a fair, stout, balding man with a new sunburn sitting uneasily on his office-pale face. The other, the government official named Hodge, was tall, cadaverous and tired. Mr. Pryde waved self-consciously to the smiling crowd, but Hodge, after perfunctory greetings to the white men, retreated to the house with Davitt. The ship's boat made two more trips to bring the crew members ashore, and the Eskimos set up a little bazaar on the beach. Sealskin rugs, boots, mittens, crude soapstone sculpture and a few narwhal tusks, slenderly spiraled as if carved by a more fastidious artist, were spread on the pebbled sand. The women sat surrounded by their wares, serene and smiling, and the crew circulated, offering money, cigarettes and glass jewelry. Even Maggie was selling, with Zeke beside her to translate — children's jackets fringed and intricately patterned, hoods of silverjar and white fox, belts of braided sealskin — all Splaine's River finely fashioned fruits of the long winter night. Among her wares were the artful carvings of that sorry old man, Saloositak Tana, remarkable contrast to the careless stonework of the others.

Michel frowned as he saw the sailors gazing appreciatively at the comely little figure, and her answering sideways smile. She sold all her goods. Michel drew Zeke aside and whispered, "Why does she have to sell? There are others."

"She looks better."

"I don't like it," muttered Michel, then laughed at himself. "But I asked for it. She could have come in her old clothes. Zeke, why are Splaine's River goods so much better than the others?"

"Our women know how to work, because they must. The women here get everything from the ship and they forget how to sew skins."

"And Saloositak Tana?"

"He has nothing else to do."

"He makes good use of his laziness. You'll do well with your own trader. Come with me, let's butter up Mr. Pryde."

The traders' representative was supervising the unloading of supplies and looked up with an uninterested professional smile as they approached. Michel proffered a hand. "I'm D. E. Michel, of *East-West Review*."

The smile turned real, creasing the plump, sun-scorched cheeks. "Mr. Michel! Why didn't that fellow Davitt introduce us? You're a long way from home. But then, you always are."

"This is home right now, Mr. Pryde. My friend Zeke would like to take us both fishing tonight. You're entitled to a few hours off, aren't you?"

"There's that infernal dance. Been to a dance every post we've stopped at. Have to attend these affairs, you know, good for business."

Zeke spoke with soft-voiced diffidence. "They will not dance before midnight. We can fish first. Char is running, fifty or sixty in the nets in one hour. I can get you a kayak."

"Kayak! That'll be something to tell the folks back home." His face fell. "Have to unload this stuff, have to assess the skins, have to have a conference with Davitt . . . The hell with it, I'll skip Davitt, give him a half hour in the morning — after all, he's only a policeman."

Michel laughed. "I see you don't know Jacques Davitt. If you can get away with it we'll pick you up after supper."

"Can't you eat with us? I'm not used to these broody northern types. Davitt isn't enthusiastic for traders — or for the Home Office either. Seems sugar ruins their teeth and tobacco ruins their lungs and government regulations ruin their dispositions. He's going to end up ruining my digestion. Come on in."

"I haven't been invited."

"I'm inviting you."

The government official, Hodge, came then and requested a word with Mr. Pryde. Michel excused himself. When he reached the tent he turned. They were talking earnestly and they were both looking at him. He let the tent flap fall behind him and stood still inside. He could hear his heart beat in the opaque white quietness.

Conversation at supper was desultory and uncomfortable. Davitt was inexplicably gloomy, Michel was tense, the government official seemed unbearably fatigued and his eyelids kept dropping. Mr. Pryde chattered in short bursts about life in the capital but his garrulity dropped into a void. Supper was cooked and served by Ide, who then disappeared into the office.

Mr. Pryde essayed again, speaking brightly against the glum silence. "Hey, you know, I'm going fishing tonight in a kayak. Do you really seal yourself in and upend?"

Davitt turned his gray eyes on the trader. "You won't enjoy upending. The ice broke just a week ago."

"Why don't you go with him, Davitt, take the police launch," said the lean-visaged Hodge unexpectedly.

"I'm going calling. Officially. This is the one day of the year I can see all the people at once. We won't need the trader . . ." His voice held a trace of scorn and Michel winked at Mr. Pryde. "But it's best if you come with me, Mr. Hodge. There may be one or two small problems and they're easier to handle on the spot than from a desk a thousand miles away." Hodge said nothing, but his face drooped even more. He was not going to get his nap. "Maybe Ide would go," continued Davitt. "We don't need him either. Want to go fishing, Ide?" he called.

The junior constable responded like a boy fortuitously let out of school, and in minutes they were dragging the big police boat down to the beach.

"Forbidding type, isn't he?" said Pryde between grunts of effort. "But he's doing a fine job up here, a fine job," he added hastily. "No crime, no illegitimate children, no starvation . . ."

"If you ask me he's gone bush," muttered Ide, and the trader glanced sharply at him.

Michel broke in, soothing. "It's just that the natives treat him as one of themselves. He loves the life, really understands them. He's fair and doesn't tolerate laziness, but I've heard tales about his generosity and kindness to anyone in trouble."

"He hasn't been so fair and generous to you, has he?" said Ide, mouth curled in his version of a smile.

Curiosity glinted in Mr. Pryde's small blue eyes. Michel abruptly turned and pointed. "There's Zeke in his kayak." The slim craft shot inshore, pivoted gracefully inches from the boat and came to a halt beside it.

Mr. Pryde looked down. "That's a pretty little toy. Never seen a skin boat before — at all the other posts they were canvas."

"So they are here," started Michel, and suddenly fell silent and stared downward, his face reddening. "But not at Splaine's River. Zeke, where did you get the boat?"

Zeke's smile faded. "I borrowed it," he said almost inaudibly.

"From his father," said Ide. "Without permission, no doubt, the way he borrowed our dogs."

"Then Nauligak came here?" Michel was still looking at the boy, but Ide answered.

"Of course, man, didn't you know. I thought they told you their innermost secrets. He came right after you last night. Spent three hours with the great white father, the both of them gibbering away like a couple of long-lost monkey brothers."

"Trouble goes with him," said Michel slowly. His eyes were fixed on Zeke, and the boy turned his head away, the pulse throbbing in his temple.

"Who — what?" Mr. Pryde's chubby face was alight with inquisitiveness. "Sounds like a fruity bit of gossip. Got to take something home to the folks besides ivory buttons."

"It's nothing," said Michel smoothly. "Nauligak, Zeke's father, is a fine hunter. This is the white whale and narwhal season, and I was surprised he'd go off in the middle of it. I guess he wanted a day on the town too. Ship day is Thanksgiving, Christmas and New Year's Eve, isn't it?"

"You said it. All rolled into one, with flags on, for twenty-four solid hours. Still, there was something you said . . ."

Ide interrupted. "We'd better get on if we're to be back for the dance. Mr. Pryde, it's your turn to borrow the kayak."

Mr. Pryde looked again at the dainty boat. "Boys, this is my first trip North, and I'll leave the acrobatics to you Eskimo types. That thing looks a lot frailer than me." He chuckled, his cheeks quivering.

"I've never been in one either," said Michel. "Can I try, Zeke?"

The boy looked up, still troubled. Michel smiled warmly and Zeke's face cleared. "Sure, Michel." He climbed aboard and held the little boat while Michel lowered himself into the waist-size hole. The kayak tipped, and icy water splashed his shoulder. He shook his arm and the kayak tipped the other way. Zeke handed him the double-bladed paddle. He swept one blade through the water and the kayak bolted like a live thing, headed directly for an ice pan. Swiftly he dipped the other blade, whipped around a 180-degree arc and was barely able to keep from piling end-on into the launch.

"This thing's not a boat, it's an unbroken colt." He looked up, to meet Mr. Pryde's gleeful regard, waved, and nearly turned over. There wouldn't be any trouble with that one, he decided, so long as he was kept amused. Mr. Pryde was essential; without the trader's good will Michel would lose his only pretext for staying on. He mismanaged the boat a while longer, then found the rhythm of the long paddle and dropped back, keeping a prudent distance clear of the launch propeller's eddies.

[113]

At Char Fork, a narrow rock-edged river two miles from the post, Zeke set up a long gill net, fastening it to rocks on either side of the river's swirling exit into the sea. While he was still working, fish leaped and the net shuddered. Michel swooped in.

"I'll clear your net, Zeke!" he cried, and seized a fish by the gills. It thrashed in the net, entangling itself like a fly in a web. Michel laid the oar crosswise and engaged both hands with the fish. The boat tipped, the oar slipped into the water, and the fish fought, but Michel finally freed it from the net and held it aloft. Exhausted and gasping, the fish glared at him with protruding eyes (rather like Ide's).

"Round one to me," Michel said. Then the fish twisted with a violence that threatened to overturn the kayak, and Michel, wet to the waist and balancing like a tight-rope walker, paddled with one hand in the freezing water to retrieve the oar. Six pounds of desperate fish in one hand, useless paddle in the other, he drifted helplessly around the small harbor pushing ice pans out of his way.

"Round two, fish. Look, guys," he called, "I've got a fish here."

"We've got twenty," answered Ide. "Keep him."

"He is good to eat," said Zeke. "I will throw you the salt." Mr. Pryde shook with merriment.

"If it takes an hour," said Michel, "I will land this fish."

"Haven't got an hour. We're going back to the dance. Goodby. Have a good sail." Ide leaned over to fumble with the motor.

"You're not really going to leave him?" asked Mr. Pryde anxiously. "He might — well — drown or something."

"Not in two feet of water. Actually we're just going on shore to make tea."

"Tea?" said Michel, and tapped the fish on the head with the edge of the paddle. "Round three, knockout." He thrust it down between his feet and glided between ice pans and rocks to a patch of sand where he beached the boat with one hand as he had seen Zeke and Nauligak do.

"You did wonders with that cockleshell," said Mr. Pryde over tea and jam. "Can't believe you've never been in one before."

"As a matter of fact I'd never been in the North before I came here to do a piece for *East-West Review* a few weeks ago. That reminds me . . ." He flushed and the freckles stood out.

"Hodge got it from Davitt that you wanted to stay awhile," said Mr. Pryde comfortably. "Start a little trading post up the sound at — where was it again?"

"Splaine's River."

"Oh yes, the old missionary place. What happened to him?"

"He seems to have gone. There hasn't been anyone in that house for some years."

"They do come and go, don't they?" He chortled. "Probably set up a new church on an ice floe to baptize the walruses. Hodge gave me the figures on the population there. Not enough to make you a millionaire. Are they industrious?"

"Very much so," answered Michel. "Their leader, Nauligak, has them out hunting day and night. They have more skins and more to eat than any of the other settlements around here. Fox and ermine traps too. Nauligak bought them years ago when he saw the profit in furs. You could help them by setting up a trading post there. Help your company too. The women there make the finest clothes, and they have a first-rate sculptor."

"They could use a post," added Ide. "There isn't much for them in a pinch — we can only manage to take care of the people who live right here. Michel brought over about ten dozen skins, fox and ermine and ringed seal, to see what he could pick up for them, and give you an idea of their industry."

Mr. Pryde nodded slowly, looking out to sea. "Sounds like a good proposition — for us. We have to find a new man every year just to spend a month on the ship touching at these backwater posts. You'd be surprised at the resistance . . ." He shut his mouth on the rest of the sentence. "I'm office staff actually, Had to come myself because last year's man begged off when the ship was weighing anchor. It's a bonanza to find someone willing to *live* here, without contacts, without . . ." He turned to face Michel. "It is curious," he said, his bright small eyes narrowing, "that a man like you, an international character, would want to bury himself alive in a white tomb."

For an instant Michel went numb; he felt the blood leave his face and cold creep up his spine. The little eyes seemed to look right through to the image that never left him, of the white stone on the hilltop.

Mr. Pryde chuckled. "Someone just walked over your grave, eh, Michel?" His round face was bland and the blue eyes were vacant.

"Something like that." Michel produced a smile. "The answer to your question is just that I *have* been an international wanderer since I was big enough to carry a portable. This seems a good place to settle for a while, and if I can at the same time help the people, whom I have come to like and respect . . . I assure you, however, that I don't plan to end my life here."

"Odd way to put it," commented Mr. Pryde absently. "End, not spend. By the way, what does Constable Davitt think of your plan?"

"He's — reserved."

"Constable Davitt," put in Ide, "is a policeman, sir, like myself. Our job is to keep the peace. It doesn't look as if Michel is going to break it."

"Actually Davitt has nothing to say in the matter of traders," said Mr. Pryde. "I'd listen to a legitimate beef but I haven't heard one yet. Trading posts are my department — with Mr. Hodge's say-so, of course. And he's already said so." Unexpectedly he took Michel's hand and shook it vigorously. "It'll take about a month for the confirmation to come through, but that's just a formality. We have enough stuff on the ship to set you up in style — on credit, of course, until next year, minus the furs you brought in. You're in the grocery business as of now, son. Congratulations."

"Thank you," said Michel gravely. "The Splaine's River people will be grateful."

"No need to put on the idealistic act with me," said Mr. Pryde with a short laugh. "Nobody stays around here unless he has a reason. This eyewash about helping the people . . . Did you know there'd been a ruckus about you in Davitt's office today? All very high-minded, of course. Davitt went on about teeth and lungs and esprit and all that. I thought Hodge was asleep, but suddenly he comes out with a quotation from Epictetus — in Latin. Something about second-class citizens, I gathered. Davitt lit into him with another quote — sounded like *Hiawatha* — and between them they divided up the future of the Eskimos. They got pretty hot in a dark calm way. It's clear Davitt doesn't like outsiders and Hodge doesn't like Davitt but can't do anything about him on account of his good record. So Hodge says you're staying, and Davitt can't do anything about that. They kept it real philosophical." He snorted and poked a fat finger against Michel's chest. "No need to point out to them the future of the Eskimos is right here, with you and me, and it adds up to just one word — profit."

Michel stayed silent.

"And that's what we expect from you, son. You'll do all right. I learned from the boy here" — he indicated Zeke, still gathering fish from the net, discreetly beyond earshot — "that you're right popular over there. Just keep 'em from going lazy. You'll bring in double the skins this time next year, I guarantee. It's in your face and it's in your record and it's in the way you acted tonight. Go-getting type."

With difficulty Michel focused. "Yes sir. I'll do my best."

He turned his face toward the burning midnight sea; his eyes were dazzled. No, he wanted to add, you office salesman, you have no glimmer of what is in my face and what keeps me here.

[117]

It keeps Davitt here too, and the handful that make the North their home.

The word is not profit. It is love.

Zeke left the boat and came to them, and Michel put an arm over his shoulder. "Now you can teach me to harpoon whales, Ezekiel Okkomikpok. I'm going to live at Splaine's River."

The boy looked up at the big man with adoration. "I will make you your own harpoon, Michel."

11

F ARAWAY accordion music floated on the thin air, and they launched the boat again. Fish still half alive quivered and leaped on the floor planks, and fell back. Mr. Pryde drew his feet under him on the bow seat, but Zeke and Ide waded unconcerned through the shining dying mass, kicking fish aside to make room for gill net and food box.

"That's a lot of fish," said Mr. Pryde. "Wasteful, isn't it? I can smell them a week from now." His nose wrinkled in distaste and he shuddered away from one that launched itself at his knee, thrusting his hands against it and closing his eyes.

"Nobody will smell them a week from now," said Ide. "They'll be eaten before morning."

"But they're *your* fish. What about you, boy, does your father let you give them away?"

"Everybody likes fish," said Zeke, softly apologetic.

Mr. Pryde looked shocked. He shook a warning forefinger at Michel, who stood ankle-deep in the water holding the boat off the rocks while Ide started the motor. "Mr. Trader, you're going to have to introduce a little capitalism around here."

Michel grinned at him. "Not tonight. I only caught one." He added quickly, raising his voice against the sputtering of the engine, "Trading goods is another matter. Your company won't lose money on me." Mr. Pryde cupped his ear, looking doubtful. "Don't worry," shouted Michel. "I'm all for profit." Mr. Pryde frowned and brushed another fish off his knee. It was not clear whether the frown was intended for Michel or the fish.

In a few minutes Michel had forgotten Mr. Pryde. He lifted the kayak into the water, lowered himself gently, and wove through the little harbor with swift touches of the paddle. The low sun threw floating ice debris into surrealist relief; beyond, the open sound was blue and gold. He paddled far in the still water until the post was a spatter of white flecks against the long rising orange hills. The sun dipped behind the crouching mountain and cirrus clouds filmed the northern sky, gleaming as if with their own fire. A glaucous gull circled high, white and incorporeal as the paper-thin moon rising. The musical drip from the paddle and the muted bubbling of the boat's wake blended with the distant accordion to emphasize the vast silence. Michel himself was part of the sunset and moonrise and shining water and iced mountains and the unending quiet northern loneliness.

This country was enchanted, hidden from all eyes except those alike enchanted. He had come on it unsuspecting and in a moment he would wake up. Tears welled into his eyes. Don't wake up, oh don't wake up! There is nothing in waking life that is like this dream.

Then he remembered Maggie and turned toward shore, paddling strongly, the pointed prow lifted. The dance music, no longer softened by distance, was off key and noisy, punctuated by thumping and shouting, and the market-day tent town was busy with running children, buzzing old men, giggling girls and boys. Gasoline drums, piled wooden crates, tarp-covered packaged goods lay in heaps around the warehouse, emptied for the dance.

Michel peered in the open doorway. The quiet sun-touched night was behind him; before him was a medieval drawing of inferno. A kerosene lamp swung from the middle of the ceiling, casting a smoky, dark-yellow glare on whirling bodies, kicking legs, waving arms. Heat thrust outward with the assault of raucous howls and caterwauling music.

Gradually the scene took on a weird semblance of life. A fast round dance was in progress. The musician sat on the floor in a dark corner, his legs crossed under him, his accordion wheezing out sounds like a medley of jigs played on two phonographs at once with the speed trebled. The player was, improbably, Nauli-gak. The dancers galloped in opposite circles, each man swinging the opposing girl off the ground. Mothers with babies in their hoods swung high, the babies' heads narrowly missing the wall; little girls danced with old men; boys lifted gray-haired grandmothers. Young men took turns leaping in the center of the circle, kicking their heels with awkward gusto, to the accompaniment of laughing shouts and clapping hands. Mr. Pryde circled sedately with Nina on his arm, a glowing Nina who had not a glance for Davitt brooding on the sidelines.

In another corner Maggie stood alone in her beautiful clothes, her eyes lowered, her body seeming to shrink into the walls. Michel pushed through thrashing arms and legs. Passing Davitt, he muttered, "You might have asked her to dance."

"I did. She wouldn't dance with anyone." He gave one of his rare smiles. "You're lucky. I'd have to handcuff Nina to keep her with me. In fact I may do just that." He stepped forward and touched Mr. Pryde on the shoulder. "If you want to take it easy awhile, sir, I'll finish this dance. Pretty hot in here." Mr. Pryde, red-faced, relinquished the girl. He looked not only hot but sorely uncomfortable.

"Sorry, old man. Business, you know . . ." He turned even redder and slid away, sidling inconspicuously toward the door like a rabbit backing out of a fox den.

Michel stood before Maggie. She looked up and her flat sad face changed bewilderingly to beauty. Taking her hand, he drew her into the circle, swung her around once, and passed her on to the next man. He could scarcely take his eyes off her. The little feet flickered; she turned and ran and swung lightly as a ballet dancer. When she came back to him she was not even out of breath. He lifted her so her black-glistening eyes were level with his, swung her around once more, feeling the bird-lightness of the small body, and brushed her cheek with his lips.

From his corner, Nauligak watched her too. The jigs seemed to pour automatically from the accordion; they had no connection with the somber, vigilant player.

The dance ended suddenly, in the middle of a phrase, and everyone sank down on the floor or wandered outside, lighting cigarettes and pipes. Michel drew Maggie's arm under his and led her down to the water's edge. The summer night peace was still there, beyond the arc of beach, undisturbed by the noisy horde around the warehouse.

"Maggie, I will stay at Splaine's River," he said slowly and clearly. "I will live in the house for always, and you will live there too, and have all the food and cloth you want." She answered, her voice sweet-cadenced, her eyes radiant. Michel put both hands on her cheeks and leaned to kiss her. They did not hear footsteps.

"She already knew," said Davitt quietly. They drew apart, unsurprised, and turned to him, still deep in the spell of each other. "Zeke told her when he came back from fishing. Come with me now, and Maggie can stay with her brother and her father until you are ready to take them home." He spoke a few words to Maggie, and she pressed Michel's hand and ran away up the beach as lithely as she danced.

They both looked after her. "I don't think she knows any English," said Davitt, "but it's possible she understands you." A brief smile crossed his face, followed by an even more fleeting trace of grief. In silence he led the way through the congested tent village, around the hill to a wooden hut out of sight of the sea. It stood alone, gray and old and self-sufficient, none to keep it company but the summer-talking river and the soaring, singing birds. Inside, feeble flames rose from the thin wick of the seal-oil dish, ritually placed at the left of the entrance. An aged woman sat straight and stern behind it, contemplating the oil as if she were reading an old familiar book. She raised her head and her faraway look went right through Michel; she seemed to see him before he was born and after he was dead.

For Davitt she had, not a smile, but the faintest softening of her skull-like face. He spoke to her, then to Michel.

"She will tell you a story. Please give her a cigarette." Michel, awed, handed her the pack. Slowly, as if choosing, she took one, put it behind her ear and returned the pack. Then she stood up and twisted her clawed hands in stylized contortion at the level of her head. She was very small, but her shadow on the wall was enormous, the hands freakishly long-fingered. Her cracked voice rose and fell with the monotonous precision of an old priest intoning the litany, and her hands moved with it in static, bizarre gestures. The weak fire flickered over the almost fleshless mask of her face, distorting it into a semblance of meaning like a primitive clay idol, and the skull shone yellow through her sparse hair.

The deliberate, unrhythmic chant grew hypnotic; the woman seemed to extend backward and forward into time, and Michel could smell the seal-oil lamps of a thousand years of storytelling and see the solemn listening faces of Eskimo children long since dead. The black-stone eyes were fixed unwaveringly on him, the old face austere, lips hardly moving; only the hands writhed in slow ritual. He felt like a bird before a snake.

She stopped speaking, took the cigarette from her ear and lighted it at the wick. Then she sat back on her haunches again and stared at the oil of the lamp, the cigarette hanging from her bloodless lips. The little river whispered secretly through the silence.

Michel stood up awkwardly. "Thank you," he said. "That was very interesting." She did not look up. "Shall I give her something else?" he asked Davitt.

[123]

Davitt seemed to wake out of a deep trance. "No . . . no, nothing. She doesn't want anything. She was old when the world was new — what do you have that she would want?" He spoke to her in Eskimo, his voice muted and kind; then they left. Michel turned in the doorway and saw her, still immobile, slow smoke curling before her unblinking eyes. She looked like an unwrapped mummy.

They walked around the hill again, to the fresh salty wind and the bright sea, and sat on a flat rock. Davitt looked far over the water, not speaking, his expression remote and melancholy.

Michel was suddenly impatient. "Well, Davitt, why don't you tell me the story?"

"It's an old story," he said slowly. "They don't tell it much any more. Too many people have told them it is foolish and wrong." He gave Michel a brief, accusing look.

"I'm not 'too many people,'" said Michel sharply. "They can tell their tales until their tongues fall out. I would simply like to know why you took me there — why all the devious mystery."

Davitt turned to the sea again and spoke as monotonously as the old woman. "There was a young girl who did not want to marry. Her father was angry. 'If you do not marry,' he said, 'you will have to marry my dog.' One night a stranger came. He had long teeth but he was very handsome. He lay down by the girl and took her to wife. The next day, when the people woke up, they found that the curse had come true. The girl had married the old man's dog. The people were angry, and took her and the dog to an island, and they lived there alone. The dog swam over to the village every day to get deer and seal meat for his wife. The girl bore a litter of many children. Some were dogs and some were humans. The old man heard of the children and felt sorry for his daughter. He decided to kill the dog. The next time it came, the old man put rocks in its pack, with meat on top, and the dog drowned. The girl had nothing to eat, so her father came in his kayak to get the girl and her human children. He brought a sharp knife for the dog children. The girl saw him coming and put the dog children in the sole of her boot. Two blades of grass were their sails. 'Go away,' she said, 'far to the south, where the old man cannot find you.' The dog children sailed away and became white men." Davitt stopped. "That's all."

"They don't think much of dogs," remarked Michel.

"Nor of white men."

"It's plain you'd rather I went away," said Michel, his face flushed with irritation, "but why the mumbo jumbo? Do you think you can frighten me?"

"The mumbo jumbo is part of one of their classical stories of the creation. It's not too much sillier than some of ours. Many of them still believe it."

"Do you?"

Davitt smiled. "I'm not superstitious in any religion. I only wanted to show you this is not a white man's world."

"You seem to get along fine here, you and Nina and Nauligak and all the old witch-ladies."

The dusky eyes dropped, and after a long pause the voice was just audible. "This is not my world either."

Michel stared at him. "Oh well, we'll struggle along somehow. I'm going back and collect my people. They've danced all night. We ought to have a short sleep and get home."

"Yes, take them home by all means. Before you go, discuss with Mr. Pryde what supplies you want him to leave. They can be kept in the warehouse here; you haven't room in your house."

"You don't need to keep an eye on me," said Michel mildly. "Zeke and I will collect the supplies and take them back with us. I'll make room."

"As a policeman," Davitt said formally, "I am concerned with the territory under my jurisdiction. The Splaine's River people are relatively untouched and more primitive than most. I'd like to see them stay that way. They're the most successful community here. The missionary brought them Christianity, which they didn't need — but it did them no harm. They're innocent."

"It isn't in my plans to corrupt them."

"Of course not. But it isn't easy — you may not understand their ways. They know little about trading and there could be misapprehensions. It's possible Nauligak won't welcome a newcomer. He keeps to the old beliefs."

"He likes you."

"I leave him alone."

"So will I." Michel spoke with sincerity, his blue eyes squarely on the policeman's. "Don't worry about me, Davitt. I'm used to being on my own."

"On your own, but not alone. Take care, Michel."

The music had stopped, and people were drifting back to their tents, smiling at each other, murmuring peacefully. In the warehouse were only Nauligak, an elderly couple and a boy Zeke's age, talking in whispers and smoking. They looked up as Michel filled the doorway and quickly looked down again, their voices stilled. Behind him Davitt spoke. They nodded unsmiling and all got up at once.

"I'm going back to their tent," he told Michel. "All beds full in the house. Good night and good luck. I won't see you before you go." He lifted one hand in a quick salute and turned on his heel. Michel watched them down the beach. They were talking again, Davitt's voice blending with the rest in earnest singsong.

Ide was alone in the office typing reports, dregs of strong coffee in a stained cup beside him. An uneasy harmony of snores came from the double bedroom. Long sonorous sighs — that would be Hodge — were counterpointed by Mr. Pryde's brisk wheezes.

"Don't you police ever get to go to bed?" asked Michel.

"It's all right, we slept last night. We only sleep every other night — or rather every other half year. When the sun goes down we sleep and sleep. It's more interesting than reading over last summer's newspapers. How was the dance?"

"I expected drums and incantations. I got jigs and round dances. The incantations came later."

"The old lady around the hill, I expect. She's Jacques's pet witch. Did she frighten you?"

"No," said Michel shortly. "Ide, could I type a radio message for you to send after I'm gone?" The policeman gave up the typewriter with alacrity and went for more coffee. When he came back Michel pulled the sheet out and handed it to him.

" 'Harold Twining, Editor, *East-West Review*, Hudsonton,' " Ide read. " 'Material rich. Will stay send you stuff projected book. Request indefinite leave. Thanks.' No wonder you want this sent after you've gone. Guess you don't want an answer."

"You don't need to rush over with it," said Michel smiling.

"Michel, I don't want to give advice like Grandfather Davitt. But aren't you rather burning your bridges? Suppose you get cabin fever. Suppose you get sick. Suppose those people over there gang up on you. Suppose there aren't any furs to trade." Michel was turning red. "Oh hell, forget it. You're as stubborn as that piece of hair at the top of your head. Go on over with you — but don't get lost."

Michel smoothed his cowlick. It sprang up again through his fingers. "Thanks anyway. You see, I know this place is purgatory to you and I know Davitt doesn't want me here. So the testimony is prejudiced. In any case I wouldn't listen, because I like it here."

"So I gathered. But why?"

Michel almost laughed to hear his own constant questions repeated. Why, he wondered, should I like a country so indefinite for a journalist, so unprofitable for a trader, so monotonous for a professional traveler — so appallingly underpopulated? Have I at last discovered that what Jacques said that first night is true, that it is less lonely here than outside?

"I don't know exactly," he said finally. "It's that I've always been an outsider — there've been too many people, too much coming and going. Here there are only a few, living intensely. I've never known such friends. I only had the memory of a house; now I have a real one. Mainly I've found time and space for thinking. Davitt said that and I didn't listen. He was right. You know, Ide, I've never thought, always lived on the edges. This is home."

"You're demented," said Ide gravely. "But you might just get lucky. I hope you find what you're looking for."

12

LITTLE WAVES danced on Michel's own curve of beach, and the house on the willow-greened terrace, surrounded by late wind-blown poppies, was weathered and welcoming as if it had been there always.

They carried the supplies from the boat and piled them in the small back room. "Tomorrow shelves," said Michel, "the next day a store. Tell them all, Zeke, that if they need anything it is here."

"They will make shelves for you, but I think they will not buy in the store."

"Why not? Too decadent?"

"They will think it is begging."

"It isn't. Their skins brought a good price and part of these goods is already theirs. The rest they can pay for with the winter trapping." Zeke's forehead creased distressfully above his lifted brows, but he did not speak. "It's all right, Zeke, if they buy or if they don't buy. I think they will when they get used to the idea. Don't worry so much."

"But the foxes . . ." began Zeke.

"The foxes won't run away because I have a store. You fuss like an old maid. Don't carry the world on your back." Michel patted his shoulder and turned to measure the walls for shelves.

"Maggie," he called. She came running. He caught her hands

and swung her around, and she laughed. "You like to run, don't you, like a little girl," he said fondly. "Get supper for everyone — please. Zeke, will you ask her? Don't forget the 'please.'"

Zeke talked and she answered. "She says she is making supper. It will be ready for all when you are ready."

"I don't have to ask you anything, Maggie. You always know before. However, I will teach you English."

"No use," muttered Zeke.

"And you will teach me your beautiful tongue," continued Michel. "Don't scowl, Zeke," he went on as Maggie ran back to the kitchen. "Your sister may be only a girl but she is my girl." Suddenly he frowned. "She looks too young," he said half to himself. "Zeke, didn't you say she is old enough to be married?"

"Seventeen, a woman — I told you."

"Is she engaged?"

"What is that?"

"Is there a boy — a man — who wants to marry her?"

"Yes. He lives two sleeps away, over there." He pointed out the window toward the low mountains on the horizon. "They were to be married when they were ready. Their fathers said so when they were born."

"And now she is seventeen, so this marriage could take place tomorrow."

"Yes."

"And she's been . . ." Michel's face darkened with anger. "Why didn't you tell me? You're as deceptive as all of them."

"Tell you what?" asked Zeke innocently.

"That your precious little lying sister," he shouted, "is on the eve of her wedding day."

"But she will not marry. I said only that she could."

Michel felt like shaking him. "If you're not secretive, you're dense. Why don't you tell me all these things at once? Why won't Maggie marry him? When does she see this man? She wants to marry him, yet she comes to me . . ."

[130]

She came to him then and put a hand on his arm, speaking with soft entreaty. He shook her off and her eyes filled with tears. She turned to her brother, questioning. Zeke answered low and anxious, and she spoke again, decisively, her little chin set, eyes flashing.

"She wants me to say all," said Zeke finally, and continued with reluctance. "My father wished her to marry, and took her from here to hide her. But she came back to you, and then he made her go to the dance. She would not look at him . . . the other. After, his father and my father talked, and they said there would be no marriage."

Michel saw again the shy figure in the darkness of the dance hall, with eyes and arms only for him; relived the moment after the dance when he had unknowingly walked in on the conference that decided her future, felt the stiff embarrassed hostility of those abruptly silent people. He looked down at Maggie with pity. "Poor little Maggie," he said. "Old enough to marry but no one wants her." The face upturned to him was alight with love. Tears still shone on her cheeks and lashes but the dark eyes were clear. Pity faded, replaced by a faint sense of awe. Those trim feet, he remembered observing, were set unhesitatingly on a straight path.

"She is only a girl," Zeke was saying, still worried. "She does not know what must be said and what must not be said. Now you will be angry with my father."

The pity transferred to Zeke. "I would be more angry if I did not know," he said gently. "Didn't Father Splaine teach you the strength of truth? Maggie, I think, is stronger than you and stronger than her father." Dangerously strong, he added silently, not dangerously young. Nothing would stop her. She had decided to be his, and his she was. He gripped her shoulder hard, half expecting steel under the snowy cloth. The dimunitive bones twisted under his hand, and she squealed, then laughed.

"You are such a child, Maggie dear. You don't know what you're doing. I'm a loner." She would not believe him but he had to try. "Tell her, Zeke, that I cannot marry her, that this is not my home forever and I will go away sometime." He looked down at her again, at the delicately modeled face with the trusting eyes of a young animal, and his stomach knotted with pain and tenderness. The sweet wide child's forehead should never be lined . . . "No, tell her nothing. She is all right as she is."

"You are not angry with my father?" Zeke's concern was light years away from the fate of his sister.

"Your father doesn't matter," said Michel. "Get that through your confused head. He does not matter one wooden nickel's worth. About me and Maggie, that is," he added as the pulse throbbed behind Zeke's tensed forehead.

"Michel, you do not know my father." The words were whispered and deadly. A cold wave rippled up Michel's spine. But he laughed.

"Neither do you. Nauligak has you buffaloed. He's no more powerful than the old lady who tells horror stories to scare the tourists." He drew Maggie close and felt comfort.

"Now, Maggie, we're hungry. Zeke, would you tell the others they can stay and eat?" The boy went outside and Michel followed Maggie to the kitchen. Bannock was baking in the oven, its odor rich and sweet, and on the stove was a pot of rice and another of canned beef stew. Strewn over the table were tins of spices and dried herbs, sharp sauces and condiments. Maggie opened them all, sniffing and wrinkling her small nose, and sprinkled liberally from each into the stew pot. She stirred and sneezed and looked up at Michel laughing, her eyes red.

"I brought you too many toys, little one. Don't use them up or you'll have nothing to play with this winter." He closed the tins and bottles and put them on a high shelf, shaking his head and pointing at himself. "I'll pick them out until you get used to them."

But the boys and girls were pleased with Maggie's stew. Sneezing, coughing and giggling, they consumed the whole pot within minutes and sopped up the remains with fat pieces of bannock. They rubbed their stomachs and belched contentedly as they lit the cigarettes Michel handed around.

He scanned the smooth happy faces. Children all — but the boys carried long knives and their harpoons rested by the door, and the girls wore plain rings. These children were hunters with their wives, none of them older than Maggie. He turned to his dainty girl with a sharp pang of guilt. She met his eyes instantly; hers were untroubled. He turned away quickly.

"Zeke," he said, "you must tell Maggie that . . ." Her small hand, warm and strong, crept into his under the table and lay in his palm like a sleeping kitten. It was too late: the fine balance had been tipped and Maggie had changed. She would now never be as these girls . . . "that the supper was perfection," he finished, squeezing her hand.

He held her close all that night, feeling even in sleep the soft-nippled adolescent breasts. She stirred early, slipping from his arms. "Stay, lovely Maggie," he said in half-sleep, and she sank back, turning her body toward him, the nipples now erect and hard against his chest, heart beating to heart, bellies and thighs pressed together, motion taking them in a slow crescendo of ecstasy until at last they both cried out with the agony of desire and he took her roughly, crushing the slight body beneath him, his teeth against her open mouth. She melted against him in a trance of passion.

"My beautiful darling," he whispered when at last they were quiet. "You will never regret your birthright. I will keep you and cherish you . . ." The words did not ring true; the bell had an unseen crack. He took her head in both hands and kissed eyes and mouth and neck, covering with affectionate caress the words he had omitted.

To Maggie it was all one; again, as the first time, though they lay close in love the paths of their thoughts ran divergent courses.

From that day on Maggie stayed, all through the dry cool late-summer days and the twilit nights, and Michel began to teach her English, using a cookbook as text and food and kitchenware as objects — spoon . . . salt . . . fry . . . breakfast . . . oven . . . chili sauce . . . These were the limits within which Maggie was leashed, with all the wide world of words untouched around her. "She is good with needles and stoves," Zeke had said. Unconsciously, because it was easier than trying to know Maggie, he accepted the evaluation. She looked at him, as he enunciated the dry directions of a recipe and pointed at tins and sacks and measuring cups, her pencil-line eyebrows raised and her widened eyes asking. Sometimes she turned to the window and spoke to it in her own singing language, although outside there was nothing but the same hillside of browned moss and yellow grass and dying poppies, traversed by twittering, swift-feeding birds.

"What are you saying, Maggie?" he asked, but she only smiled and picked up the cookbook to trace with one finger and speak slowly the hard-learned words, her expressive eyes again lowered.

The days were busy with building and painting and the two hours, measured to the minute, which Michel imposed on himself for writing. The slow deep-blue nights were bewitched with love. But unease built in him as Zeke stayed away. Had he fallen under the spell of his father's hostility? Was he hurt by his friend's blunt words? The wind bore the distant shouts of the whale hunters, and kayaks bobbed and spun far out on the water, but none came near.

"Maggie, why doesn't Zeke come?" She answered in a lilting flow, her straight look unconcerned with any but him. "Tomorrow we will go and find him," he said, consciously stiffening his spine against the small prick of fear. "Both of us, Maggie. We are not exiles."

But that evening Zeke came, cheerfully apologetic. "My father is very stern," he said. "All must hunt, in the day and in the night. Between day and night I made your harpoon. Then I slept, for two sunrisings without stopping. Today there are no whales, so I have come."

The harpoon was of walrus ivory, its barbed iron tip bound with strong leather, its handle spiraled with a strip of silver-furred seal-skin, a thong wound loosely from tip to handle, with a dried inflated seal bladder at one end. Michel held it in one hand; it was heavy but perfectly balanced, seeming almost ready to throw itself.

"Beautiful and vicious," he murmured. "Thank you, Zeke. It is a good spear, but I hadn't realized before that I shall never use it." The boy did not answer. His face went sad, with the young-old look, and his shoulders drooped. Michel explained quickly. "I'd like to go hunting with you, Zeke, but you must do the hunting. I've never killed anything before the young seal and the old bear, and they made me cry."

"You were very brave, Michel. It is easier to kill a little whale."

"I'm not afraid of a little whale. I only don't see why it should be killed by me."

The boy looked up then. "You are a great man. Already the grandmothers sing to the babies of you. I myself will tell my little children, and they will tell theirs."

"It's very important to you, isn't it? You own the hero. All right, Zeke, I'll go with you, and I'll try not to miss. The legend must go on." His tone was light, and the acidity of the words did not change the glow of relief on the young face.

"Come tomorrow. I will have a kayak for you."

"And the whales will come running when they see my new harpoon?"

Zeke laughed like a child. "Yes, they wait for you now, hiding because you are not there yet."

Zeke was a solicitous guide. About a mile from land the water was roiled as a line of whales surfaced and sank like a huge serpent, and he showed Michel how to cut one out and drive it gradually inshore. The boy's kayak, darting and spinning, was an extension of his body, and Michel felt clumsy in his wake. The whale leaped and turned in the midst of the leap, its heavy tail fluke thrashing before it disappeared toward deeper water. In less than a second Zeke was at the far side of the still whirling water, and a moment later the whale surfaced beside Michel, its large surprised wet eye on a level with his. Michel stared back and unwillingly lifted the harpoon. He threw — too late — and the whale was gone in an eddy of dark ripples.

Zeke touched the water with one hand. "Go in peace, little white whale."

"Now can we go home? You see how I am."

"You have never thrown the spear before. Next time will be easy."

The next time was too easy. Zeke caught one in the side of the neck and it streaked out into the sound, the inflated seal bladder flouncing behind. They went after it, their wakes white stripes on the flat blue. The whale slowed, and bubbles came up where it wallowed, struggling with its wound, in the deep water. At last it surfaced.

"Take it!" cried Zeke.

"I don't want to lose another one."

But Zeke leaned on his spear, his eyes, darkly shining, fixed on Michel in unswerving, hypnotic adoration. The whale, agonized, asked to be killed, and Michel drove his harpoon into the pain-reddened eye. The animal gasped and sank, bubbling blood, then rose again in a last convulsive leap, to land, white belly up, beside the kayak. Michel's left eye ached abominably, twitching as if a small barbed spear were caught there.

They towed it back to shore, where Zeke extracted the liver and handed it to Michel. The whole village followed, admiring, as he carried the bloody burden on his outstretched palms, like a crown, to offer it to Nauligak. The old hunter stood inflexibly silent before his door. Aitu, just behind, gave him her beautiful smile. On impulse Michel passed Nauligak and handed the prize to her.

"For you, lovely mother of Mauyak. I would offer you jewels, but this, I think, you like better."

Zeke's voice echoed the tenderness of her answer. "You are as one of my sons."

Then Nauligak spoke, his voice solemn as his face. "We will feast now, and thank Takanaluk Angaluk for sending us the whale and for guiding your spear to its eye." Zeke repeated the speech, turned abruptly and walked down to the beach. He did not look up when Michel followed and touched his shoulder.

"What's wrong, Zeke?"

"He should not have spoken those words."

"I thought they were very polite words."

"He knows well," said Zeke angrily, "that only our good Lord Jesus can tame the whale and send the spear straight."

Michel laughed. "Is that all? The old names still come more easily to his tongue, Zeke. You must not blame him. Besides, you've got it wrong too. Jesus may have performed miracles, but his legacy was love, not magic."

"He should not have said that name," repeated Zeke sullenly.

"Don't be sulky. The liver will taste as good whoever was responsible for it. By the way, who is Takanaluk Angaluk?"

"She is nothing. Before we knew about the Christ Child the foolish people believed that she married a dog and then the bird of storm. They said her children with the dog were the first people, and the seals and whales and walruses were made from her fingers, and that after she was dead she ruled the sea and the land. My father knows it is a baby's story. He has not spoken like that since . . ." He broke off and stared rebelliously out to sea.

"Married a dog . . ." So Nauligak was one of those who really believed the preposterous legend. For a few seconds Michel was caught in a web of nightmare, and the washed pebbles and the

[137]

clear cold sea and the white-gold mountains threatened him with unknown terrors. He shook his head violently. "Let's both forget it, Zeke. Superstition isn't catching."

A sweet call floated on the calm air. It was Aitu, smiling in her doorway, summoning them to dinner.

13

THE SUMMER DAYS, ever shorter, slid by. Hunting grew fever-
ish; every day kayaks sped nervously back and forth over the gray
sound and the hunters' cries answered one another like the calls
of anxious birds across the cold quiet water. Michel did not hunt.
When one hunter or another slept after the long hours of chasing
the elusive little solitary seals and the rare column of whales,
Michel borrowed his kayak and went out to watch. He kept near
Zeke, and the boy, eyes restlessly scanning the watery desert, told
him of the habits of sea mammals and the ways of hunters. In
the midst of a sentence he would be gone, toward a distant ripple,
and Michel followed to help herd the wary animal to the shallows.
But he left his harpoon at home.

"You don't need me," he said. "Tell the others, if they wonder,
that they are the hunters and I am only the storyteller. They will
do great deeds and I will keep them on paper. I don't care to kill
wild animals, and I've already done my bit for the grandchildren."

Zeke turned worried eyes on Michel. "You are strange, Michel.
But they all know you are brave, so you can be strange too." He
gave a small laugh that did not touch the lines of concern, and went
back to his unquiet vigil.

"Narwhal!" he called suddenly, and plunged his paddle into the
water. Beyond the streaking kayak was a slow stately procession,

dead-gray bodies arching ponderously out of the water, elongated teeth like enormous knitting needles dipping and rising. The two boats broke through the line and cut one out. It circled toward the dangerous shallows, deliberate even in its attempts to escape. It was pathetically easy to kill. Even watching is too much, thought Michel as the heavy helpless creature rolled over and the long tooth, carved and delicate and useless, pointed for a moment at the sky, then dipped for the last time into the water.

The pale stout body, touched with red, seemed alone in the still sea. It was large, it was calm, it ate only small fish; there was nothing in its innocent world that it need fear. Yet an unknown enemy had made of land and sea and air a sudden horror, and the quiet elements of its wide-spaced home had dissolved into pain and blood.

Zeke rested on his paddle beside Michel. He also gazed at the narwhal, and his eyes were still anxious. "We need many like this. There is not much time."

"But it's still summer."

"When the storms begin summer goes fast, and all the whales go then too."

Michel followed his glance at the cloud-rippled sky and the yellow in the southwest where the invisible sun neared the horizon. "Sunsets," he mused. "Just like home." For a moment, staring at the sulphurous sky, he was unaccountably depressed. "Zeke," he said quickly, recovering himself, "you have mountains of seal and whale in your storehouses. Why do you always talk as if you would all starve?"

"The meat goes quickly. There are many of us."

"Then come to my store."

"Perhaps it will be necessary," said Zeke gloomily.

Michel laughed. "You're as dolorous as a soap opera. Of course it's necessary. What will Mr. Pryde say if I don't sell so much as a pack of cigarettes?"

[140]

"Do you want the tooth?" Zeke was still frowning down at the narwhal.

"Not specially. Is that what we were talking about?"

"It is a good one, longer than you are. It has been told that white men like them because they are magic."

"Sailors used to sell them as unicorn horns. I'll tell you the unicorn story while we all eat the liver. We're having the usual feast, aren't we?"

Michel told the legend of the unicorn and was given the tooth. It stood between his windows, white and narrow-twisted, next to the unused harpoon. It did not look like a tooth, and Michel could sometimes forget that it had been part of a live animal. Meanwhile the hunting went on.

The terns were hunting too, with the same concentrated haste as the men. Their voices floated in Michel's window on the sea wind. He stopped typing to listen to them. The calls that sounded over antarctic seas in the long southern summer day now rang over the tundra ten thousand miles north. Theirs was the voice of the icy regions of perpetual sunlight. The cries were hoarse and sad; these terns did not seem to enjoy eternal sun. Michel left his sterile page and stood by the window, the fur curtain billowing softly against his face.

Maggie was at the edge of the beach where the river joined the sea. The slim-winged swallow-tailed birds circled around her, banking steeply and darting at her head. She walked slowly, stooping now and then and holding the long front of her parka in a cup. Michel understood that she was gathering eggs. He sighed and went down to her.

"No eggs, Maggie," he said carefully. "They belong to the birds." He began to take the eggs from her and to lay them haphazardly on the beach. With a smiling head-shake Maggie picked them up again.

"No, child," he said more sharply. "Give them to me." But she was searching the ground. Gently she laid two mottled eggs in a shallow depression marked only by random feathers. They blended into the pebbled sand and were invisible a yard away.

"How did you find them?" he asked when she had replaced the last egg.

"Birds tell me." She walked away from him, watching the circling terns. Two separated from the rest and swooped toward her head uttering high harsh cries, passed her with a rustle of wings and nearly brushed the ground before they rose. She knelt and laid her hand where they had been. One egg and one immovable beach-colored chick nestled in the small shelter of a willow shrub.

"The birds could tell the foxes too. I hope these terns find the South Pole again. They're better off there." She raised her eyebrows in a question. "Never mind, Maggie, you already understand too much." He touched the willow. Its furry blossoms had long since gone to seed, leaving yellow-headed dry stalks, and its leaves were brittle. Then he pointed to the chick. "It is late."

"Late," she echoed. "They all die." She swept her hand over the desolate beach. "No food."

"The ocean is full of fish."

She nodded, then shook her head, her sunny face momentarily grave as if a small cloud had crossed it. "Fish no good."

Michel laughed. "You just wanted an excuse to collect eggs. We'll leave these where they are anyway. Maybe the fish will get better. Or there will be Indian summer."

They left the terns to their hopeless circling. The forlorn cries followed them into the house.

One windless morning there was a thin elastic cover of ice on the sheltered cove below Michel's house. The slow trickle of the river, already frozen far up in the foothills, could not break it. It was dissipated by the late-rising sun and the push of the tide but formed again in the night. All at once birds were everywhere, calling nervously, fussily gathering their scattered young into tight flocks, eating with frenetic haste. There were too many of them; blindly busy, they barely evaded Michel's feet. They were disturbing, almost disgusting. Go, go, he shouted silently. The birds were a reflection of an obscure malaise that came on him with the too-early sunsets.

A storm came down from the polar seas, and for three days there was no sun as the blizzard swept over the unprotected land. Fingers of ice tapped at the windows and the roof shook under titanic gusts. It was impossible to stand outdoors. Crouched low, Michel crept to the river for freezing, silt-laden water. The rolling brown hills, the mountain, the long stretch of sea had disappeared in a frenzied whirl of sleet and snow. The house was invisible from the river, and disembodied waves crashed high above the beach, breaking on the rocks of the promontory and sending their salt spray to mingle with the sharp snow that stung his cheeks and eyes.

When the sun rose on the fourth day, pale yellow, far to the south, the world it shone on heatlessly was silent, swathed in white. No bird called; even the river was soundless, hidden under a ragged pall of new ice. Tides moved the inlet ice, and every night Michel heard booming and crackling as the cover formed, ever thicker, and the currents broke it and thrust it far up the beach. That was, these days, the only sound.

He wished the birds back.

The terns had gone, their eggs and chicks lost under the snow. Just within his porch Michel picked up a snow bunting, a flash of black and white in his palm, now stiff as wood, its wings frozen outspread at the moment of seeking shelter.

Remembering the sweet derisive song of summer, he visited the graveyard. A tall dirty mound of snow had formed on the missionary's stone. It moved; yellow eyes flickered, and the big brown-flecked owl flapped slowly away, soundless as a drift of snow. Atavistic fear gripped him, and he hurried down the silent threatening hills to his warm house.

Maggie sat by a window sewing a hood on the sealskin parka she was making for him. The silverjar curtains framed her coronet-braided hair and her welcoming smile was gravely sweet.

"You don't laugh any more, Maggie," he said, "or run like a little girl." Her eyebrows lifted at the surprise in his tone. Uneasiness possessed him as he regarded this creature who had made an indispensable niche for herself. Maggie was his to keep and cherish — but did he want to?

He shrugged, giving way to the unresisting fatalism that overcame him more and more these strange short days. The sense of fate deepened to depression as he looked out at the slow, inevitable twilight. Write, he thought despondently; that's what you're here for. But the typewriter repelled him. He turned to the organ and began methodically to take it apart. With minute dedication he mended the broken pedals, tacked a narrow plank along the back where the old wood had split, cleaned and oiled the action, scrubbed the yellowed keys with vinegar. The leather of the bellows was dry and cracked.

He sat down amid the pieces of the dismantled instrument, suddenly hopeless.

Maggie was at his side, unasked, fingering the ruined leather. "I make new," she said softly.

"You read my mind, little one. But only part of it." He lifted out the bellows and handed them to her. "It's too damned peaceful here," he said.

One day the sun did not rise at all. A tantalizing glow on the southern horizon moved with the long hours from east to west, and Michel, pacing restlessly, watched, it, demanding the sun. When the glow dimmed early in the afternoon he was incredulous and angry. Maggie served him supper and he snapped at her. "Too much pepper. I don't like pepper." She crept fearfully around the house while he sat by the window watching the stars that had never really faded all day and now were bold and numerous, like flies on an unresisting sick body.

"For God's sake, child, walk, don't creep." She tiptoed into the kitchen. "Didn't you hear what I said?" he shouted, then was silent, not ashamed but despairing.

Maggie came back and sat in the big chair that was hers, mending in her lap, eyes down, flat face sad over the busy fingers. He walked over and looked down at her, abruptly exasperated by the yellowish skin, the humble motions, the troubled devotion in the oval eyes now turned to his. Did he really want a lifetime with this small animal? Cold knowledge informed him: he did not. He remembered the girls of the cities, the lively, nervous girls who never did what you wanted.

"Go home now Maggie, there's a good girl. I have to work alone for a while." He spoke gently, but the distaste was in his voice.

"Michel," she began, then continued in her own tongue. The cadences rose and fell, entreating, comforting, loving, unhappy. She lifted her hands toward him and dropped them again before the tall unmoving figure and the face of inward despair.

"Go. I will come for you — sometime."

"I come back."

"Not until I tell you." His voice rose. "Do you hear? Do you understand? Be off now." He was almost screaming. Maggie went swiftly without another word, not looking back.

Michel picked up the pages he had written. He leafed through them, shrinking at their dry futility. There were embers in the stove and he thrust the thick mass in and closed the door. The papers took a long time to burn, and he sat with his hands over his ears against the horrible, monotonous crackling.

It died down at last. He snatched the cover off the typewriter, rolled in a sheet of paper so hastily it creased, and began to type.

"Dear Sandra," the fingers pounded out. "No doubt this will catch you at a late breakfast, your head aching from the dancing and the drinking the night before. You will look at the envelope

and open the other letter — the one inviting you to a football
game next Saturday. Maybe you'll come back to this later, maybe
not. If you do you'll learn something you don't want to know,
that one man at least can manage to live without you. I'll tell you
how that's possible, my dearest spoiled brat. It's possible because
this very big, very cold hostile country demands everything of a
man, leaving him not even his own soul. It has its compensations.
They are not for your delicate ears but you are going to hear them.
I went hunting by kayak — before the sun went down for good.
The inlet was frozen thinly but it had cracked into patterns like
a jigsaw puzzle. A seal's head showed for an instant black against
the ice-whitened water, then disappeared. We separated, my companion taking the way the seal had gone, I farther out to drive it
inshore if it tried to escape. It couldn't escape. He killed it and
we dragged it back to the gray beach. It looked like old putty except for the blood. Do you know the quantity of blood that comes
out of a dead seal's eye? Or the amount that gushes out of the
belly when you slash it open? Most of it was on our hands when
we had finished, and the thing on the sand was a mass of dark
red chunks with the stench of old death — one meal for the dogs.
Beside it was a clump of late poppies ethereal as the early morning sky, nodding in the freezing wind."

The letter went on, page after page, written in longing haste, as
though he would die in the morning and had to talk his heart out
before the final silence. But even as he wrote he knew in a small
sane corner of his mind that the letter would never be mailed, that
he was only reaching for a world where the sun rose each morning.
There was no Sandra.

An unmeasured season he stayed at home, afraid of the large
outdoors, the iron ground, the crumpled, still sea, the silent, dusty-
white owls. He walked back and forth the short length of the
house, too uneasy to sit down. He ate standing at the kitchen sink,
heating cans over the primus and dropping them on the floor

when he had finished. He watched the daytime dusk with staring intensity; he tore open the cartons in the storeroom to find bolts of flannel, and cut strips to cover the windows against the merciless stars when the day's brief promise died.

Sometimes he read Splaine's books, but the words had no meaning. They were ephemeral; they belonged to a world denied to him.

"Sandra," he wrote. "My mind has become a lump of ice and I see with frozen eyes." Ripping the sheet out, he flung it on the growing pile, then picked them all up and started tearing. He stopped in sudden horror, and the half-torn papers fluttered to the floor. Carefully he gathered them again and put them in a drawer. Sandra was his only reality.

Time was lost. Days were short and gray, nights miseries of sleeplessness. The house was airless and cold. There had not been a fire in the stove in the mindless eternity since Maggie had left.

There were footsteps on the porch. Michel backed to the wall, speechless with terror, while the door slowly opened. It was Zeke, but not the Zeke he remembered. This was an ashen-faced frightened boy who looked like a sick child just awakened from a fever dream. The two stared at each other across the room, trembling. Then a small smile turned up one corner of Zeke's mouth. Michel smiled tentatively in return. They started toward each other and met, hands clasped, relief overflowing in laughter and a tangled spate of words.

When they had quieted enough to understand each other Zeke said, "Mauyak made me come. I was sick, I was afraid of the dark. She pushed me out and held the harpoon so I could not go in again."

The vision of gentle Maggie driving her brother with a harpoon made Michel laugh again; then the dread came back. "I thought I was losing my mind. I drove Maggie away."

"I know. When the sun goes our thoughts go south with it. Our heads have nothing left in them and we are like dead. We want to be alone as if we were spirits from the bones."

"Does it happen to everyone?"

"Only a few. Here only me, and now you. I do not know why. I get sick every year like this and they have to push me out. It goes away."

"Davitt likes it," mused Michel, looking at the covered window. Panic touched him again as he thought of the inexorable darkness beyond it. "This must be what he meant about solitude. I'm not very good at it." Zeke looked a question. "I have to get out of the house, Zeke. Far away, for a long time. Night or no night."

"I go to lay my fox traps. Will you come?"

"I think so." He touched the door and drew back again. Then determinedly he pulled it open, stepped out of the house as if into cold water, and saw a world of outer space.

The earth lay silent as a planet that had never known the sun; the farthest curves of this pale globe were clear as pen lines in the arid chill. The southern horizon, mountains clearly black against it, was transparent green, shading to midnight blue overhead, stars enormous as if there were no barrier of atmosphere. The sea was shadowed with motionless waves; its tides deep buried. The round hills, their outlines blurred by snow, lay like frozen foam around the base of the glittering mountain.

"Why didn't someone tell me?" breathed Michel.

"Tell you what?"

"What night was like. I've never seen it before."

14

ZEKE had brought his dogs; they huddled on the snowy beach, noses in their flanks, until he called them. They rose with alacrity, ears alert, and as the men jumped on the sled they ran out on the sea ice, lines taut, the sled rolling and pitching behind them. There was no need to drive them. They raced one another, scooping bites of snow as they ran, tails high, ears cocked. Zeke grunted at them occasionally and snapped the long whip in the snow, as if to remind them he was there. For two hours they seesawed through the humped ice, seeking out valleys formed by tide and wind, the men often hopping off the sled to push it over a concave ridge into the next precipitate valley. When they stopped for tea Michel was breathless and exhilarated.

"The dogs must have had cabin fever too," he said. "They act as if they'd just been set free."

"They like winter. Now they grow up quickly, not like summer when they have nothing to do. Do you want dogs, Michel?"

"What would I do with them?"

"I will show you how to make a little sled, for two dogs. There are good pups. By Christmas they will be ready to train."

Ahead of them the mountain jutted into the sea. Its sheer cliff loomed dark, shining with icicles and twisting rivulets of snow. At its foot ice floes twenty or thirty feet high had been driven against the rocks by the unseen tide. Michel gazed appreciatively at the waste of rock and ice. "Thank you, Zeke. I would like dogs and a sled. I will take them up there."

Zeke looked astonished, then grinned. "You could, Michel. You could grow wings."

"If I reached the top would you believe I grew wings to get there?"

"I would say it to all."

Michel looked at him curiously. "But would you believe it?"

"It would be half true, like all our stories."

"Like the killing of the bear," said Michel bleakly, "or the girl who married a dog. You half believe that, don't you, Zeke."

"Michel, it is cold to sit so long. We have far to go."

"By all means let's go. Talking is a trap." In silence they gathered the primus and the food and pushed the sled out of its frozen ruts, diving for it as the dogs started at a dead run. Zeke led them out to sea, giving the cliff a wide berth.

"Maybe open water there between the ice floes," he explained, "and bears. You do not need to make a legend twice." He smiled, and Michel relaxed.

It took two days to get around the mountain. They slept on the sea, making a snug tent out of the sled and a caribou skin and wrapping themselves in more skins. Michel asked where the caribou skins had come from.

"I haven't seen any tracks," he said, "and all your food comes out of the sea."

"The deer come from people in the south. It is a long way, all the winter, to go and come back. Our people go no more. The last time there were no skins and the deer people were hungry. Many were dead." He stared gloomily at the warm light of the primus. "We are lucky. But maybe not so this winter. There is not enough meat. The cache will be empty before the sky gets light."

"You can always get seals."

"Yes," said Zeke doubtfully. "We need a seal now for the dogs. Will you help?"

They stood for an hour over two blowholes, unmoving and silent, a freezing freakish wind blowing ice flakes in eddies around them. Wrapped as he was, not an inch of flesh uncovered except his aching eyes, Michel felt the cold creep from his fingers and toes numbingly through his whole body. At last a dim shape, blacker than the water, shattered the reflection of the stars at his feet. He stamped and the nose disappeared.

"Seal!" he called, and Zeke twenty yards away stiffened into the killing position, knees slightly bent, body forward, arm raised with the spear poised toward the hole. He stood thus for a full minute, darkly monotoned against the pale ice, motionless as iron.

The hunter arched suddenly and the harpoon struck with a sound like a smothered hammer. He pulled the limp body out of the hole and leaned over it. His knife glistened in the starlight and blood spurted on the snow. Michel moved slowly, needles in his feet, but the boy did not speak or look up. He stared down at the dead seal, dripping knife in his hand, and Michel stopped, enveloped in fear. Had the boy's winter fever come back, out here in the black wilderness? He felt cautiously for his own knife and approached again.

The animal lay flat, skin falling in empty folds at its sides. The eye sockets were deep and the snout and skull were prominent as a dog's, the bone structure clear. It was starved, little left but lusterless fur hanging loosely on a skeleton.

Michel touched the hunched shoulder. "Bad luck, Zeke. We'll get another one." Zeke did not answer but dug again with his knife into the seal's open belly and brought out an object that Michel did not immediately recognize as a fish. It was eel-thin and its fins were large on the fleshless body.

For the first time he recognized the enormity of food. His horror nearly matched Zeke's "Maggie was right," he whispered. "The fish are no good."

At last Zeke spoke, his voice a monotone. "The seal was very hungry. He swallowed this in one piece. If I cut again I can find many more like this. They are not food, they are bones."

"What's happened to the fish?"

"I do not know, but they will be like this everywhere. I have not seen it before, but my father has told me. Then the seals go away to the south, or stay here and die. The people die too."

"We'll have to go after bears after all," said Michel lightly.

"There will be no bears. They eat fish and seal. They go where they can eat."

"Never mind. You have a storekeeper now. No one will starve while I'm here."

"You will be our father," said Zeke bitterly, "feeding the little children who are not big enough to hunt."

Michel was suddenly impatient. "All your people wanted me to stay. What did they think I was staying for — to study butterflies?"

Zeke's voice held the entreaty of a misunderstood child. "Please, Michel, do not be angry. We want you to live here because we love you. We have never had a store and do not understand about it."

"It is easy to learn," he said shortly. The boy turned and hunched unhappily over his seal. "Here, I'll help cut it up," said Michel, repentant. The dogs finished the lean meat in less than a minute, then tore the skin to shreds and trotted off with the bones, snarling with discontent.

The next seal was better. It was half grown, born late, Zeke said, when the snow was already soft and the sun high, and it still had much of its baby fat. But it was the last seal they found.

The third day they left the sea and drove far into the deep-cut river valley behind the mountain. Snow had drifted waist-high in the gorge and they took turns breaking trail, the dogs floundering in their footsteps. Tall rock cairns marked the sites of Zeke's trapline. Near each he baited fox and weasel traps with frozen whale-meat, set them, and sifted snow lightly over them with his mittened hand.

While he worked Michel studied the mountain, powdery under a cloud-filmed moon. There were no cliffs on this side. From the top snowfields sloped roundly into the valley. It was not a high mountain. Gauging the contours and picking out the easiest slopes, Michel estimated that they could descend in less than an hour on snowshoes; it would take longer if they had the dogs.

"What is the mountain's name?" he asked.

"Nothing. Just mountain — kingak."

"It should have a name. It's a landmark for miles."

"It is only a mountain, that has to be gone around, like bad ice in spring."

"You could make life much easier if you went over it. The trip would take one day from your village."

Zeke glanced fearfully up at the mild rises. "No one goes over it."

"Would you go with me one day? Without dogs."

"We must have dogs. They are our feet when we are tired. They are our eyes when the snow comes."

"All right, with dogs. Would you come?"

"I do not know." He looked up at the fogged moon. "We must go home quick."

"Think about it, Zéke."

But Zeke was already turning the dogs, speeding them on the back track. Halfway to the sea Michel turned again toward the mountain. It was not there. Stars and moon had disappeared too, and though he could not see the cloud he could feel it. It was clammy-textured, like a dead hand on his face. There was no wind, but a half hour later it started, fitful gusts playing first on

[153]

their faces then on their backs, whipping the powder snow into small cyclones.

When they reached the sea the full force of the gale hit them all at once, knocking them down. They blundered up and ahead blindly, encompassed by a riptide of snow whirling from both sky and earth. They could not see the dogs; they could barely see each other, and walked beside the sled, bent low, each gripping one of the upcurved runners.

Zeke did not call to the slow-moving dogs, either with encouragement or command, and Michel opened his mouth to ask why. The glacial wind struck down his throat savagely and he dropped his head, covering his ice-torn lips with a numb hand.

He protected himself somewhat by walking doubled over, eyes closed, head down. Slowly accustomed to the battering of the storm, he became aware also of its extraordinary silence. There were no trees to bend and sigh, no waves to crash. Snow fell soundlessly on snow and the wind swept mutely over an unresisting earth. A dog howled, and the sound was torn away in the instant of expression.

No less eerie than the storm's hush was its timelessness. As so often in the past months Michel lost touch with the current of day. But this was a tumultuous timelessness; the wind whipped the seconds out of their minds.

They kept close to the shore. The ice there was high-piled and treacherous, but they could guide themselves by the veiled darkness of the mountain. In its shade the wind was less fierce, and they could take turns going ahead of the dogs, testing with the harpoon the abrupt valleys between the tidal floes.

They struggled steadily, almost without volition. Then — after a day or an hour — Zeke touched his arm. "Tea," he mouthed. Together they tugged on the main trace to stop the creeping dogs. Under the overturned sled, in the shelter of a hide, they lit the primus stove and warmed their hands while the water heated.

Zeke grimaced as the hot tea touched his cold mouth, and his chapped lips split. He put a hand to his face and it came away bloody. "My mouth will be big when we get home. Big enough to swallow a whale." Michel joined in the laughter, feeling his own lips crack. They chuckled over bleeding mouths, frost-touched noses, wind-burned eyes, while the storm raged inaudibly around them and the dogs curled in snow-grizzled spheres.

The wind dropped and the snow ended its dizzying dance and lay decently on the ground. The dim line of the horizon could be seen, a difference in grays, and an occasional star appeared, hidden the next moment in a wisp of frost smoke, then bright again. Following the blizzard came the cold, so deep that they did not feel its intensity. But its insidious narcosis lulled them.

"We must get away from here," said Zeke in a slow sleepy voice. He rose, almost falling, and pulled Michel to his feet. Michel's eyelids drooped as he stumbled around the sled helping to pack and untangle the harnesses.

"Try to run," said Zeke with effort. They headed out to sea, away from the shifting shore ice, running with aching feet beside the sled. The pain in Michel's hands was agonizing as he clapped them together to bring back circulation. Zeke urged the dogs, calling constantly, cracking his whip in the snow.

On the still, open field of the sea ice time was with them again. The short glow of day moved from southeast to southwest, and Michel, following its progress and watching the stars, measured two days and two nights before his own promontory was darkly outlined above the pallid ice.

During those forty-eight hours they had not dared stop to sleep. Cold was not the only threat; more dangerous were the dogs. "If we sleep they will eat us," said Zeke. "You first. They know me."

"They'll eat you first. You're tenderer."

Meals were quick. In the minutes of waiting for the stew to heat or the water to boil they played children's games — leapfrog, hopscotch, tag. Breathless, laughing and momentarily warm, they

[155]

sipped the hot food and regarded each other with unspoken affection.

Michel's house was hot and the stove purred like a well-fed cat. Maggie, shy and smiling, fed them curried chicken. Zeke's eyes closed in the midst of eating but flew open when Michel asked him to stay.

"I cannot. The dogs are hungry." In a few minutes he was gone.

As he wavered on the edge of sleep, the hours and days and minutes of the trip shone briefly in Michel's mind like little candles in the wind. The perilous tidal ice, the hungry dogs, the fatal lure of cold, the soundless blizzard — the children's games and the timeless gaiety of spirit — the little candles went out one by one. The last lighted a despairing boy kneeling before a dead seal.

Winter divided itself in two for Michel: the time for Maggie and the time for Sandra. Except for occasional visits to her mother, Maggie was always there, but he could divorce her at will.

"I do not love you, Sandra, but I can talk to you," he wrote once. "There is no one here to talk to." He made efforts to learn Maggie's language but was baffled by its fluidity. The sharp-spaced English words in turn frustrated her, and their conversations were short and practical. In evenings made bright by the diaphanous shimmer of the aurora borealis they sat close to the hissing stove laboriously exchanging words. What a pretty picture, he thought, and how dull. Charming, obedient child, if only you had a bit of Sandra in you.

Against the stilted limitations of the meeting of their minds in the daytime lay the ecstatic freedom of the meeting of their bodies at night. He never tired of her fiery lovemaking, nor of the soft outpouring of her low lovely voice in the darkness. He did not speak then, nor even think, but caressed her while the song of her love entered his unknowing mind.

In the mornings she was dismissed as if she did not exist, while he communed with his typewriter. Quietly she kneaded bread in the kitchen or sat over her sewing, head down, the furs shaping under her expert fingers. He forgot her.

"Death may speak through the polar gale," he wrote Sandra, "and they laugh in its face, lips cracked and bleeding, eyes nearly blind. Danger may stalk behind an ice floe — they play games in its shadow. I can never be like them. This is the most formidable country to live in, and they live in it the most easily. Coming from a different world, I find difficulties. Davitt doesn't, yet he is not like them either. I marvel at his deliberate aloneness. He likes it!

"Winter madness took me — all the time I was deranged I could stand aside and watch my mind slipping. It was terrible, worse than unconsciousness, worse than downright lunacy. But it's inevitable, they say. No one knows why a few get it, most don't. It may be an extra vulnerability, a slight, unnoticed unbalance of the emotions, a fear of solitude — or simply that the craving for the sun is inherently stronger in some than others. Maggie didn't have it, but then she is just a . . ." He stopped. Maggie had no place in letters to Sandra.

Without the sound of the typewriter the silence was remarkable; no rustle, no breath, no click of needle or knife hinted that she was still there. He turned to look at her. She sat totally still, the shining fur untouched in her lap, her eyes faraway and unseeing, sorrow and fear etched in lines around her mouth and the painful twist of her brows. Michel was unreasonably disconcerted. His safe-made small winter world showed a dangerous crack, and in a moment it might lie in shards around him.

"Maggie?" he said tentatively, afraid of her pain, of her ardors and longings, of all the facets of Maggie that he had deliberately blinded himself to.

Her eyes came back to him and her face glowed with immediate happiness. "What was wrong, Maggie?"

"You go away," she said carefully. "I fear." She smiled as she spoke, and Michel misunderstood.

"Little one, I will go away sometime, a long time from now. But we can be happy together. Isn't that enough?"

The cloud passed over her face again. "You go away *now*, Michel, while I am here."

He took her hands and pulled her up and against him. "Everyone wants to be alone sometimes. It is not strange, it is not to be afraid of." He stroked her hair and the back of her neck and she sighed. "All right, Maggie, not afraid any more?"

She spoke against his chest. "I am afraid for you." Her voice was muffled and he could hardly hear. He lifted her face. No smile was there and the bright eyes held tears. He kissed eyes and mouth.

" 'Grief melts away like snow in May,' " he said gently, " 'As if there were no such cold thing.' Remind me to read some poetry to you tonight. We've had enough of cookbooks."

But he had forgotten by suppertime. From that time he never looked around at her again when he was writing to Sandra.

15

THE TRAPLINE had to be visited and Zeke came by for Michel.

"Let's go over the mountain," said Michel.

"My father says no one goes that way. It is not possible."

"How does he know, if no one has ever climbed it?"

"He knows."

"Therefore you know too." Michel looked straight at him and Zeke's eyes slid away. "I'm going to talk to him." Distress showed on the averted face. "Don't panic, Zeke. We won't fight. This is simply a matter of reason. Father Splaine taught you that, didn't he, to look for reason, not just take what's handed to you?" And where's Father Splaine now?

They rode the sled back to the village. Nauligak, sitting on his furs, his lined face indifferent as a Chinese idol, listened to the careful explanation.

"I have climbed many mountains. There was ice and snow, as you have here, and I know which is good ice and which is bad ice, and how to find the cracks. When I look at a hill I know where the snow might slide and bury us and where it is safe as walking outside your house. There are rocks on your mountain and we will not go on them. I think they are dangerous and will break easily from the hands and feet. We will go on the glacier where your river starts. It is not difficult." Michel felt as if he were talking to a deaf-mute. "Here is how we will go." He took a notebook

[159]

from his pocket and sketched the mountain with dotted lines to show the route. "We will be back in less than three days," he concluded, "with foxes."

Zeke traced the lines with one finger as he translated. His father suddenly swept the boy's hand off the paper and spoke definitively, in a flat monotone. Zeke's face registered respect, fear, anger and rebellion in rapid succession.

"My father says I am a child who thinks he knows everything and will no longer listen to the wise ones. The mountain is bad. There is a bad spirit that lives at the top." He grimaced in disgust. "He knows better than the silly man from the south. He knows all the spirits by name and can call them." His voice rose. "He reads the Bible every Sunday and sings your beautiful songs of God and still he talks of dead old grandmother's stories. He is wrong and evil. God will punish him!"

"Easy, Zeke. Tell him you are a man now and not a little boy. Don't say anything of God or the old spirits. Just say we are going over the mountain."

Zeke talked defiantly. Nauligak waited until he was finished, expressionless as weathered wood, then raised a hand in dismissal. As they went out he spoke again, low and apparently to himself. Zeke shrank as if hit and looked up at Michel with terrified eyes.

"Don't be afraid, Zeke. He is only a man, like us, but older and not so strong. It is hard for him to imagine climbing a mountain and harder to change his old beliefs. His legends can't hurt you."

"It is not that," whispered Zeke, and said no more.

They packed the sled, harnessed the dogs, and were up Splaine's River out of sight of the village before Michel tried to pierce the shell of silence. "We can slide down the other side," he said, "sitting on a skin. It's like flying." Zeke did not respond. Hunched low, eyes riveted on the front of the sled, he seemed sunk in a private dread.

"What did he say?" Michel demanded.

Zeke finally faced him. "He said he had lost a daughter and that now he would lose a son. Okkomikpok and Mauyak are dead."

"Did he mean you would die on the mountain? Or did he mean that you like me?"

"I do not know. I am afraid. Sometimes I remember the old stories, then I forget God and Father Splaine."

"And me," added Michel smiling. In the light of the rising full moon Zeke's face darkened. He might have been blushing. "Mountains are just piles of dirt and rock and ice, Zeke. There are no spirits in them. And when we come back with your sled heavy with skins your father will know he still has a son."

"You are my friend," Zeke said fervently, then added doubtfully, "Everything you say is different, but I believe you. I do not believe my father — but I think there is a bad spirit in me, one of the old ones."

"It's hard to be two people at once."

Zeke stared at him, uncomprehending, then laughed. "I need two heads."

The mountain, washed with moonlight, was more clearly visible than on a summer day. Michel had no qualms as they crossed the round foothills to the broad highway of the inland glacier. The talus was rough with fallen ice and snow-covered stones, and the going was slow. When they reached smoother ground Michel tied himself to the sled with his climbing rope and walked ahead, testing the snow with his ice axe. He instructed Zeke to walk behind, tied with a length of leather stripping, ready to throw himself to the ground and dig in with his harpoon against the slope in case Michel hit an invisible crevasse. They threaded a tortuous course between the wide depressions where the snow had sunk into cracks, and before they were halfway up the white field their shadows were long behind them. The great moon shone directly into their eyes between the two peaks, and the headwall pass at the top of the glacier was already a dark blue shadow. As they neared it, the dogs panting, the men walking ever slower, their legs caught up to the knees in snow, the moon disappeared behind the mountain. In the abrupt darkness the stars shone unnaturally large, winking in the black sky like crystals turning in a light wind. There were no shadows, and Michel moved with exaggerated care, testing every step.

The glacier steepened precipitately where its top arc met the mild incline of the headwall. In five minutes they would reach the flat pass between the peaks. Confidently Michel leaned into the slope, the rope taut behind him — and all at once there was no slope. His feet at the edge of a black gap, he jumped backward so quickly that he startled the dogs, who milled around him whining and growling.

"Get them back, Zeke, quick!" he called urgently. Zeke tugged on his line, jerking sled and dogs downhill in a tangled cluster. Once they were straightened out and had calmed themselves into dark heaps on the snow, Michel turned to hand Zeke a cigarette. The boy was trembling and in the dim light his face was gray with terror. He did not lift his hand to take the cigarette.

"What did you see?" he whispered. "Is it — alive?"

"There's nothing there, Zeke," he said cheerfully, and the irony of his words hit him. "*Nothing*. No spirits and no animals. Just a little difficulty with the ice. Let's eat."

Zeke seemed rooted to the ground, his staring eyes fixed beyond Michel on the place where the footsteps stopped. Nauligak's baleful words echoed in Michel's head and he too shivered. Here in the high lonely darkness the old hunter's curse was a reality. Determinedly he set about making tea. He lifted Zeke's hanging hands and closed them around a cup.

"You'd better warm up, boy, before you freeze to the ground. I'll explore later, by myself. The ice won't bite me."

He ate and drank quickly, then rolled Zeke in a caribou skin, tied all the lines together and fastened one end to his waist, the other to the sled, whose runners he rooted deep in the snow. It was foolhardy to go alone — he looked at Zeke, helpless on the

[162]

snow — but less irrational than dragging a stupefied boy to pitch into the gap behind him.

The glacier was about three hundred yards wide, and along its whole length it had parted from the snow-covered rock of the pass in an opening varying from five to twenty feet and probably hundreds of feet deep. They were walled between narrow serrated ridges on either side of the glacier valley, so precipitous that even snow could not cling to their sides. The ice between the rock walls was slipping relentlessly down the mountain, forming a true moat before the headwall. This was Nauligak's bad spirit.

The makeshift line did not reach the rocks, and Michel loosed himself and crawled to the nearest to look for a possible way up, probing before him with the ice axe. The cliff was an overhang, in deep shadow. He did not notice until he was within a few yards that it was not granite. He picked a shard from a crumbling ledge. It was only slightly darker than the snow. White stone . . .

Slowly he traversed close to the edge of the gulf, searching for an ice bridge. There was none. Back at the sled Zeke lay where he had been left, still fearful.

"The ice is cracked all the way across," said Michel flatly. "There is no way up the rocks on the sides. We'll have to go back. By the way, your father has been here."

"My father . . ." Zeke sat up, alarmed.

"Where did you think the missionary's marble stone came from?"

"I was young and did not ask." His voice was hardly audible as he added, "No one asks my father."

"And why did Nauligak make up stories about spirits? Why didn't he tell us about the crack?"

"I do not know these things, Michel. He thinks in a different way."

"He just about thought us into an unpleasant death."

"No — no, you are wrong. Please, Michel — a crack in the ice is nothing. We will cross it with the sled, the way we did the day you shot the ravens." He laughed shakily as he unfastened the main trace and thrust his harpoon through it, deep into the snow so that the dogs were chained where they lay.

"We will not cross it with the sled. Your father said you might die. I'll be blamed."

Zeke walked, boldly now, to the edge of the chasm. "It will fit here. If I die you will die too. Then there is no one to blame."

"I don't get you, Zeke. You were afraid of a spirit and you're not afraid of this thing."

"It is only a little crack." He dragged the sled to the gap and upended it, shoving the runners far down into the snow.

"It's a little horror," said Michel, baffled by the easy courage that was Zeke's birthright. "But we may make it. I'll go first. Hang on while I get this thing across." Zeke squatted, his heels dug in, and Michel pushed heavily at the raised front. The runners thumped down on the other side with barely a foot to spare. There was no more than a foot on the near side.

"It may be undercut," said Michel. "Stay well back." He drove his ice axe into the snow behind the sled, angled downhill, and knotted the rope strongly around it. "You sit on this and don't move until I'm across. If the bridge doesn't hold, jump for your life. When the stake pulls out of the snow it will throw you right into the crack." He was tying the other end of the line around his waist as he spoke.

Zeke took Michel's hand off the rope and untied it. "I will go first. I am little, like a fox. You are too fat. Over there I will dig the sled in the snow and sit on it. Then it will be safe for you." He fastened the rope around himself.

"I got you up here and I won't sit here and watch you fall in a hole. Besides I'm not fat," he added childishly. Then he let go the rope and laughed. "You're right, of course. This is no place for heroics. Go ahead. I'll tie you double." He unfastened the lead dog's long line and knotted one end around Zeke's waist, the other around his own. Then he sat down on the buried stake, dug his heels into the snow, and kept both lines taut while the boy crept out on the sled, cautious as a cat. In a moment he was on the other side and digging deep trenches with his knife under the sled runners. These he piled with snow and stamped on them. Walking a few paces back, he dug holes for his own legs, burying himself up to the thighs.

"Come across, fat man," he called, tugging lightly on the line.

"You don't look so good yourself. You look like a cooking pot with a face on it." Michel threw all their equipment over, then followed on hands and knees, glacing back at the underside of the glacier. There was no reflection there of starlight on snow. The undercut ice broke off about a foot from the top, and below this crust was a vast empty cavern whose floor was so far down that not the faintest gleam of light illumined it.

His legs were shaking when he joined Zeke. "The ice is rotten. We'll have to leave the dogs. If we go across again it will break."

"The dogs will die there." Zeke was already at the sled.

"Let them die."

"They will be good dogs," said Zeke reproachfully. "They are young but already strong."

"Do you want to kill yourself for five useless dogs?"

"I like them."

"Go ahead then. But they will all fall in, one after the other."

Zeke was already on the other side. "Not my dogs." He pulled out the harpoon staking them and threw it across the gulf, then tied them in single file. Flicking his whip toward the lead dog, he shouted hoarsely. The dog sniffed at the edge, then crawled on the sled, tail down, nose touching the wood. The others followed with reluctant docility.

Michel laughed, relieved. "They look ashamed to be riding on a sled. Come back quick, Zeke."

The boy stepped lightly, surely on the sled. There was a deep rumble as the uncertain ice finally gave way and the sled, Zeke clinging to its end, sank slowly. Then the ice axe leaped from its moorings on the far side and Michel fell forward, the lines biting

[165]

into his ribs. He threw himself back, legs deep in the holes Zeke had dug, and gripped the lines with all his strength. They held, but he could do nothing. The sled swung in the gulf, then bumped massively against the underground rock of the headwall, wrenching his arms cruelly at the shoulder sockets. His fingers weakened under the strain, but he willed them to hold fast. Neither motion nor sound indicated that there was anything at the other end but a dead weight. He stood for a lifetime, eyes shut, mind closed, hands like iron on the unmoving lines.

"Michel!" It was a husky whisper, startlingly close. Michel's fingers loosened with the shock, then clutched again as his eyes flew open and he saw first a head then shoulders ease over the wall, and Zeke slowly crept out of the abyss. The lines were still around his waist, attached to nothing, cut raggedly short. Michel stared, disbelieving. The boy should have been hundreds of feet down in a black cave of ice.

"We lost nothing, no dog, no sled, no ice axe. You are very strong, Michel. Not fat." He laughed.

Abruptly the reaction came. Michel's frozen hands slipped off the lines, which seized at his waist. He swayed forward, almost fainting. Zeke threw himself on him, took the lines and dragged the sled up over the edge.

At last they sat together, well back on the placid slope of the pass, and gazed, wordless and exhausted, at the still night world. An expanse of rolling hills, withdrawn under the snow, rose from the coast high to the inland mountains, peaks rounded with ice-caps. Moon-touched clouds drifted under immense stars, and far below their moving shadows billowed the sea.

Slowly the two turned their heads and looked at each other. Michel essayed a smile. "For a minute I thought you were that spirit. I nearly dropped you down the hole. What happened to the lines?"

"They caught around the back runners when I fell, so I cut them with my knife and climbed up the sled." His round innocent face had lines of laughter at the eyes and he spoke as lightly as if he had been describing an escapade on his father's roof.

Michel was shocked. "That was a crazy stunt . . ." Then he realized the extent of the boy's courage and spirit. "What really happened," he said slowly, "was that you cut the lines so I shouldn't be killed too. You were ready to give your life for mine — and not tell me."

Zeke laughed again. "The mountain does not need two more spirits. We would not be bad ones, but it is better not to be any kind of spirit."

But Michel was grim. "If it hadn't been for you we'd both be down there. We shaved it close, Zeke. I still wonder why your father didn't tell us."

His thought hardened. Nauligak had seen the undercut ice shelf. They were both to have fallen, one helplessly pulling the other after him. The boy was to have been sacrificed so that the outsider would perish.

It was only a guess. He would never be sure. He shut his eyes against the suddenly hostile mountain night.

"Your hands are cold," said Zeke quietly. Kneeling, he pulled off the wet mittens and massaged the stiff fingers with hands almost as cold. Michel watched the intent face, so easily moved to laughter at danger, now lined with concern over his friend's discomfort. At this moment he was like Maggie, undemanding and solicitous and faithful. A fleeting perception lighted Michel's mind: these two friends were more important than hypothetical enemies and conjectural hostility.

But introspection was foreign to him and the insight was, as always, short-lived.

He withdrew his hands. "I'm fine now. Let's have tea." As soon as they had drunk they loaded the sled, harnessed the dogs and started down. Shallow ravines and sloping terraces spread below them. No ridges or glaciers interrupted the long curves of mountainside.

"Let the dogs go their own way," said Michel. "We'll slide."
Boulders from the peaks littered the pass. Michel dug one out
with his ice axe and fastened it as an anchor to the end of the
sled. Then he took a caribou hide from the sled box. Zeke
snapped the whip in the snow, calling his dogs, and sat beside
Michel on the hide. They flew down the first slope, snow spray
in a cloud behind them, and landed heads down at the bottom of
the ravine. Shaking themselves, stamping and laughing, they
climbed to the next ridge and sailed away again. Choosing the
steeper slopes and avoiding the terraces, it was less than an hour
before they stood breathless with speed on the lip of the valley
where Zeke had laid his traps. Far above them the dark spots of
the dogs moved back and forth, traversing downward at a prudent pace, the weighted sled swinging easily behind them.

Zeke pointed to the south, yellow with day. "We left when the
moon came up. Not one sleep from home. We will always go
this way."

"What will you do with the crack? Fill it with pebbles?"

"We can go on the other ice. The short one with rocks at the
top."

"It's probably worse."

Zeke grinned. "We crossed one ice. Another is only another.
My father made up the bad spirit like a story to frighten babies."
Death might never have yearned up at him from the cavern.

Michel shivered. "Let's leave the mountain to the storytellers,
Zeke. We'll try your second ice this time but not again."

They let the dogs rest a few minutes, then descended to the
valley. The first trap, now buried in snow, was empty. Zeke
brushed it off, put in new bait, reset it and sprinkled snow over
it. The second held an elderly weasel, its skin loose over its
frame, fur fallen out in ugly patches. He frowned and threw it
far away so the dogs would not fight over the meatless carcass.

The next traps were empty, but from the last came gasping
squawks. Zeke, grim-faced, uncovered a raven caught by the leg,

blue-black feathers ruffled and dull, thin neck twisted, beak gaping. As they watched, the bird died. Zeke opened the trap and picked up the desiccated body. Loose feathers fell back, exposing a breastbone thrust sharply against skin. The whale bait in the trap was untouched. He dropped the bird, reset the trap, and strode back the way they had come, speaking no word. Michel, following, saw a dog pick up the raven, worry it for a few seconds, and drop it. The other dogs sniffed it and passed on.

At all his trap areas Zeke left Michel with the sled and trudged in widening circles, head down, searching the ground. Finally, back near the first trap, he came to the sled and sat down, sunk in apathy. Michel made a meal. Zeke gazed blankly at the food as if he didn't know what it was, then looked up with an embarrassed smile, very young.

"You think this is my first trapline and I am a child who thinks foxes will walk into his house when he calls them."

"Of course not."

Words poured out now. "The raven is a quick bird. He thinks like people. He never takes a trap, only if there is nothing else and he is dying. There is nothing else, Michel. No tracks in the snow — no fox, no weasel, no rabbit, no owl, no bear, no mice. It is true I am a child. I am so young that I never knew a winter like this. The old ones speak of it, as if their life was harder than ours and they were braver. I thought they made up stories to fool little boys, now they are old and cannot hunt."

There was a glimmer in the back of Michel's mind, lit by the mention of the raven. Something had been said and erased quickly — erased with a practical joke about ravens. "There was a winter like this," he said finally. "The time your father had to eat tiggak out on the ice. You told me, remember?"

"I only heard of it." Zeke's voice was low and sad. "Many people were dead when I came back from school. My baby sister, my grandfather . . ." The words trailed off and Zeke looked away across the barren snow.

"All the crosses," murmured Michel, "on Father Splaine's hill. Tell me, Zeke, did Father Splaine die then too, after he had buried the others?"

"Yes. In the spring," he said, faint-voiced.

"On a hunt with your father, when your father had to eat tiggak — which no outsider can eat?"

"I was not here."

Michel looked directly into the haunted eyes and Zeke turned his head away. Neither spoke. There's probably nothing in it, thought Michel. But I will never know. They'll all see to that.

He straightened his shoulders. "It's time to try the mountain," he said briskly. "When we come again there will be foxes in your traps. You can't tell from only one day."

Zeke brightened. "There will be foxes. Maybe not here, in my traps, but somewhere. They will not all leave us."

By the time the moon rose they were around the seaward of the two peaks and facing down a waste of rocks to the steep glacier. They fastened the dogs single file again and wound slowly downward, often retracing their steps to find corridors wide enough for the little caravan. Michel, tied to the lead dog, went ahead, and Zeke, also tied, stayed beside the sled, lifting it over boulders, balancing it on slippery iceways.

The rocks became fewer, with wide stretches of snow between them, upward-reaching fingers of the glacier. The grade grew steeper, then there was only snow. Michel stopped, tired, but there was no resting here. The glacier dropped percipitately into an invisible valley; one slip and they would fall a thousand feet. The snow of early winter was firm but not icy. There was no wind and the air was calm and very cold. An avalanche was unlikely.

Michel smiled back at Zeke. "You picked the one day of the year we could come down this way."

Zeke answered the smile, his eyes shining in the moonlight, his face no longer despondent. "We slide?" He made a motion of diving but held fast to the taut line, his heels deep in snow.

"Yes, if you want to end head down in the river. Keep the line tight and the sled sideways to the hill." They tacked from one side of the glacier to the other all the way down the glistening path. The moon was high when they reached the river. Warm and exhilarated, they rested only a few minutes, then sat on the sled and let the dogs carry them home down the round hills.

16

OBLONGS of warm light lay on the snow. A hazy line of smoke floated from the chimney and there was a smell of meat and spices. Maggie ran out and helped unharness the dogs, rejoicing on her face. But they were almost too tired to speak. They fed the dogs a frozen seal Zeke had left inside the porch and stumbled up the steps. The house enfolded them, and a few minutes after eating they were both asleep, the lamp, turned low, still burning, embers in the stove shifting softly.

A few hours later Michel awoke from a dream of dead ravens, his heart thudding, his body damp with fear. He sat up and looked distractedly around, expecting weasels, white stone, Nauligak's disembodied face.

Gradually the peace of the room asserted itself, fur curtains shining in the lamplight, polished wood of the organ, crude furniture he had made from leftovers — a lamp table of a barrel, every other stave removed to give it a look of lightness, a bench of boxes along the windows, covered with baby seal pelts, two stools of smaller barrels, their open tops laced with leather thong. Lying on the bearskin, Zeke snored gently. The stove fire was purring. Michel, relaxing, decided to ask Saloositak Tana to make a carving of a young seal and its mother for the lamp table. The mother would have a fish in her mouth — a fat fish.

Today, when they went to show Nauligak he hadn't killed them yet, he would ask the old man.

He slept again, easily and deeply.

Maggie built up the kitchen fire and made coffee, but still he slept. At the sound of bacon spitting in the frying pan he finally opened his eyes. Zeke was at the table, yawning into a coffee cup, and Maggie, seeing Michel awake, brought him coffee in bed. As he propped himself up to take the cup she slid a finger down his cheek in a light caress. Traces of vigil showed around her eyes, and her cheeks were hollowed with tiredness under the broad cheekbones.

"You didn't sleep any more than we did, Maggie."

"I look at you on the mountain." She pointed to the binoculars. "You go high but not so high, then I cannot see you." She had lost them at the cirque, Michel realized, where they had nearly lost themselves. "Then I look more, and wait. I do not see you again until you are here." Her voice in English was monotonous and copybook careful but the blue-smudged eyes were eloquent. He touched them and she leaned against his hand for a moment.

"I'm glad we got back, Maggie. You would have been sleepless a long time if we'd fallen in that hole."

"The mountain is not good," said Maggie gravely.

"So your father told us." She nodded. "You knew?"

"Yes. He go there for white stone."

Michel stared at her. "Then why in hell, girl . . ." But she could not have kept him from going up the mountain. "Maggie, tell me truly, why did your father forget to warn us?"

"He says do not go. He says bad spirit there. Then nobody go."

"Impossible. The man's not that simple. He knows I don't believe in spirits. It's likely he doesn't either."

"Zeke maybe believe. But Zeke not care about holes in ice."

"Maggie darling, you know more about all of us than we know about ourselves. There remains a small question." Maggie's own eyebrows made a question mark. "Which one day I'm going to find the answer to." He smiled to cover the grimness in his voice.

The dogs were howling, and before they got to the village Nauligak's house was filling. Maggie had told the night before about their safe return, and all eyes were on them, admiring and wondering. Zeke told the story; as before it was a piece of theater. The audience gasped, laughed, groaned, laughed again. At the end Nauligak turned to Michel, made a short formal speech, shook his hand and said in English, "God bless you."

"He thanks you for saving my life," said Zeke, "and for showing us that there is no bad spirit on the mountain."

Michel looked directly at the old hunter. "Your son also saved my life. All we showed about the mountain was that no one must go over it again. As you know." The opaque eyes did not waver as Nauligak spoke again.

"He says you made us all wiser and your name will stay alive."

"I'd rather my body stayed alive," murmured Michel.

"What is that?"

"Nothing. With the food shortage your father had better omit the usual feast."

"Of course we feast," said Zeke, surprised. "This is a happy time."

"Did you tell him about the starved animals?"

"He knew before."

"I see. Rejoice today, rue tomorrow. It doesn't really matter, though. There's all that nasty canned beef stew at my place."

They feasted largely and long, on crackling whaleskin and hot seal fat stirred into snow. During the meal Michel asked Saloosi-tak Tana to carve him a seal. Zeke frowned as he translated, and a look of avarice crossed the fat man's face.

"Do not pay him much," said Zeke.

"I'll pay what I think it's worth. Or maybe he'd rather have store goods."

"No," said Zeke quickly. "He will live on your porch."

"He will not. I'm only asking him for one carving."

"He is like the fox that always follows the bear. The bear cannot catch him and cannot lose him. You should not have asked. You will have him perpetually."

"I'm pretty tough."

"So is the bear." He laughed. "But you are tougher."

The sky trembled as Michel and Maggie walked home. Green light flickered in the north, then spread upward in rhythmic waves, the few stars infinitely distant behind them. At the zenith a cloudy ball of green fire formed. From it pulsated blue, yellow and red in ever-increasing brilliance, until the whole sky swung with color, reflecting from the snow, lighting the ice of the mountain.

"The mountain is on fire, Maggie."

She gazed, not at the mountain or the sky, but at him. "Not mountain. Michel." He looked blank. She swept a hand toward the peaks. "Name Michel, for you. My father say it."

"I've done it again!" he said with dismay. He regarded her, a barbaric little princess clad in furs, her wide-spaced eyes alight with love.

"Bother," he said.

At home, ignoring her, he wrote to Sandra. "Do you know what it feels like to be a shade? There's said to be a spirit at the top of the mountain. Well, dear, I'm it. I tried to prove to at least one of them that the spirit business is phony. As a result, in future generations, it will be my spirit that lives at the top waiting to spring on the reckless. The present, living Michel is only a tale to be told winters when there isn't anything else to do. It's stagy, the whole deal — the feast to celebrate the sensational new legend, the aurora borealis, even the mountain itself, at this moment apparently going up in flames. I don't understand these people, but maybe they have to be the way they are, to fit into the Wagnerian drama that surrounds them. Sometimes I sit here at the window and look at the glamorous scenery and long for ordinary people — talking over the hum of city traffic, streetlights in

[175]

their eyes, arguing about politics, listening to progressive jazz, watching a Western. Everything here is significant. I get lonely for the busy little futilities . . ."

He let his fingers slide off the keys. "Maggie," he called, "let's have coffee." The rest of that long night was hers.

Constable Davitt came to visit the day before Christmas. Michel was wrapping presents awkwardly with brown paper and skeins of colored wool, and the air was heavy with the smell of baking. The men greeted each other with wary friendliness and Maggie served them supper. She moved like a woman now, sure, slow, graceful, a little heavy, and her glance at Davitt held no coyness.

"You're lucky," he told Michel. "I hope you have the sense to take her with you when you go. You won't find many like that, here or outside."

"Maggie's a little dear — here, where she belongs. What in heaven's name would I do with her outside?" What, he added to himself remorsefully, are you doing with her here? Spoiling her future, depriving her of her heritage. Fool, Michel, to think that you two could share equally so much as one hour of your disparate lives! Angry at himself, he added defensively, "She can't learn anything."

"What have you tried to teach her?" asked Davitt. "She defied her father for you. Whatever you think of her mental endowments — she's as quick as her brother, by the way, and not half so mixed up — you owe her at least loyalty. She loves you."

"She only thinks she loves me because I'm here. She didn't defy her father. The young man's family turned her down."

"You got that from Zeke. He doesn't think much of the local females. His wits are addled by having two fathers, and now a big brother who teaches him to climb mountains."

"Why not? At least he's getting some new ideas. Do you want him to live in a superstitious backwater?"

"He'll die on that mountain," said Davitt quietly, "unless he dies sooner trying to prove something else of your way is better than his father's." He watched Maggie as she poured more coffee. "I wish my girl . . ." He caught himself. "Nina is a marvel. She can shoot a seal at a hundred yards, travel weeks in the winter with cold bannock and raw fish, make a pot of tea in a blizzard, put up a hide shelter and live in it like a cat on a cushion. But at my house she pulls the curtains so she doesn't have to see her own country and keeps the radio going to drown out the birds. She has one thought in her head — to get out of here. She wants to wear spike heels and put dimes in a jukebox. She'd die of illness and loneliness. I can't make her see it."

"Why don't you marry her?"

"She won't have me unless I promise to live in a city. I'd do it, but she wouldn't stay with me two weeks. I don't want to take her away from here and watch her destroy herself. Sorry. Seeing Maggie so happy set me off. Be good to her."

"I don't intend to turn her out in the snow," said Michel stiffly.

"She'll need you even more when the baby comes. Her family will try to take her away. Eskimo women are supposed to give birth alone."

"Baby!" He smothered his confoundment. "Yes, of course, she'll be all right. What was it you came to see me about?"

"The Splaine's River people. They're having a hard winter and it's going to get worse. All the settlements here are suffering and we're trying to see they don't starve. You'll get recompense from the government for whatever stores you have to give without payment. It's not likely you'll get many furs to trade."

"Yes," said Michel, not listening.

Davitt rose to go. "Thank you for agreeing," he said as they shook hands. Michel had no idea what he had agreed to. As soon as the door was shut he stamped back to the kitchen. Maggie was up to the elbows in dough, eyes frowningly concentrated on a spotted cookbook. Aristotle she would never read, and that was all right. But a baby . . .

"Maggie," he began sternly. She turned her head sideways and up, a smile touching the corners of her mouth. At sight of the tight face her eyes widened. She turned quickly and tears spattered the brown dough. "No matter, I suppose it wasn't your fault. But we can't keep it, you know. I have no interest in being a father. I'll probably be gone before it knows me. Have you any notion what I'm talking about, Maggie?" She shook her head dumbly, tears still falling. He was suddenly ashamed.

"Just as well." The rest of the afternoon he wrapped presents with fierce attention, hating himself, while Maggie worked silently in the fragrant kitchen. The last gingerbread man was arranged on the wooden platter Michel had carved from an old plank, the last cake received chocolate frosting and a sugar angel, the last present went under the small tree of green-painted cardboard and tufts of white cotton. Maggie pulled her fur parka over her head, wriggled into her embroidered boots, and slipped her hands into sealskin mittens.

"Where are you going?" Michel demanded. "It's the middle of the night."

She smiled uncertainly. "I go home, help my mother cook."

"Are you coming back?"

"You come to my father for Christmas church, then — are you angry?"

He sighed. "No, little one. I shouldn't have scolded you. You're just a little girl pretending to be grown up. Now you've got us in a real grown-up pickle and it was my fault. I'm not angry, Maggie. I want you to come back. Please?"

"Yes," she said doubtfully. He watched her go, her figure slight on the immensity of snow. Mauyak — soft snow, he remembered. She was springtime, plants already budding beneath their melting cover. Guilt mingled with a first stirring of pride.

Christmas morning, as on Sundays, Nauligak conducted a full prayer service, including the reading of the Nativity. The house

[178]

was dark in the corners, but a kerosene lamp lighted Nauligak's imperturbable features and the calm aging beauty of his wife, and shone dimly on the attentive faces of his five children seated in a decorous row at the edge of the sleeping platform. Saloositak Tana, as usual, crouched by the entrance. Christmas had made no difference in his appearance; indeed, he was untidier than ever. His sparse-haired cheeks hung in folds and his small greedy eyes were mesmerized by the meat in the cooking dish. He did not look at Nauligak or join in the responses.

At the end of the long service they all came alive, launching noisily into the familiar Christmas songs. Nauligak's accompaniment on the accordion was only a little slower than his tuneless jigs, and the singing had all the gusto of the dance.

"Zeke," said Michel after dinner, "everyone is to come to my house tonight. I have presents and cakes and cocoa and we'll sing again. Maggie and I have fixed the organ and it sounds like the seraphim." Zeke told his brothers and they scattered like windblown birds to spread the news.

All the thirty-six people of the village crowded into Michel's house later. They knew his songs now and gusts of laughter met every earthy line. They joined in the choruses, drowning out his big bass. Then there were tests of skill — juggling, balancing, arm wrestling, seal-hopping races on hands and toes, leg kicking in the manner of the *pezotska*. They were less self-conscious than children. Nauligak fell on his face in the seal-hopping race and laughed as loud as the rest. Zeke dropped the pebbles he was juggling, grinned and tossed them to Maggie, who could keep four in the air at a time. Her bright eyes laughed as she concentrated on the pebbles. She glanced at Michel to see if he was watching, but the stones kept flying. In a corner Saloositak Tana fussed with a piece of string, his thick gnarled fingers swiftly weaving it into cat's cradles. Two young men sat before him watching as if their futures depended on learning the intricate patterns.

There were no tomorrow and no yesterday, no undercurrents of jealousy, fear, enmity. It was Christmas, and time had stopped for a while in the night, waiting for the northern earth to turn back toward the sun. Saloositak Tana droned unmelodiously as he wove the ancient pictures of owls and wolves and bears and fish, the same his people had made for thousands of years, even back to their forgotten Asian ancestors in the first home of man. It seemed that they were back there now, racial memories alive in their dark gleaming-eyed faces, in their thoughtless and timeless celebration to welcome the rebirth of the sun.

The games slowed, then stopped. Dreamily they sat watching the fat man's quick ugly hands. His humming had words to it now, quiet-flowing like a slow river through pastureland. The sound was as hypnotic as the voice of the old woman telling the dog story, but the singer was not stern. He seemed to be dreaming of another world far away and long ago, and a sleepy smile played at the corners of his mouth. Saloositak Tana had eaten well.

The song ended unnoticeably. Murmuring filled the room; there was motion as children went to the table for a last cake and parents hunted for small boots and mittens in the pile on the porch. Zeke slipped outside and returned with two large adolescent pups on leashes. They blinked at the light, snarled, dropped their tails and headed for the door. Zeke dragged them up short and presented the leashes to Michel.

"They are for you, Michel, from all of us." Everyone turned toward him, awaiting his joyful reaction. The dogs regarded Michel with dislike and he returned the look with misgiving. Quickly he arranged his face into a glad smile.

"Thank you all, my friends. I have little presents for all of you, but they don't make up for the handsome dogs." He handed out presents at the door as the people left slowly, carrying sleeping babies and pocketfuls of cake and chocolate. Each one, down to the smallest child, formally shook hands with him and uttered courteous words. Maggie went with her mother and father, and did not look up as she said her polite good-by. She looked little and lonely, her young face lost in the big fur hood. Michel took her hand and brought it to his lips. "Thank you, Maggie, for the lovely Christmas party. Come back soon." Her eyes lifted and she whispered a sentence that was like a melody. Nauligak waited impassively, but Aitu gave a slow, beautiful smile.

He followed them out. The morning was no brighter than yesterday's, the air silent and frosty, the black sky cobwebbed with stars. Spring might be forever away. But there was a mirror image of life-giving light in the southern sky. Maggie's baby, he thought — my baby — will be born in April, when the sky is light blue and the sound of running water mingles with the songs of birds.

Zeke and his friends Kooluk and Lalinga and Itarvak were still in the house, and Michel asked the meaning of the fat man's song.

"I want to go a long way away, to the land of the birds, where there is no winter, and I will return to this land in the spring," quoted Zeke softly, the lilt of his own language in the English words. He stopped, his lips curled in disdain.

"Go on," said Michel. "It makes me remember spring."

"No. It is a foolish song and it is too long. Saloositak Tana only remembers long songs. They take more time. He has nothing to do but make things of stone and sing long songs."

"Someone should sing and carve."

"He eats too much."

"Is that a sin?"

"Yes," said Zeke seriously.

Lalinga took a mouth organ out of his pocket and played the first line of "Eddystone Light." The others lit black pipes and Michel lay on his bed. Tobacco smoke circled lazily around the lamp and spread near the ceiling. Its smell mingled with that of sweet cakes and the oily odor of sealskins that was the pervasive smell of the North. The player changed to "Silent Night" and

[181]

Michel sang softly in harmony. The song died away and the three men talked idly, their voices an echo of music. Michel closed his eyes and felt the earth turning under him calmly, carrying him into morning, into spring. Someone put a fur robe over him. "Merry Christmas," he murmured. He felt a brief touch of cold air but did not hear the door shut as his last guests departed.

17

WHEN HE AWOKE, the world had disappeared in a chaos of snow. There was no hope of Maggie's coming back that day, so Michel, halfhearted and sleepy, swept papers and crumbs and string into a corner, put cups and dishes in the sink, dismantled the Christmas tree and tore it in strips for kindling.

Howls and whimpers came from outside. He opened the door and was nearly swept off his feet by a gust of snow-laden wind. "Who's there?" Holding the door frame for support, he peered into the gray maelstrom. Nothing was visible, but the howls were loud and demanding.

"Oh you," he said, dismayed. "I'd forgotten you. Come in." Nothing happened. "Blasted dogs," he muttered. He closed the door, built up the fire, and dressed himself as if he were going on a long trip. Then he slipped out into the eddying storm, fastening the door behind him. The dogs were tied to boulders on the hillside above the house. They strained at their heavy leather lines, protesting.

"Why don't you curl up in the snow like ordinary dogs?" he said irritably. He unfastened them and pulled on the leashes. The dogs planted their forefeet stiff in the snow, raised their haunches and refused to move. Michel carried them one at a time into the house and dumped them in the corner behind the pot-bellied stove. After his own breakfast he got from the porch the half carcass of a seal Zeke had left, sliced off a few frozen chunks, and threw them to the dogs. Sunk in the corner, slitted eyes following his every move, they would not even extend their noses to the meat.

There they remained for three days of the storm, deeply suspicious, unmoving except for the wolflike eyes, refusing to eat, curling their lips when he went close. He opened the door several times, inviting them to depart and leaving the way free. But they stayed where they were and he had not the heart to throw them out.

On the morning of the fourth day Michel awoke enveloped in disgust. The house showed the inevitable sloppiness of a man accustomed to depending on a woman's housekeeping. The saucers he used as ashtrays were clotted with ashes; the sink held an inexhaustible fund of dirty dishes — though he washed a few at a time he could not bring himself to tackle the entire greasy pile; the garbage box was overflowing, the lavatory can unemptied. The dogs, lacking normal exercise and the rough cleansing snow, smelled like the menagerie of a bankrupt circus. The odors assailed him in a concerted wave, and suddenly it seemed that the blended stench came from himself. He jumped up, donned layers of outdoor clothing and ran outside, slamming the door. Wind hit him and drove him back against the wall. He fought it, stooped and moving slowly, head down, blinded by snow. His feet found the slight declivity of the river shore and he slid down to the river itself. Here he was protected. Upstream the shores steepened and he could stand upright. He found himself counting the twists of the stream and struck upward, battling the wind, to the place where the crosses stood. They were not visible, and he thought he had mistaken the spot when he tripped and fell full length. He lay there a full minute, catching his breath. Then the oddness penetrated. The cross he had tripped over, knocked flat by the gale, was free of snow. As far as he could see in the swirling darkness the hilltop cemetery was swept almost clean. Patches of snow lay in hollows, but last summer's gray grass and brittle willow lay naked on the iron ground. In the fierce wind no crosses stood.

On hands and knees he crept to the edge of the hillside, where the missionary's stone was still upright but leaned to one side. A narrow crack showed beneath it where the snow buntings had nested; snow had settled there and turned to ice. The grave was opening.

Reasonless fear struck Michel, and he crawled over the exposed graveyard until his hands and knees touched snow again. Then he stood and ran downhill, careless of direction, oblivious of wind and cold. A remnant of common sense told him to keep the wind on his right. He slid down the last ravine to the flat ice of the river and was home quickly. Once inside with the door shut he leaned against the wall and closed his eyes until the terror receded. The room was malodorous but the smells were those of the living.

The dogs still lay sharp-eyed in their corner, but one mangled boot and the sole of another lay on the bearskin, which had a hole gnawed raggedly in its side. The baby seal pelt was torn, tufts of yellowish fur spread all over the floor. They had started on a curtain but evidently his coming had surprised them. Only a lower fringe was gone.

Michel wrinkled his nose in unconscious imitation of Maggie and set about cleaning up. He picked up each dog in turn and dropped it outside in the lee of the wind. The dogs snarled, then dug themselves holes in the snow and curled in tight balls, their eyes shut probably for the first time in three days. He filled two large pots with snow, and swept and dusted the house while they heated. Then he attacked the dishes with angry energy. Garbage box and lavatory can he carried down to the sea and emptied on the high-piled tidal ice well away from the house, then scrubbed them thoroughly with snow.

The house finally clean, he sat down at the typewriter. "Of course what happened was that the wind picked up the snow and put it somewhere else," he wrote Sandra. "There's not much snow

[185]

falling, even though your footprints disappear as soon as you take your feet out of them. What is true of the graveyard hill must be true of all the hilltops. And the cold — the sea ice must be a dozen feet deep by now. It expands underneath and cracks at the surface from its own pressure. The frozen earth would crack as well, particularly in exposed spots.

"But there is something wrong about the missionary's death. This is a town with a secret. The people have agreed on silence. Everyone knows a certain vital fact but me. I don't think they've consciously decided not to tell me — it's a fundamental instinct of social protection from an outsider. He was not pushed off a cliff or knifed on a lonely hill, because then Davitt, prejudiced as he is, would have had to take over and the whole thing would have been public. The deliberate mysteriousness frightens me — so much that I've taken on the local superstition, running from a grave before the corpse has time to sit up." He scanned the lines; his fear seemed tenuous. "That damned stone," he wrote. "Why do people put up gravestones to plague strangers?" Ripping the sheet out, he balled it and walked to the stove. He hesitated over the embers, then smoothed the paper, turned and slipped it furtively, as if he were being watched, into the drawer under the other letters. Someone who was friendly might find it, afterwards.

On a fresh sheet he wrote in longhand: "To Ezekiel Okkomik-pok, son of Nauligak of Splaine's River, I bequeath this house and its contents, abandoned by its former owner and made mine by right of occupancy, also my two dogs. To Mauyak, daughter of Nauligak of Splaine's River, I bequeath $1000, in addition to the royalties accruing from the publication or other use of all material written by me up to the time of my death. This money is to be used for the support of herself and our child and the education of said child so far as is practicable.

"If I should die here I wish to be buried in Aurora Sound without religious rites other than those customary to burial at sea.

I do not wish a gravestone or any other commemorative monument. Repeat, emphatically.

"As executors I appoint Jacques Davitt, at present date Senior Constable at Aurora Sound Police Post, and Harold Twining, at present date Managing Editor of *East-West Review,* Hudsonton. I direct these two to act on this testament without regard to its technical irregularities according to the dictates of their own good sense and their knowledge of my true wishes." He signed the holograph will and thrust it into the back of the drawer.

Maggie came back, and for a short while Michel remembered the peace and hope of Christmas night. But winter had truly settled in. The inlet boomed like an old-fashioned battleground, snow fell, wind blew, the days were obdurately dark. The North moves far too slowly, Michel thought irritably, looking out at the blank sea ice. He wrote letters to Sandra and constructed a small sled, the runners soaked, then upcurved at the ends over the opened kitchen stove, the crosspieces laced with leather thong.

Still he was bored and lonely. The two were alone in the house, talking little, seldom separated, outdoors only to fetch snow and feed the dogs. Michel regarded her indulgently, if indifferently, as a stray kitten that had lost its wildness and settled in by the stove. Her shyness had left her. Tenderness was outspoken, and every word and motion conveyed her deep-growing love.

She loved him because he was here, Michel repeated to himself. Marriage was not only impossible but unnecessary. The baby would be provided for, and when he left she would forget him as easily as she now accepted him. It was unrealistic to feel guilt or acknowledge responsibility. She was sweet but shallow-minded.

He could not see that Maggie was too gentle to demand anything, too innocent to tie Michel to her, too much in love to know anything but immediate joy and the moving life within her.

Their frames of reference were different; they were unable to sense how far adrift they were.

Draggle-tailed Saloositak Tana was the first to come to him for food, on a day when Maggie was in the village helping her mother. The fat man said nothing but stood in the porch and fumbled through his ragged garments. He held toward Michel a grimy swollen hand, palm up. On it lay two gray soapstone seals. One held a fish in its mouth. The other, smaller, lay on its back, head inclined sideways, rear flipper twisted up in an attitude of lazy play. Michel took the appealing little sculptures and Saloositak Tana started to follow him into the house.

"Stay there," ordered Michel, raising a hand. "I'll pay you." The old man stood where he was, greed and apprehension warring on his face. Michel came back with his wallet and counted out bills. Saloositak Tana pushed the money away, speaking in a thick voice which seemed to originate in his stomach.

"All right, you can have stores," said Michel, and grudgingly led him into the storeroom. He counted out cans and boxes and shoved them over the counter. Everything disappeared into the no-colored bundle of rags within seconds, but Saloositak Tana looked hardly fatter than before. He departed without a word and Michel left the door open to get the smell out.

The next day he was there again with an ivory bear. The miniature, fat as its creator, yet conveyed a sense of power and split-second coordination. It was crouched, head low, one paw hooked downward as if to scoop a darting fish from under an ice pan. The narrow blackened eyes seemed to have their own life and the black-tipped muzzle practically twitched.

Michel, blocking the doorway, was embarrassed. "Thank you, thank you," he muttered, and thrust some bills at the artist. Saloositak Tana took the money and dropped it at his feet. His pendulous cheeks trembled as he shook his head, and there were tears in his eyes.

"Oh hell," said Michel. He moved from the door and the fat man sidled around him as swiftly as the bear and was in the storeroom before Michel. Again food vanished into the interstices of his noisome garments, and again the man left without speaking.

The seals were on the lamp table and the bear on the organ. Maggie had mended the skins mauled by the dogs. His house was complete; it was lived in and loved. Yet suspicion and unease nagged him as he regarded the fine-wrought sculptures.

When Maggie came back she wrinkled her little nose. "Saloositak Tana," she said. "No good." Michel showed her the figures. "No good," she repeated emphatically, and set about cleaning with intensity, using the broom as if she were sweeping the old man out of the house.

A week later she went again to her mother. Michel walked with her. The aurora borealis undulated across the sky and the snow held shadows that were not darkness but motion. It was so cold and clear that frost particles quivered in the air. They took the short cut over the hills, a snow path between drifts, packed deep by the tread of Maggie's feet. Breathless in the icy air, eyes dazzled by the sky display, they walked in silence until they came in sight of the village. The houses huddled in the river valley, low-built, with snow massed almost to their roofs, looked like a group of boulders rolled haphazardly from the mountain glacier. Only an occasional square of dark yellow light in a gut-covered window showed there was life under the snow and rock.

Michel kissed Maggie's hand — the gesture from another world always pleased her immoderately. She laughed low, her eyes sparkling like the frost diamonds, turned and ran down the hill to her father's house. Michel watched her disappear into the shadowed rock. It was as if the earth had swallowed her, and he felt an instant's apprehensive sorrow.

He had not been back in his house five minutes when the door opened and Saloositak Tana was there. "Go away," said Michel, alarmed vexation sharpening his voice. The fat man whined incomprehensibly, his voice like the grind of a dull-edged saw, and held a little ivory owl into the light.

"No," said Michel distinctly. "Go away." But he stood still, his shapeless face sagging dolorously, the minute carving a contradiction in his deformed hand. Michel gave in, wishing Maggie were there. But of course she wasn't. She never would be. Saloositak Tana had waited outside, hidden, until he knew Michel was alone. He would wait again.

Fear compounding with annoyance, Michel pushed the man out of the house. He felt the edge of food boxes through the greasy clothing.

It took him an hour to make a wooden bolt for the porch door.

18

No one came, not even the fat man. Michel arranged his store, the most tempting wares, chocolate and tobacco, on one side of the counter, cloth and bright-colored skeins of wool on the other, boxes and tins attractively geometric on the shelves. The only one who saw them was Maggie. She dusted the spotless supplies and swept the unmuddied floor every day. There was little else for her to do. Michel sat writing or reading or looking morosely out the window. He seldom walked; went outdoors only briefly to get water and throw frozen seal meat to the dogs, who gobbled it without looking up, then curled again defensively in the lee of the house. Soon the seal Zeke had left him was finished and the dogs fed on scraps. They were uninterested in what they ate, or how often. They had as little interest in their owner unless he approached too close, when they growled and backed away. Bored, as he was — and as useless.

But Michel was nervous as well as bored. All his young fears of being hurt had come back. What had happened to his friends, who no longer seemed to be friends? Perhaps they had never been, and he was, as always, the outsider. Perhaps, used to being an onlooker, he had not taken an unconditional part in his new home life. He watched the window often during the short twilight of day. It was unrewarding; no human passed his view on the sea ice, no animals or birds showed against the fields of snow that rose toward the mountain. The emptiness was scornful, the total stillness a mockery of his hopes.

"Where are they all?" he asked Maggie, breaking the long silence of supper.

"They look and hunt," she answered stiltedly, then rose and ran to the window. "Michel, come!" she cried, turning to him a face animated for the first time in many days. It occurred to him, as he joined her, that this life might be equally hard on her. He discarded the thought. After all she had made it abundantly clear that she didn't want to be anywhere else.

The snow was light under the stars and two sleds were silhouetted. One man ran beside each, shouting at the dogs. Mounds on the back ends of the sleds were indistinguishable, but they were too large to be sled boxes.

"Furs," said Michel. "At last." The spell was broken; soon they would be in, and he could treat the children to chocolate and the men to tobacco, and sing again as at Christmas, and talk with Zeke.

The next day they did not come, nor the day after, and Michel's depression sharpened into anger. On the third day after he had seen the sleds Zeke appeared, empty-handed, his eyes shadowed with fatigue. Michel greeted him with reserve and Zeke said little as he ate supper with them. He gulped the food as if he had not eaten for days.

"Was it you who went by?" Michel asked finally. "With your sled loaded?"

"Yes. With my father. We were out long." He lapsed into silence again.

"You had many skins with you."

"Some seal and some other skins, all bad."

"Let me be the judge of that, Zeke. Why didn't you stop here?"

The room was still. Zeke looked up, then dropped his gaze to the table.

"Why don't you answer?"

"We were tired," said Zeke hopelessly, then brightened. "To-night we take your pups out. They are ready to train."

"By all means. It's better than sitting here evading each other."

They harnessed the two short behind Zeke's five dogs. In turn they kept a close hand on the newcomers, and Michel learned to use the whip as Zeke did, a hard snap in the snow accompanied by a shout of the dog's name. Sun and Shadow he called them. Sun had reddish fur shading to pale yellow on the belly and the backs of the legs. He stepped out like a veteran, pulling his weight, domineering, snapping at the dogs ahead of him, already a leader at seven months. Shadow was light gray and dark gray, with narrow paws and large eyes. He couldn't do anything right. He ran out to the side, his trace slack, until Michel called him back in line. The loose trace caught on a runner and the pup went under, howling. He was disentangled and put back, trem-bling, begging Michel with his midnight eyes, tongue licking nerv-ously at the slender muzzle. Instead of running forward he went to the side again, bumping into Sun, who bit him. Shadow howled again and fell on his back, and the trace snapped. He shook himself all over and leaped ahead of the team. Facing it, he barked happily, front paws low, rump high, daring the others to come and play. They came on, docile and earnest, and he was not quick enough to get out of the way. For the third time he was run over and his cries were piteous.

"That dog cheers me up," said Michel. "Someone made a mis-take. He should have been born into a circus."

Zeke, fastening Shadow to a line at the back of the sled, shook his head. "He will be good. Very smart. Only too young — here." He pointed to his head.

Michel considered his handsome pup, tail and ears now alert. Ignominiously tied behind the sled, he stepped out nobly as if he were leading the team. Michel laughed. "Not so young and not so smart. This one is fighting the system, and that's the fight you can't win."

He looked at Shadow again, proud and wrong, and his observation sobered him. Maybe I'm fighting the system too, he thought. Remember the sleds, high-piled, that wouldn't stop, the fat man who came unasked to the store, all the others who didn't come at all. But I don't know what their system is. Have I, like Shadow, found myself in the wrong world? The beautiful North, that I love, does not appear to love me back.

"Saloositak Tana was at my house begging for food," he remarked. "He had hidden until he knew I was alone."

Zeke's nose wrinkled but his face was grave. "Hungry. He is always hungry, but now he is more hungry."

"Will you tell him I'm not giving away any more food, and if I want carvings I'll order them."

"I will tell him." Zeke spoke shortly and he frowned.

"What's the matter? Do you think he has a right to beg? None of the rest of you come in, even with furs to trade."

"We will hunt now," said Zeke, and occupied himself with the sled box.

"All right. And tomorrow you'll come in to trade. You're hungry enough."

Zeke, unwinding the thong on his harpoon, appeared not to have heard. "We will go hunt," he grunted again, and stumped away over the ice, withdrawn, all Eskimo. They found blowholes covered with thin ice. Zeke broke the ice and waited, poised, with his harpoon high. Within a few minutes he struck. The seal was gaunt, and Zeke, standing over it, was stern and impassive as his father.

Michel broke a long silence. "I'd forgotten about the seal and the starved fish." Zeke nodded without speaking and set about flensing the animal. Michel's thoughts went into a random sequence like a fable: the seal ate the fish and the man ate the seal and the man died because he was too proud to beg.

Only they were not too proud to beg. They were staying away on purpose.

"Zeke, you all have credit at the store. When you bring your furs in you'll have more credit. You'd be surprised at how much better that is than going hungry." He was almost pleading.

"Perhaps . . ." murmured Zeke. "But the winter is long . . ." He laughed. The dogs were fighting over the meager flesh. Two masterful animals, Sun and Zeke's lead dog, were trying to snarl each other into submission over a lean rib. Shadow slipped between the bared teeth, picked up the bone and flashed away, tail down as if he had been whipped, to gnaw it on a distant ice hill. Too late the big dogs realized they were quarreling over a space of empty snow. They glared at each other suspiciously, growled once more to cover embarrassment and stalked off to assert their dominance over more reliable cowards.

"He beat the system!" exclaimed Michel.

"I said he was smart. Our dogs all fight to see who is stronger and they are stupid. They fight to death sometimes. This one will never fight. He will live long."

Finished with the bone, Shadow circled the group, well out of reach. The dogs, a noisy rabble, were tearing the skin apart. Before they were through Shadow had gathered all the discarded bones and carried them separately and swiftly, not to the far ice hill, now indefensible, but to the side of the sled where Michel and Zeke sat. Michel reached out a hand and touched the dog's silky head. Shadow snarled unconvincingly and settled down to eat behind the protective shield of his master.

Zeke speared another seal and they turned toward home, the loose-skinned body flapping under the cords at the back of the sled. Zeke was glum, not even smiling at Shadow's antic non-cooperation. In the warm house, over coffee, Michel again urged him to come to the store and bring his friends. Zeke's "Thank you" was short.

"Take Sun for a while, will you?" said Michel as the boy was harnessing his dogs. "I want to train Shadow alone with my sled."

"No good. He must run with the other dogs — he will not learn alone."

"He doesn't seem to be learning much in society."

Zeke gave in, disapproving. "The dog will go bad alone," he said, but put Sun in the team. He did not wave as he left, but stared straight ahead, hunched dismally on the sled. Michel was glad to see him go.

Shadow regarded him with distrust as he approached. The ears flattened, the tail went down, and a low growl rumbled in his chest. But he allowed himself to be touched. Michel filled a dish with scraps and set it within the porch door. He went into the house and closed the inner door. A few minutes later he heard the tap of claws, then for a while nothing, then retreating taps as the dog went down the outer steps. He opened the door. The dish was empty and Shadow was not in sight.

For several days he fed the dog on the porch, and at last he heard the sound he had been waiting for, the thump of a body on the wooden floor. When Maggie went to fetch snow the dog snarled. Michel ran to the door, to see her step nonchalantly over the raised hackles and bared teeth as if Shadow had been a stone in her path. He smiled to himself. Maggie was not allowed to feed or touch the dog, but the two had developed a wary tolerance. It would not be so with strangers. The next time Saloositak Tana came . . . the dog would not fight, perhaps, but he would threaten. That was all that was needed.

In the days that followed, Michel trained the dog to the little sled. Shadow was quick and willing, and a signal once heard was known and obeyed. He pulled only light loads because he was not to be a sled dog. He was to learn obedience to one man, to be outside the dog society and unfriendly to every human except his master. For now, after six weeks of virtual isolation, Michel himself felt the corrosion of distrust, and the void of the winter night was ominous.

Still he watched the window, and one day two figures appeared over the hill beyond the river. They carried harpoons and they looked behind them and to all sides as they approached. Michel saw danger in their weapons, their hesitant steps and backward glances. He strode to the door and called Shadow. The dog came instantly and was tied in the porch, close to the wall, a rope noose around his neck. By the time the visitors were at the steps he was in a ferocious temper, snarling and gasping, straining at his choke collar, each jerk of the rope making him more frantic.

The two men halted and looked up at Michel, puzzled fear on their faces. They were Kooluk and Lalinga, and they had just come from hunting for the smell of blood hung on them. They carried burdens on their backs. Abashed at his reasonless panic, Michel stepped into the porch and put his hand on the dog's head. Shadow subsided, the growl still deep in his throat, while his master gestured the two inside.

They slid along the wall, their motions uncertain, no smiles on their dark round faces. Michel tried to cheer them, but his dog had started the visit wrong. Before long it was evident that they were disturbed by something more than the dog. They unwrapped their bundles with an air of embarrassment. In the weak light of the kerosene lamp Michel saw that the fox furs were patchy with mange, and the seal hides, still bloody and unscraped, were almost hairless. They shook their heads and murmured at him.

"Never mind," he said heartily. "If there are some there will be more. I can't credit you with these because I know Pryde won't take them . . . Maggie, come and help translate . . . But you'll get food, whatever you need." He pointed to the shelves and the young men shyly helped themselves, not taking much. Everything went down in Michel's neat ledger, and the hunters watched his writing with alarm.

He laughed at them. "Don't worry, it's only numbers. You've broken the ice — this is the beginning." Only why the continuing fear, he wanted to ask, and why the uncured sealskins fresh from the water? He kept his thoughts out of his face and gave them each a tin of pipe tobacco. "Come and have coffee, now you're here."

They sidled back toward the outside door and Michel repeated his invitation in a louder voice. "Maggie, please tell them to stay. They don't understand me."

Maggie spoke softly, and their glances slid away from her, toward each other, then to the floor. They shuffled their feet like children and moved again toward the door.

"What's wrong? Maggie, tell them it was a mistake about the dog. They can come any time." He went to the organ and played a few bars of "Barnacle Bill," looking around at them. Their expressions were disconcerted. He turned back to the organ and sang with it. When he looked again they had gone. His hands dropped from the keys.

"My fault," he said. "Maggie, they hate me and it's my own fault. I must be going queer; I'm frightening people."

Maggie came to him and touched his cheek. "I am not afraid, Michel, you are very good."

He pulled her head down and kissed the back of her neck. "You are very good also, my dear. But be careful. I may frighten you too some day." He laughed, but there was a catch in the laugh. His profession, his music, his mountain-climbing, his deliberate sociability and even more deliberate itinerancy had all been devices of his adult life to avoid the fearful isolation of his childhood. None of them worked now. He had nothing left with which to defeat solitude.

He stared over her bent head to the dark square of window and wondered at the sudden force of his misery.

Later the same day Michel saw Saloositak Tana. He did not skulk until he saw Maggie leave, but came straight to the door. Michel was before him, to tie Shadow, all his suspicions back in full force at the boldness of the old beggar. Backing into the house, he coldly watched the fat man cower against the porch wall while Shadow, furious, lunged the short length of his rope. Saloositak Tana mumbled piteously and brought from under his clothing three ermine skins.

"Quiet, Shadow," commanded Michel, his hand on the dog's head. "Let's see what kind of rascality this is." Shadow dropped back but the growling was low thunder in his chest as Saloositak Tana inched past, clinging to the opposite wall.

They were not only real ermine, they were thick-furred and healthy. He called Maggie.

"Where did he get them?" She kept a distance from the old man, her nose wrinkled, as she spoke. He grinned toothlessly without answering, and pointed to the supply shelves. Maggie grimaced with disgust. "All right, girl, you don't have to stay," said Michel.

"Give him nothing," she said.

"Don't be foolish. He must be paid."

After the old man had left she said, "He no trap — he take."

"You mean he stole them?" She nodded. Michel enunciated carefully. "From whom did he steal them?"

Maggie spread her hands. "All. He take from all."

"He must have a houseful of furs. Why don't the hunters take them back?"

"He hide them. He no good. We give him food, he come to you, get more food."

"Maggie, if Saloositak Tana took furs there are furs to take. Your people must be hiding them too. Why?" He closed his eyes and saw the face of the grim hunter, and knew that Nauligak was trying deliberately to frustrate him. He opened his eyes wide and stared at her. "Possibly on orders from your father."

Maggie shook her head, confused. "I'll find out," he said, "if I have to look for them myself." He was more perplexed than she. What does the man want, he wondered helplessly, what can he gain?

Then, early one morning, he saw his suspicion confounded.

[199]

Aitu came over the river. Deeply relieved, he went outside to greet her, the dog decorously beside his left heel. Her gracious smile was ready as ever, but her eyes were apprehensive as she showed him two white fox skins.

"Nauligak?" asked Michel, and she followed her nod with a flood of her own language. The tone was anxious. Michel took the furs to the light and examined them. They were shining, thick, newly cured.

"Maggie," he called, "please tell your mother these skins are fine. She needn't worry."

Mother and daughter talked. "She not sad about skins. She know they are good."

"Then Nauligak must bring more. Also the others. That's the only way I can stay here. You know that, Maggie?"

"Yes," she said, and spoke again to her mother. Affection mingled with concern in their glances at him.

"Don't baby me," he said impatiently. "Just see that Nauligak gets his crowd working. You have good credit, Aitu. I'll give you whatever you want. Come again soon."

She did, often, but without skins. Once in a while some of the others came with her, but they were distant as before. Michel became severely businesslike, conducting his trade stiffly, braced against the silent timidity, entering the purchases in the ledger with frowning exactitude. There was no singing, the organ was silent, no children came for chocolate.

Saloositak Tana was the only one to bring skins to trade; in the neat ledger it was finally his entry alone that showed a credit. He always came by himself, sliding warily past the dog, whom Michel still tied in the porch when he saw anyone approaching.

For Michel's doubts were growing monstrous within him. Suspicion alternated with misgivings about his own rationality and he trusted no one, least of all himself. The result was a nameless, lonely fear. It might be imagination — it might not.

Once Aitu brought her little sons with her. They looked big-eyed at the chocolate on the counter but refused, wrinkling their inconsiderable noses, when he offered it. Hurt, he turned to Aitu. She did not smile; her face, turned from him, was infinitely sad.

When she had left, Michel asked Maggie why the children had refused. She thought hard and spoke with effort. "My mother get too much. My brothers must not eat."

"You mean they mustn't eat candy?" He was incredulous. "I've always given it away, Maggie. There must be another reason."

"I not know," said Maggie honestly.

He looked at her intently but her eyes did not waver. "Maggie, why does your mother buy more than anyone else?"

"My father give to people." She spoke simply, no hint of accusation in her voice.

"I don't, you mean. Heaven knows, my dear, I've tried. They don't like the taste of my gifts." There was acid in his voice.

"My father is chief. All come to him, always."

"Your father is running out of credit, Maggie. You'd better tell him not to be so generous."

After that day he watched Maggie in all her comings and goings, and counted the food every evening after supper, distrust nagging at him.

Zeke had not been to see him in several weeks, and when he finally came Michel, his loneliness almost intolerable, welcomed him fervently.

"My friend, I thought you would never come back. I can't talk to the others, can't even give them coffee or sing with them. They're afraid of me. Sit down, sit down!"

"Yes, Michel," said Zeke dutifully. "First I must buy nails. May I?"

"Anything you want — your credit is always good with me." Michel got the nails, conscious of troubled eyes following him. When he returned from the kitchen with coffee and cake, Zeke was standing uncomfortably in the middle of the room as if he had never entered the house before.

"You too?" said Michel, his spirits fading again. "You're still allowed to sit at my table. What's wrong with you?"

Zeke sat, looking at the floor. "Not me," he said. "You."

It was not to be endured. "Why do you come at all then? You can send your little brothers."

"I come to see you, Michel. You are my friend. I always hope it will be the same as before. But now you are not happy."

"I'm as happy as I want to be," said Michel sharply. "What's not happy about me?"

Zeke gestured. "The door with wood to keep it closed. The big book with all the food written in it so carefully. The dog . . ."

"The dog is fine," Michel interrupted. "Not like your brawling huskies. Leave the dog alone."

"He should have run with other dogs. Now he never can. He is a one dog, all alone." He added in a whisper, "Like you, Michel." Tears shone in his eyes and he turned his head quickly, the temple pulse throbbing.

Michel stiffened as if an electric shock had gone through him, then quickly groped for words. "What are you making with nails?" Zeke sipped coffee carefully. Swallowing seemed painful, and seconds passed before he could answer.

"Fixing a sled," he got out finally, with effort.

"But I saw your sled outside. It looked in good shape."

"Not my sled. My father's."

"I see. Your father has had good hunting, and very much, to break his sled. Whenever he is away your mother dares to come here. Right, Zeke?"

The boy's averted face was distressed and he did not answer.

"Have you had good hunting too, Zeke? How are your fox traps?"

"You saw them, Michel. They have not changed."

"Oh. Foxes come only to your father's traps, not to anyone else's."

"My father went far away for a long time. There was not enough to eat and his sled broke on the ice hills, so he had to come home. He only caught two foxes."

"I know about the two foxes. I don't know about the only." Michel's tone was pitiless. "Your friends have brought me poor furs. But Saloositak Tana has brought fine ones. He does not hunt: ergo, your friends are hunting and they choose not to bring the catch to me — perhaps, as you pointed out, because I am an ogre."

"Please, Michel, they still like you. They are not afraid. It is only that . . . they cannot . . ." He stopped suddenly, stood up and said formally, "Thank you for the food."

"Just a minute. Tell your friends they've run over their credit. There are good furs. Saloositak Tana has found them. Your father has trapped them. Your own sled was probably piled with them when you passed my house by. Where there are some there are others. You'd better bring in the furs you're keeping in your houses. I'm a storekeeper, not the Salvation Army."

Zeke winced as if he had been slapped, and remorse stung Michel. "It isn't Pryde's profit motive," he said gently. "I don't care about making money, Zeke. But I won't be allowed to stay on here if I have nothing when the ship comes. I'll leave under a cloud and I'll never be able to come back."

"We will bring what we can." Zeke's voice was almost inaudible. Michel watched him out, watched the chill darkness swallow him, and turned back into the house, unspeakably depressed.

They did not come. Michel started taking long walks with Shadow, far back over the dormant hills. The dog, vicious in all other eyes, was his secret friend; when he felt the shy touch of the cold nose and looked into the bright direct eyes, he knew also it was his only friend.

[203]

On his return home late one night he saw Saloositak Tana crossing the river on the track to his house. Michel stood at the top
of the bank waiting for him. The dog, held close, growled. The
fat man looked up at Michel, gigantic above him, and cringed
backward as if hoping the narrow river canyon would swallow
him. I must look pretty menacing, thought Michel with satis-
faction.

"What do you want, Saloositak Tana?" he bellowed, while
Shadow threatened beside him.

Saloositak Tana fumbled two fox skins from his rags and held
them up. They caught the starlight and shone brighter than the
snow.

"Where did you get them?" The man mumbled, still cowering.
"You can't speak English but you know what I mean all right.
Show me where you got them." He started down the hill, Shadow
straining ahead of him. But Saloositak Tana turned and scrambled
up the bank, and when Michel reached the top he saw the man
stumbling across the snow back toward the hills, leaving hysterical
shreds of sound in the cold air behind him.

Saloositak Tana's panic triggered anger. "I don't want your
furs, you terrible old man!" shouted Michel after him. "I know
where you got them and I'm going after them."

In spite of the acute cold he was hot and red-faced when he
reached Nauligak's house. He stood square in the low doorway,
scowling, legs spaced well apart. The peaceful scene within was
immobilized, and for a full minute the room was still as a photo-
graph, the woman's hand halted in the air with the threaded
needle, the man with a hammer raised above a splintered sled
runner, two children stark in the midst of play, another with a
jam-soaked cracker halfway to his mouth, the boy holding a tattered dog harness. The only motion was the slow drip of jam
between the child's fingers.

"Nauligak, you have skins. You lied." He moved through the
stunned silence to the back of the sleeping platform and searched,

throwing patched clothing, threadbare boots, worn caribou skins in confusion around him.

"Michel . . ." started Zeke, but Michel stalked out without a word. A deep sigh, the collective breath of the household, reached him through the door he left swinging open.

He visited every house in the village, searching with unabated ferocity, leaving fearful children and shocked parents amid the holocaust of tossed clothing. From the houses he went to the shed where they kept the cache of frozen meat and fish. The supply was dangerously low but he did not see it. He looked only for the gleam of white fur in the icy dusk.

Frustrated, he strode back along the line of houses. He shook his fist. "You've got them somewhere!" he shouted. "I'll find them. I'll follow you until I find them, whatever cave you've hidden them in." His voice battered against the closed houses and lost itself over the deadened sea and ice-wrapped hills.

For hours he walked in the foothills, anger keeping him warm, looking for footprints in the snow, caves in the rocks, finding nothing. Wan winter daylight came slowly, and still he walked, now hopeless. A sense of eeriness entered his vacant mind and he stopped uncertainly, his eyes still fixed on the ground before him. He was looking at his own shadow. He lifted his head toward the mountain. It shone against the green sky as if light burned inside it. Turning, he saw the edge of the sun and long shadows of hills stretching toward him. Daybreak and nightfall met, and in a few minutes the new shadow-giving light was gone.

He stared at the afterglow and tried to remember how he had longed for this day. Sun, what good are you to me, he said to himself. You show me my failure. When you are high and warm and flowers grow and Maggie's baby is born I will be gone from here, unlamented. As long as winter lasted there was hope, but when spring comes the long inconclusive experiment will be over.

The air vibrated with a deep hum. A plane circled, reflecting the sun, and disappeared low over the ice in the direction of the police post. They are coming for me already, he thought, and his heart sank. Instead of the beginning, the coming of the sun is the end. They will take me out tomorrow.

His thoughts hardened: But not before I find the answers to my questions.

At home Maggie, small and frightened, tiptoed around the house until Michel snapped at her to stop creeping. She contrived to look even smaller. After supper she went for her outer garments, but Michel was there before her, blocking the door.

"I suppose you're going to help your mother."

"Yes. I come back tomorrow."

"Well, you can help me too, girl. Tell them they can have food, if they need it, when they bring the skins they've stowed away."

"No skins," she said sadly.

"There've got to be." He examined Maggie's pocket and hood and shook out the sleeves, then handed the clothes to her. She shrank from him and the clothes dropped. He pointed. "Take them and go." Snatching them, she ran outside, past Shadow's automatic growl. The door shut quietly behind the frigid starlight and Michel went straight to his store. He counted everything. No box of food was missing, no tin of tobacco, not so much as a spool of thread, yet he counted again.

At last, exhausted and depressed, he dropped on his bed still dressed. He could not sleep. Thoughts ran in his head like rats in a cage. Why am I cruel to Maggie? Am I losing my reason? Where do the furs come from that the dirty old man brings? Where did Aitu get her furs? What had been on Nauligak's sled, piled high when it passed his house? Why didn't they come to his store? Why did he frighten them so they would never come? He lost consciousness at last, but it seemed only a minute later that he was roused by the smell of smoke. Maggie was in the kitchen. He ran past her into the store to count everything once more.

While he scrabbled feverishly in the dark room the plane hummed again. Slowly its sound faded. They had not come for him. He was, after all, to be ignored.

Depleted and obscurely frightened, he crept out of the room into the false morning brightness.

19

ONLY MAGGIE was left. Michel had turned taciturn, and she responded with a quiet loving tact so subtle that he did not notice it. As the days lengthened and the sun began to give its first warmth, she grew much heavier and moved slowly. Desire no longer touched Michel. Adrift on his own sea of uncertainties, he accorded her only a vague, tolerant kindness.

Walking into the kitchen one morning, he surprised her in an attitude of despair. She leaned on the window sill, shoulders drooped, eyes fixed unseeing on the snowbank on the hillside, high as the house, where Michel had shoveled the drifts away from the wall. Shadowless morning light lay on the shrouded earth. Everything was pale gray; it was more disheartening than the cold constant starlight of winter.

When she heard his step she straightened and spun around. Her face, drawn in old woman lines, changed instantly. It was Maggie's face again, smiling and young, too young for pregnancy, too young for haunting distress.

"What is it, Maggie?"

Her sloe eyes sparkled. "Nothing, Michel. Come quick, go quick — like you say about grave."

"Stranger walked over my grave?" The words loosed undefined dread, and her smile died as she saw him forget her. She turned back to the half-kneaded dough on the table. He looked at her back, unseeing, then scraped his hand over his eyes as if to twitch off a cobweb.

"Maggie," he said softly, touching her shoulder. The face she turned to him was tender. "I'm pretty dreary company these days. If you'll just bear with me awhile . . . Things are bound to come better . . ." If only they wouldn't ignore me, he added to himself; if only I hadn't frightened them. Which came first? He gave her a reassuring pat and went out with his dog.

Daily he searched for caves, found only the ice-paralyzed foothills. Shadow, the projection of his joyless isolation, was always with him. The dog stayed close, never running after the rare mouse tracks, ignoring occasional ravens and owls. When Michel stopped Shadow stopped too, his nose touching the loved hand, waiting for a casual caress.

Sometimes they passed the graveyard. The crack under the missionary's stone was widening, and Michel peered into the ice-filled gap with morbid fascination, expecting fingerbones, toes, scattered vertebrae, not sure he would find anything.

It was the middle of April when he saw it.

There had been a week of thaw, false spring. Snow melted on the hills and they smelled of mud. Michel imagined roots stirring under the elastic ground of March and the cautious purl of water under heavy river ice.

Then an ice-laden gale had roared down from the north. When it cleared the weather was cold as January and the bright sky a pretense. The gray grass was brittle, the bared mud frozen in humps, the spring smell a thin memory.

The swift changes had created small upheavals. Here a boulder had slipped, leaving an open depression where one day flowers and grass would grow high and geese nest protected; there melting snow had found a new track that would become a riverbed. At the gravestone the ground had split wide.

The bones had shifted under the slow violence of successive

thaws and freezes, but they were all there, so near the surface that Michel wondered why they had not come through before. Then he remembered. The stone had been carved under Zeke's direction, and Zeke had been outside at school until mid-June. Splaine's body had been preserved until the earth could be dug deep. It had taken these three years to rise, inexorably, to present its hollow face to Michel, the only one who looked for it.

In the cavity of the rib cage lay a small rusted metal strongbox, evidently once clasped decorously in the corpse's hands — perhaps instead of weapons, to assure his well-being in the Moon Man's country. Michel picked it out gingerly, trying not to touch the bones. The body must be left exactly as it was, for the police to judge the manner of death. Yet he winced when the back of his hand scraped over a rib and it fell with a small clatter.

"I'll give it back," he said out loud to the listening soul of the dead. With a pocket knife he pried open the rusty lock. Within were a Bible, a hymnal, some letters in envelopes addressed to Father Splaine and a plain leatherbound notebook filled with closely written penscript. Michel turned the damp-stained pages to the last entry:

Sunday, February 20. The sun rose yesterday for the first time, to gladden our hearts at last. After the service I read the 19th Psalm . . . "In them hath he set a tabernacle for the sun, which is as a bridegroom coming out of his chamber and rejoiceth as a strong man to run a race . . ." But few of my people were here, most being too weak with sickness or hunger to leave their houses. Those who came, half-starved, listened to my words with a brightness of spirit that only made my spirit lower. I cannot feed them any longer with God's words alone. I have given them the last of my food; for two weeks I have eaten, as they do, only the bony cod and the fleshless seal. My strength is ebbing, and before

I am quite helpless I must find help for them. Nauligak has offered to take me to the Aurora Sound Post — but I fear the good Constable Davitt has nothing for us either. He has not been here in over a month, and then he said the whole region is starving. I await Nauligak and we leave at once, even with the threat of a blizzard before us. If we wait for fair weather we may never go out again. I am not afraid and neither is Nauligak. He is the only hunter I trust to get me through that most fearsome of all dangers, an Arctic winter storm. God will ride with us.

Michel read and reread this devoutly innocent document, bewilderment mounting. What now of his suspicions? Father Splaine was a trusting man. He was probably right. Michel was a doubting man. Had he been cruelly, capriciously wrong?

Slowly the ice in his heart melted. Whatever had been the truth of the missionary's end, he had given the people food while he lived. Now they were starving again. Michel put the diary into the box and replaced it carefully in the grave. He ran home, to find the house cold and unlighted. Maggie had gone. He would load his small sled with food and take it to her people, and bring her home again.

He lighted the fire, made a quick supper of beans and coffee, then went to the storeroom. Dogs howled outside and Shadow answered once from the porch, then was quiet. Michel went to the door to find him quivering in a corner, ears drooping, tail low. Jacques Davitt's big team was on the beach and the constable was coming up the rise. He walked heavily and looked old. Michel stood in the porch with his hand on Shadow's head, feeling the dog tremble.

"What's that?" asked Davitt, peering into the corner.

Michel stood in front of his dog. "Just a dog — my dog."

"Seems to be frightened half to death. Bear get him?" He

didn't wait for an answer but walked into the warm room and dropped his coat on the bed.

"There's supper left," said Michel. "Are you hungry?"

"Yes, thanks." He sounded listless. The big handsome face was hollow-cheeked and the eyes sunken as if he had not slept. Michel made conversation with effort.

"Have you enough to eat over there?"

"No, not really. We'd given away most of our food when the plane came . . ." He flinched as if an open wound had been touched, and fell silent.

"I heard it," said Michel uncomfortably. "Did it bring food?"

"Some, maybe enough to last until the seals start birthing — if they do."

"You can take some of ours."

"I may. Good you still have plenty. Your people are luckier than some I've visited." Michel reddened. "Where's Maggie?" asked the constable suddenly.

"I don't know. Helping her mother probably. Why?"

"Only wondering." Davitt's gaze wandered vaguely around the room, then the pain-filled eyes met Michel's. "Nina's left. Went out with Ide on the plane that came to pick him up. He claimed sick leave. Burned eyes . . . He must have made her some sort of fake promise. He'll drop her when the plane lands. I was on patrol when she left. She didn't say good-by. She'll die out there . . ." The monotoned sentences trailed off.

"Why don't you go and get her back?"

"Hopeless. By the time I could get out of here she'd be lost. I'm a policeman — can't walk off the job." His eyes were sad over the transient smile. "Can you see me going in and out of juke joints the rest of my life looking for a lost kid?"

"You could get Ide to watch out for her."

"He doesn't like her. He only took her out to spite me." He smiled again, painfully. "You've seen our seamier side, Michel. I've gone a little bush. It's unavoidable here — this is the lonesomest country in the world. I like being alone, but it's changed me because I've stayed too long. It's too beautiful to leave — everything here seems just at the beginning."

Michel's spirit lightened for an instant. "I've felt that too, as if the world was made yesterday." He paused. "You didn't come here to tell me about Nina."

"No — yes. Supposedly I came to check on the food supply."

"You can see we're all right," said Michel quickly. "I'll give you enough to see your people through."

"But mainly," Davitt went on, "because there's no one to talk to at Aurora Sound. We should have been friends from the first. It's no good going it alone here."

"I didn't know we weren't friends. What was the hitch?"

"Nothing concrete. I liked you, but you seemed too much on the surface to be able to take solitude. This was just another camping trip. I didn't think you'd manage with the Eskimos; they can be damnably obscure if they're not sure of you. Mainly I didn't want a case of cabin fever on my beat. I tried to scare you off with the old woman — it's an uncouth story, but they believe it so implicitly it's oddly convincing. I misjudged you. You made it very well."

"You wanted me to be scared off by old Splaine too. Letting me think he was murdered."

"What?" said Davitt, surprised. He stared at Michel for a moment and continued, now reserved and alien. "Whatever you thought was your own idea."

"I decided I was mistaken." But what's the matter with the man, he wondered, acting like a hostile witness? "Why didn't you tell me Nauligak was with him that day when he tried to get to you for supplies — the day of the blizzard three years ago?"

"You know about that? I kept it from you because from the beginning you've had peculiar ideas about the missionary and I thought you'd take the accident wrong —as you have. I suppose Zeke told you."

"No one told me. I read it in Splaine's diary from the grave. The corpse sat up."

Davitt gave a short laugh. "Of course. They do around here. Even a dead man can't keep a secret. Well, when they got to me Splaine was already dead, of starvation and exposure. That's in the records in case you want to look it up. Nauligak was in bad shape. They'd got caught in the storm and gone around in circles for three days. Nauligak speared a tiggak but Splaine couldn't eat it."

"That was the winter Zeke's father had to eat tiggak," said Michel half to himself. He looked straight at Davitt. "Zeke thinks his father killed Splaine."

"That's the worst mixed-up kid in the precinct."

"He was my friend," said Michel unhappily. "Now I know he was wrong but he doesn't. He's obsessed by it — doesn't want to tell on his father but sure he's right. He managed to get me feeling haunted too. Like the day on the mountain, when I thought Nauligak had tried to get me killed." He told the story of the climb.

"You've got an imagination. Comes of being a writer, I suppose. You don't know these people as well as I thought. They never tell the exact truth. They say what they think you want to hear, or to create a dramatic effect, or to prevent you — as in Nauligak's case — from doing something dangerous. Don't believe them, just sift. There's always good will behind it."

"More like collusion behind it," said Michel slowly, trying to arrange his disordered ideas. "Splaine was a good man. He was liked. I wouldn't have had two consecutive thoughts about him — except that he died here and everybody's agreed not to say how." His perplexity came into focus. "How am I to know what really happened out on the ice? From what I've seen of Nauligak, he's too smart to go around in circles by mistake."

"He was nearly dead himself."

"Yes, of course . . . but you must admit that to a greenhorn like me" — he smiled boyishly — "who is also a journalist, the lack of enlightenment was tantalizing. Particularly on your part. Why did you go secretive just now when I mentioned Splaine?"

Davitt looked puzzled. "I don't know myself. It may have been a protective feeling toward Nauligak, that he shouldn't be misunderstood. But that doesn't make sense, does it. He doesn't need protection — quite the contrary." He seemed surprised at his own words, and added, "Well, we've cleared it up now. I'll get on over to see the people."

"They're all right," said Michel hastily. "I was just getting some more food ready to take over. No need for you to waste the time."

"It's my job," said Davitt, smiling. "Gives me a chance for a gossip with Nauligak."

Michel went with him, hoping the Eskimos' fear would keep them quiet. It did, disastrously. They sat on their sleeping platforms gaunt-faced and spiritless, and answered the policeman's questions in monosyllables, their eyes moving from his face to the tall frowning man behind him. Only the eyes seemed alive, glinting and darting in the darkness of their cold houses. In one house a baby cried weakly, but the mother did not give it her breast. All the time they were in that house the baby continued crying.

Davitt glared at Michel when they came to Nauligak's door. "They're too frightened to speak, but it's clear they have nothing to eat. Now I'm going to find out why."

Nauligak and his family were as apathetic as the others. Only Zeke raised his eyes from a fishnet he was tying, and looked at Michel sorrowfully. Davitt's words seemed to drop into a hole. At last he stopped, and through the heavy silence Nauligak spoke with slow dignity. At the end Davitt turned to Michel.

"It seems that you gave them food at first, then refused credit, so Nauligak told them not to bother you." Michel flushed with irritation. "He's proud," continued Davitt. "He told them they'd been hungry before and they knew how to wait. He said that if he had only a seal flipper and a stranger was starving he would give it to him. But he doesn't blame you, because you didn't know they were hungry. How about that?"

"I was right — the old witch doctor wouldn't let them come to the store. How did I know they were so hungry?"

"*You* kept them from coming — did you see their faces when you came into their houses behind me?"

"But they have furs . . ."

"You must be deaf, dumb and blind. There haven't been any furs all winter."

"Ask Nauligak about the pile he passed my house with," said Michel stubbornly, "and the foxes his wife brought in when he was safely away."

Davitt questioned Nauligak and the hunter answered at length. "This is the worst winter he remembers. None of the skins he brought home that day he passed your house were good enough to trade. They were all starved seal. He's trapped two foxes, and you have them."

Michel made a pretense at reasonableness, but his voice was sharp. "You sound right — it seems unlikely there are furs. But there are, Jacques Davitt. Ask him again. Saloositak Tana has been bringing me stolen skins — fine ones. He's found their cache. I haven't, though I've looked. I will yet."

"Saloositak Tana is a scoundrel. We haven't pinned him down yet. Undoubtedly he picked up a cache he'd stolen last year." He spoke briefly to Nauligak, who nodded. "He hides them in different places when no one is looking. We'll get him one day."

"You're lying like the rest of them," said Michel coldly, mistrust denying reason. "You're protecting them. You don't need to. I'm not going to hurt anyone. I am a trader. I will give credit to a hunter who hunts, but I will give no credit to hunters who hide skins."

Davitt stared at him intently. "This isn't cabin fever. It's insanity." He said a few more words to Nauligak, then strode to the door. It opened before he got there and Maggie stood in the entranceway. She saw Michel and went toward him, hands out. Nauligak's harsh voice stopped her but, luminous eyes still on her lover, she talked to him, the lilting, singing talk he had heard so often. He took her hand to draw her outside with him. Her mother spoke gently and she slid her hand slowly out of his. The radiant smile faded, the lovely voice ended on a downward cadence.

"Come on," said Davitt curtly. Michel followed him out, head turned, his eyes still caught with Maggie's, until someone closed the door, and even then he felt her look like a ghost accompanying him.

Davitt stumped ahead of him and he spoke to the uncompromising back. "What did she say?"

"A sentimental adieu," said Davitt bitterly. "What else?"

"That's what I'm asking you."

Davitt turned, grim-faced. "What good does it do to tell you anything? You twist it and mock it and don't believe it. You don't deserve her and you're not going to see her again."

Back at Michel's house, Davitt went into the storeroom and unceremoniously emptied the shelves, piling his big sled high. Michel watched, not helping. At the end Davitt went back into the living room and talked, biting off the words. "You'll be compensated, eventually. Before that, as soon as I can get a plane in again, you'll be taken out of here. Now we're both going back to the post."

"If you can tell me anything I've done that's against the law I'll come with you."

"You're not safe alone. You're halfway round the bend now."

"Isn't that my problem, Constable?" He looked out the window to the promontory, where stubborn new willow shoots thrust out of the hard ground, and beyond it, across the rippled sea ice, to

[217]

the remnant of daylight green at the edge of the sky. "I like it here."

"How are you planning to eat?"

"I'm taking a little food off your sled. My food, which you are illegally removing." He walked outside and came back with an armful of cans. "If you care to engage in a wrestling match you might be able to tie me to that sled and take me back. Or you might not. In any case I wouldn't be much company for you, and you might discover when I took it to court that you'd exceeded your duty."

Davitt scowled and Michel smiled tightly. "Don't worry. When I hear the plane I'll be over. There's nothing left for me here now. Evidently I won't even be allowed to see my baby. I would just like to enjoy the house a little longer. Don't ask why." He looked out the window again. "Maybe because I like my curtains better than yours."

Davitt shrugged angrily and went to the door. "How will you get over the ice?"

"I have a sled and a dog." Shadow cowered back into the corner when Davitt passed him and the policeman looked down contemptuously.

"That?"

"He can pull a sled and he's obedient."

"What did you do to him?"

"Nothing. He's a little afraid of other dogs."

"Bushed too. Everything you touch . . ." He turned abruptly and went down the stairs, calling his own dogs. Michel watched until they disappeared on the dark ice. He could still hear the grunting and howling of the dogs. Then there was nothing but the empty hush of the cold spring night.

20

WHEN MAGGIE went, Sandra went too. He could no longer conjure up the astringent girl who had caught the overflow of his lonely mind. Instead the sound of Maggie's voice haunted him asleep and awake. He hated the long nights and brought Shadow inside as soon as daylight was gone. At first the dog was distrustful. Used to obedience, he followed Michel, walking stiff-legged, tail down. He sought his old corner and couched there uneasily, eyes following his master. For two nights he refused to move from his dark place until morning, when Michel called him outside. Then he scuttled through the door as if swept by a broom. On the third night Michel was already asleep when the cold nose touched his hand. He stroked the dog's head and heard through half-sleep a thump and a short satisfied sigh as Shadow settled on the floor beside his bed. A nudge woke him in the morning and he turned to see the bright eyes fixed on him and the plumed tail high. Shadow wanted company too, and followed him outside when he fetched snow for coffee and washing, and inside again, close on his heels. He lingered in the kitchen while Michel fixed breakfast and settled down to his own meal close to the table. While Michel smoked a cigarette with his coffee, Shadow sat on his foot and looked up, waiting for a word or a touch.

That night Michel opened the door to call and saw him standing expectantly just outside, tail waving slightly. From then on it was a routine. Shadow followed Michel while he performed the chores, then they walked over the still wintered hills, watching for the sun to show and turn the gray world to pale long-shadowed gold. It gave no heat but an unearthly light like a promise in a dream. The two wandered also like dream figures, creatures in isolated suspense, knowing neither before nor after. They trudged the brown and white hills without destination or purpose, seeing but not noticing the tough stubs of new plants, the river water cutting caves in the rotting cover ice, the brooding changeful mountain now losing its snow in blistered streaks on the glaciers, cascades on the higher rocks.

At the end of the day Michel was tired from the number of steps he had walked. He fixed his meager evening meal, then went to the door to let in the waiting dog. The two sat still as wax images by the stove at night, Michel with a book in his hand, Shadow by his feet, touching him, eyes wide open.

Often Michel awoke with Maggie's voice in his ears or the scornful sound of Davitt's last words. He lay awake in suspense, waiting for the dream to go, yet knowing that the real dream was the one he walked around in all day. One night Shadow woke him. He thought it was a dream again; it had been many days since his dog had made a sound. Eager whimpering came from across the room by the door and was punctuated by the imperative scratch of strong claws.

"No, Shadow," he commanded. The dog knew "No" as well as his own name, and stopped. But he was still at the door, his fur faintly gleaming in the darkness, nose touching the wood, ears pricked forward. Michel watched him uncomfortably. For a half hour the dog was silent; then a small sound came, a suppressed bark, and one paw touched the door again.

Michel went to him and Shadow was instantly on his feet, eyes moving from the man to the door and back. "No, Shadow," he

[220]

said gently, his hand soothing the tensed ears. "You wouldn't get anywhere near her, little friend. The others would tear you to pieces first. Come back." Shadow followed him and sat, nose on his master's thigh, eyes begging. "Lie down." The dog subsided, unrelaxed, and Michel closed his own eyes conscious of the other's on him.

Suddenly Shadow was on his feet again, and the whimper this time was imperious. She must be very close. Michel picked up a lump of coal and opened the door, holding Shadow. Moonlight lay on white patches of snow, the hollows that could hide a dog or a man were in deep shade and the black rocks could be waiting figures. Nothing moved and the silence was absolute. "Get away!" he shouted, and flung the coal. It flew in a wide arc, landing loudly on a rock and slithering to the ground. There were no answering sounds, no flurry of motion. All the shadows stayed where they were.

He locked the door against the hostile emptiness, lighted the primus and boiled coffee. Shadow paced the room, clawing the door briefly as he passed it, back and forth, inarticulate sounds deep in his throat, until Michel, exasperated, lashed out as if the dog were human.

"Quit it, Shadow, shut up! You're not getting out. Hear that? *Not getting out.*" Shadow spared him a glance and went on pacing. "Oh hell," said Michel and went to the door again. He had to let the dog go or be imprisoned here himself, perhaps for days. Shadow would not fight. One sight of the bitch — so attractive from safe inside the house — surrounded by pugnacious admirers, and his dog would be home again before he heard the first growl.

He opened the door and Shadow streaked past him. In less than a second he was over the hill, and the disappearing flash of the shining tail in the moonlight was the last Michel saw of him.

He left the door open the rest of the night and slept lightly, one hand over the edge of the bed, expecting the touch of the cold nose. In the morning he searched the beach and the hills behind

[221]

the house for signs of a scuffle, a smear of blood, a scatter of torn fur. The ground was untouched.

That night and for several following nights he left the door open and stayed awake long. During the days he walked, calling and searching far into the foothills. Once he came down over the village and stopped on a hilltop scanning each house with his binoculars. The houses were shut, no child played outside, no man worked on a sled or boat, though the day was bright and warm. The dogs lay motionless by their stakes; none of them was Shadow. The still village was curiously frightening — its inhabitants might all have died. Then Michel caught a motion as a door opened a crack. It closed at once and he knew why the village seemed lifeless. They had seen him and hidden. He crept away, an outcast feared and hated.

Back at his own threshold, he stared at the quiet room. No stove hissed, no voice spoke from the kitchen, no wet muzzle touched his hand. He could read old hopes and loves in every inch of the perfect little house and the lonely grandeur seen through the windows — someone else's old hopes and loves. Slowly he went to the typewriter, pulled the cover off and rolled paper in. He wrote deliberately, not pausing until he had come to the end.

"Dear Sandra — I write to you for the last time because I am leaving soon. I know that you never existed, and since I am not anyone either now, you are the ideal correspondent.

"Since I left school — too young — I've liked to move. No place or person attached me. I never gave myself except in small doses, never allowed anyone to give to me. I made out well but was always on the outside. When I came here and found Zeke and Maggie and saw this house, abandoned and still beautiful, I knew I had to stay. Home was never for me, I had told Davitt. But I found myself part of this wide wild land as I'd never been part of any place. This is home — and I don't know whether I can take it. Home is something you have to work at. For a while I seemed to be living on the inside, but now, at the end, I find I was still on the outside, all the time. Davitt is an enemy, Maggie and Zeke have gone, Shadow is lost, Nauligak wants me out. (Curious how the outlandish legend of the girl who married a dog has been haunting me lately — Nauligak believes it, and I am the white man, the dog, who must be killed — do you think I'm losing my reason? — I've seen it in his face every time he looked at me.)

"I'm leaving a mystery behind but don't care any more. The missionary may have been done in. He starved to death within reach of his own house and a police post, with a hunter known for his skill — a hunter who is still alive. It doesn't seem likely, but they're all very plausible and nothing can be proven.

"The situation frightened me for a while. Splaine's fate wasn't an abstract puzzle and his death was not an ending. They were twisted into my life. His past and my future were of the same cloth, with Nauligak woven in darkly. I felt threatened by the grave on the hill, the sly fat man, the confused boy trying to protect his father, the cagey policeman — above all by the implacable hunter. I became brutal to the natives because I feared them — feared their silent, inexorable withdrawal from me.

"But I was loved too, and I think I loved a little in return.

"Now I feel neither loved nor threatened. None of this I've written matters any more. I'm thrown back on myself, just the way it always was. But there is a terrible difference. I see myself. Never look in a mirror, Sandra, because you will see nothing. I don't know why I'm alone now but I do know with stark sureness that it is my fault.

"I'll start moving again, and forget the blank when I looked in the mirror. I'll be glad to go away from here."

He dropped his hands from the keys and stared into the patchwork past — the past before he had come to Aurora Sound, that he was going back to. Isolated scenes lighted his darkened mind. He sat with two trappers in a lean-to of fresh-cut jackpine. It was almost dark and loons called across the lake still light below them. The smoke of the big campfire was in their eyes and noses. "Knew a fellow who shot a bear," said one. "Walked up to him thinking he was dead and the bear got up on his hind legs and mauled him." He paused. "Measly little guy. That bear didn't have much to be proud of." They all laughed, someone threw another tree on the fire, and they went to their sleeping bags in the pine-smelling shelter. He never saw them after that trip. The practiced mountain climber ahead of him on the rope stopped at the top of the knife-edge ridge. Michel, climbing behind him, fingertips raw from clinging to minute protuberances on the bare cliff, called to him to tauten the rope. The mountaineer, pulling the rope with one hand, put a finger of the other to his lips. Scrambling to the safety of the ridge, he looked over. Below was a small hanging valley, rock towering on three sides, the fourth a sheer drop to fields two thousand feet down. Yellow poppies grew in the dry sand, mountain rhododendron bloomed on the uncompromising rock. Three mountain sheep stood among the flowers, their heavy horns swept in backward spirals, their large eyes fixed on the strangers. "No one's ever been here before," whispered the mountaineer. They looked at each other and smiled, then carefully withdrew from the ridge. The last thing they saw were the curly horns still motionless. He never went back. The girl opposite him wore too much lipstick, her hair was blonde and shiny and her eyes were shiny too. She had had too many glasses of watery beer and so had he. Someone put a dime in the jukebox and a sentimental tune rolled out. A middle-aged man in an undershirt danced solemnly by himself in the middle of the floor and fat Armenian women sat in kitchen chairs on the sidewalk outside calling their children over the roar of the elevated train. The girl opposite him was suddenly beautiful, and he said, "Whenever I hear that song I will remember you." The city summer was beautiful too, and the girl said, "Have we got another dime?"

Michel couldn't remember the tune. He looked out to the darkening mountain and Maggie's voice ran through his head. "Dear, dear Maggie," he wrote in pencil at the end of the letter to Sandra.

The days crept past and the sun grew stronger and still Michel stayed, waiting, listening for the plane, unwilling to go far from his house. The snow was melting brownly and the river was covered with bared ice. He had to go up the hill to find fresh snow behind the rocks where it had drifted all winter. Even there it was eroded, his own footprints fouled it and he had to find a new drift every morning. Inching between two rocks one day in the search for unsullied snow, he found a muddle of tracks. They were old and had melted, frozen and melted again. There were a lot of them — but the small space would not hold more than one man or animal. He backed out, climbed the smaller rock and looked down at the space. A few enlarged, rounded footprints separately visible at the edges could only be human, and the hider had had a dog with him. The prints ended at the entrance to the sunless crevice. Beyond that the snow had melted and the springy mat of dead grass showed nothing.

Someone had come with a dog — a female dog in heat — and waited here at night. If Shadow had not been let out that night, the watcher would have retreated and come again the next night. Someone wanted him to be without Shadow, helpless in his own house. Fear crawled up his spine. The empty spring landscape was menacing, and he turned his head a dozen times as he retreated down the hill.

At home he cleaned, oiled and loaded the long-unused rifle. The feel of the smooth butt in his hand and the dull shine of the barrel gave him a measure of courage as he set out long-strided for the village. But he paused before crossing the last hill. He would be an easy target alone in a village of closed houses. Anyone could come up behind him. A long detour took him around to the other side, where he found a rock that shielded him from curious eyes, and sat down to wait as the unseen watcher had waited for his dog.

The people were out today, busy in the sunshine. They were not in range, but as soon as one of them came near enough he would shoot — close enough to frighten, not to kill — then go down and face Nauligak. They would meet on his terms. A man, even Nauligak, doesn't argue with a rifle. He would confront him with the theft of Shadow, find out where the fur cache was, then take dogs and a sled and go alone to the police post. He smiled a little at the thought of presenting proof to the doubting policeman.

The sun shone warm on his head but he did not feel it. On the sea ice melted puddles glowed turquoise between white ridges, and open leads were purple. At his feet a willow shrub showed furled new leaves and a saxifrage bloomed pink beside a shelf of old ice. A bee flew out of a lemming hole and fussed among the flowers.

Michel saw none of this. For an hour his eyes focused unwavering on the houses below him, and his thoughts were in a narrow tunnel.

An indistinguishable figure detached itself from the group, but not in Michel's direction. The man or woman loitered on the beach, moving aimlessly out of sight of the village. Then it cut briskly back into the hills, casualness gone. Michel, from his height above the houses, saw the purposeful motion and backed down from his hiding place. Running on a wide detour to avoid being seen, he lost the figure behind a hill, then caught it again higher up. The rolling tundra began to climb steeply toward the inland mountains and spring was left behind. The ground was heavily snow-covered and sprinkled with boulders hurled slow-motion from the mountain. Some, caught endwise in their fall sea-ward, resembled monolithic gravestones, some were tipped as if they would fall at a touch, some were sunk into the frozen mud like hippopotamus in quicksand.

For the last ten minutes Michel had lost sight of his quarry; now he stopped and looked around the unworldly colorless land-scape. The sky had clouded murkily, grayer than the snow. Here were no birds, no flowers, no bees, nor ever would be. He was closed off from the sea by high hills; to his right he could see the top of the mountain, black against the ashen sky.

He walked slowly in long zigzag lines, looking for tracks. It was almost dark when he found them, and the line between hills and sky was lost in mist. The single line of footprints led deeper into the labyrinth of rocks, where even the landmark mountain was hidden. Whoever walked ahead of him did not court visitors. He took the rifle from the leather case slung over his shoulder.

The tracks rounded the flank of a tall hill and descended abruptly into a narrow hidden ravine. At the bottom two upended boulders had been covered with a hide to make a crude shelter. A heap of furs gleamed in the dusk, and yellow light showed between the rocks.

Michel moved along the side of the hill until he could see the open front of the cave. Saloositak Tana sat beside a primus stove flensing a fox. Frustrated anger rose in Michel. The fat man had probably never trapped a fox in his life. This was the cache of a thief and Michel had walked straight into a dead end. But the skins were new — he could smell them. He would take them to Nauligak and demand an accounting. He turned back to find a place where he could descend without being seen — and saw Nauligak and Zeke coming around the hill. They walked easily, as if they knew this place, and headed openly for the shelter. So, thought Michel with bitter fury, they were all in it together. The fiction of the old man's thefts was just another thread in the web of conspiracy.

He plunged down the hill, legs caught by the heavy snow, fell head first over a hidden rock but managed to hold his rifle clear. Lurching to his feet, he looked back and saw the two not more than a hundred feet behind him and now hurrying. He reached the entrance before them and stood for a moment looking at the opened carcass, fur down, parts of the flesh gouged out, and a scattering of bones on the wet earth floor. Something was very wrong, but he was too angry to think.

He shouted. Saloositak Tana looked up, saw the rifle and above it the fierce blue eyes. His loose face seemed to fall apart and he backed away from the raw carcass, mumbling. Another voice, authoritative, spoke behind Michel, and the quaking man drew even farther into the corner where he hunched, apparently paralyzed with fear.

Michel swung the rifle toward Nauligak and said clearly and coldly, "You've been hiding skins. This is one of the caches. Tell me where the others are."

Zeke stepped forward, his hand reaching toward Michel, his voice entreating. "Michel, please, you are wrong." His father snapped a curt command and the boy withdrew. Nauligak spoke rapidly, addressing himself to the abject man cowered against the rock.

"Get me the skins," Michel interrupted, "or I will kill you." He raised the rifle to Nauligak's chest. His hand was loose on the trigger; his only purpose was intimidation. But before Nauligak could move or speak the boy had hurled himself between them, crying in an agonized voice, "No, Michel, no, no — *dog!*"

The word rattled against Michel's mind like a gunshot. Dog — white man — for an instant he was back in the old woman's hut hearing the ritualistic voice intoning the ancient insult. His fingers convulsed and the gun exploded in Zeke's face. He stared, stunned, at the hand that had, without conscious direction from the mind, pulled the trigger, and Nauligak stepped calmly over his dead son and thrust his knife into Michel's heart.

Nauligak took his son in his arms and walked slowly down the long hills. The fat man followed at a distance, footsteps lagging, looking in all directions as if to find a place to hide, though hiding was finished for him. At the door to his house Nauligak laid down his burden and covered the broken face with his parka. He motioned Saloositak Tana to go before him, and the man slipped sideways past him and crumpled at his usual place by the entrance. The hunter spoke quietly to Aitu and handed her the long knife.

Her tears fell on it, and her husband laid a hand on her head in brief tenderness.

It took him a long time to cross the sea ice to the police post with his hunger-exhausted team — only three dogs, all old. In the meantime the body lay in the place where no animal or bird came. Its warmth melted the snow around it, then it grew cold, and the blood froze on the sealskin jacket Maggie had made.

21

"**I** KILLED HIM," said Nauligak to Davitt as they stood beside the body of Michel in the hidden ravine. The words were quiet, but anger and sorrow contorted the still face, and the hunter turned away.

Davitt spoke casually into the tense silence. "You'll have to come back with me. Help me load this."

They tied the body on the end of the sled, and Nauligak led the way out of the desolate valleys down to the sea. Davitt walked behind him, his hand on the long sheath at his belt. They drove swiftly back across the sea ice — a corpse, a killer and the policeman with alert eyes and a ready knife. An unwilling fourth passenger was on the sled — the one who ate young dogs.

Halfway across, when the cove of Splaine's River was blue in the distance and the police post was a cluster of dots lost between ice and tundra, Nauligak finally talked. "I told my son not to come with me. It was better that I meet that one" — he jerked his head toward the wretched fat man — "alone. I was not afraid of the white man. He was not dangerous. But when we saw him go over the hills my son wanted to go too. The white man was his friend, and needed to learn the truth about the fat one eating dogs, so he would not be unhappy any more." He looked directly at Davitt. "My son made him angry by mistake. He did not mean to kill. I saw his eyes when the gun went off. There was no killing in them."

"Temporary insanity," said Davitt. "You acted in self-defense. Anyone would have done the same. You will be questioned as you were when Father Splaine died. First I will write down everything you have told me and you will sign it. Then you can go home. When the police judge comes with the boat you will come back and say it once more. That is all. As for *him* — I'm keeping him here in police custody. At the least he will be sentenced for thievery and left with me. I am not kind to a lazy man. Saloositak Tana won't bother you again."

"It does not matter," said Nauligak in a flat voice. "My son is dead."

It was evening when they came to the beach; in the light of the slow-setting sun the white house gleamed and the young willow shrubs threw long shadows. Davitt and Nauligak took the body of Michel to an empty warehouse and wrapped it in canvas, to await decision for burial.

Then Davitt went into his house, pulled back all the curtains and opened the windows. The smells of stale tobacco and coal smoke drifted out on the cool air, and with them, at last, went the spirit of Nina. I couldn't have held her, thought Davitt, any more than Nauligak could hold Zeke. Changed by the civilization they could not understand, they made their own fates, followed their own tortuous trails to inevitable destruction. We too, Michel and Ide and I . . . I must not stay here much longer.

Jacques Davitt sat at the table in Michel's house, reading the letters to Sandra, record of a man's losing struggle with loneliness. It was a week after the deaths, and the second time since then that the constable had been there. On the first visit he had searched for and found the will; the letters he had seen and dismissed as the wanderings of a disordered mind. Now he felt the necessity, as a police officer, to read them more carefully. The last letter was on top, and he read it first, then read it again. Leafing through the sheets, he chose several others and pondered them. A pattern began to emerge.

He was considering the last letter again when a soft voice said, "Constable Davitt?" Maggie was standing in the open doorway, the sun striking black lights from her hair. "May I speak to you?"

"Of course." He had seen her only once since Michel's death; that was when they let the canvas-shrouded body into the sea, far out, where tides had opened the ice. Her tears had flowed silently as the water closed around him, smooth and dark, leaving no ripple to show where the grave was. Then the baby had cried, and she had taken it from her hood to feed it, her eyes still wet, her face pensive. The baby, satisfied, had opened its blue eyes and stared into space with the half-smile of the newborn. She had smiled back at it, suddenly beautiful.

Today she looked older, serious and sad, but her face did not reflect the ravage of grief. Maggie, he thought, could live with suffering.

Low-voiced, she spoke in her own language. "My father wishes me to ask you if he can bury my brother on the hill, next to Father Splaine."

"I've just seen him," said Davitt, surprised. "He said nothing about that." Nauligak, in fact, had hardly spoken at all. Davitt had stopped in for a few minutes on his way to Michel's house, to assure him again that he had done nothing wrong. The hunter had greeted him briefly and retreated into silence. Aitu looked anxious and talked too much, hovering over her husband with food and tea and tobacco. Davitt had left quickly, saddened.

"He will not talk to anyone but me," said Maggie. "He told me Zeke would have wished it."

"Tell him I think it is right and proper. If he wants it I will say the service."

"Thank you. He thinks too much of the dead. Perhaps when this is done he can bury them in his mind as well."

Davitt looked down at the paper still in his hand, frowned, folded it carefully and put it in his pocket. "What are you going to do, Maggie? Michel has left a will, and you will be rich — maybe richer, if these are published." He gestured at the letters. "It's an interesting record. He knew the North better than he thought he did — the way it enchants and terrifies at the same time, and takes your soul and leaves you only scenery. We're all of us alone here. Do you understand, Maggie?"

"No," she said doubtfully. "Do I have to?"

"Of course not. I'm only talking to myself. All you need to know is that you can live anywhere you want."

"Was Zeke to have this house?"

"Yes. It belongs to nobody now."

"May I have it?" she asked shyly, her voice almost a whisper.

"Why, Maggie?"

She turned to the window and traced one finger down the silverjar curtain. "It was our house. Here he will never be dead. I can try to read and play the organ — learn all the things he knew and teach them to our son. When he is old enough I will take him outside in the winters, to school. I will go to school too. Then we will live here all the time and I will teach my people."

"I think it's a mistake. The boy is Michel's son too. He is not one of your people. They may not want him here."

"This is where we live," said Maggie, quiet and determined. "It is not happy now — but everywhere sad things happen. Is any other place happier?"

Davitt took a deep breath. "Maggie," he said, "your father took you away from Michel. Don't you think he might . . ." he paused, uncomfortable . . . "separate you from your son too?"

"My father did only what he thought was right. I must give birth alone, and live for a little while afterward away from my husband. It is our custom. If I want to stay here I must do as all do. Only I wish Michel had seen his son." Tears filled her eyes, and as if in echo the baby whimpered. She reached back and brought him out of her hood, and smiled. "He is not hungry. He only wants company." He lay contented on her arm, pink-skinned and blue-eyed, with his mother's black straight hair.

"What is his name?"

"Douglas Ewen Michel," she said with demure formality, pronouncing the strange syllables painstakingly.

"Of course. I don't know why I asked. You will probably do what you please, Maggie, and you'll probably be right. You usually are. But please do one thing for me — for Michel. The plane came in last night that was to take Michel out. Let it take you out instead, with the baby and all Michel's letters. They are yours. Go to the editor — his name is on the will — and he will take care of you."

"I am not ready to go out." Her eyes dropped to the baby on her arm, and a pang went through Davitt at the vulnerable youth of her fine-veined, almost transparent eyelids. "He is too young. He must know his own people before he knows those outside."

Davitt sighed. He took the folded letter from his pocket and handed it to her. "I was going to keep this, but I think you should have it."

She put it, still folded, into her belt pocket.

"Read it now, Maggie. The last word he wrote was your name."

Embarrassed, she looked at the floor, then sideways at him. "I cannot read, Constable Davitt."

"I'll read it to you . . . No, I won't; it wouldn't change you. Maggie, my dear girl, was there any one thing you liked about Michel more than anything else?"

Her face softened and her eyes were liquid as she looked straight at him. "He kissed my hand sometimes." The eyelids dropped again and her ivory skin was touched with pink.

He lifted her strong small hand and touched it lightly with his lips. "Maggie, please go on the plane." She nodded without speaking, tears on her cheeks.

He took Maggie back to her village and saw her on to the sled that would take her and her baby and Michel's record to safety.

"What will you do?" she asked, already seated with her back against the box.

"Right now I want to see your father again, maybe go hunting with him — it would do us both good. After that . . . I don't know. I like this country. I don't think I can live anywhere else, but I'll try it for a while. I'll see you again, Maggie." He waved and turned quickly away.

All the young hunters, with their wives, went to see Maggie off on the plane. The sea ice was alive with dogs and sleds, and laughter still hung on the air when the figures were small over the blue ice.

Nauligak watched them out of sight, his dark face melancholy.

"You can't hold them back," said Davitt gently.

The two men took Davitt's big team. They went far out on the sound, looking for open water. For an hour neither spoke. Then they stopped for tea near a lead.

"You can talk now," said Davitt conversationally. "There are just the two of us, and in any case nothing can be proven."

Nauligak looked at him gloomily. "There is nothing to say."

"Then I'll talk for you." He spoke musingly, as if thinking out loud. "Michel did not lose his mind all by himself. He was helped. You exiled him. You told your people not to go to his store, though they wanted to. He was to be alone. Then you took Maggie away to make sure he was really isolated. You knew Saloositak Tana was killing dogs and would sooner or later get to Shadow, the only friend Michel had left. You knew where his hiding place was too, but you wanted to see that Michel got there first — outcast, thwarted and resentful, in a threatening frame of mind where anything might happen.

"Michel guessed from the beginning that Splaine's death was not precisely an accident. He knew that a similar fate was planned for him, but couldn't avert it. You played too well on his fear of solitude.

"The death of the boy may have been a mistake, but more likely it was a necessary sacrifice. He'd changed too much, and also he knew too much. He was to have died earlier, on the mountain." He stopped. Nauligak said nothing; he was intently scanning the ice.

"You've been valuable to me, as a policeman. That's why I didn't know sooner. Your village is a model. You've kept your people together, kept them hunting, kept up their spirits and their skills, taken care of them in bad winters — kept them safe from *us*."

The hunter turned to him then, his eyes sorrowful. "My people do not think as yours, Constable Davitt."

"And your people must go on thinking as they do, or they will be destroyed. Is that it?"

"Yes," he said sadly, and looked over the ice. "I must go after that seal. The seals will be good this year, but we are still hungry."

He was going, and Davitt spoke to his back. "It's a losing fight, Nauligak. Your people liked Splaine and Michel. They like me. They'll like other outsiders."

"We were here before you," came the hoarse voice, muffled by the seal shield.

Davitt watched the inconspicuous figure stalking cautiously over the ice, harpoon lightly held in his right hand, shield in his left. Nauligak had been changed too. The impact of two civilizations — how unswervingly well-intentioned, both of them — had made of the proud hunter a devious contriver of fatalities.

He would not kill me with the harpoon, thought Davitt; that would be too obvious, and Nauligak didn't intend to be suspected.

When Nauligak came near the seal he whistled shrilly. Davitt had just time to realize it was his dog whistle, not his seal whistle. The dogs jumped up and started running toward the hunter. But the ice was undercut close to the lead, and dogs and sled fell in the water as the thin cover broke. The policeman rolled off the sled too late, hit his forehead on a jagged ice fragment, and went down with the rest.

Two of the dogs also drowned. It was a small price to pay, smaller than the life of a son. When they got back to land, Nauligak was as wet as the others.